Allen & Bill

Gary Hope

"Allen and Bill," by Gary Hope. ISBN 978-1-949756-96-8 (softcover). (softcover).

Published 2019 by Virtualbookworm.com Publishing Inc., P.O. Box 9949, College Station, TX , 77842, US.

The longer I live the more beautiful life becomes.

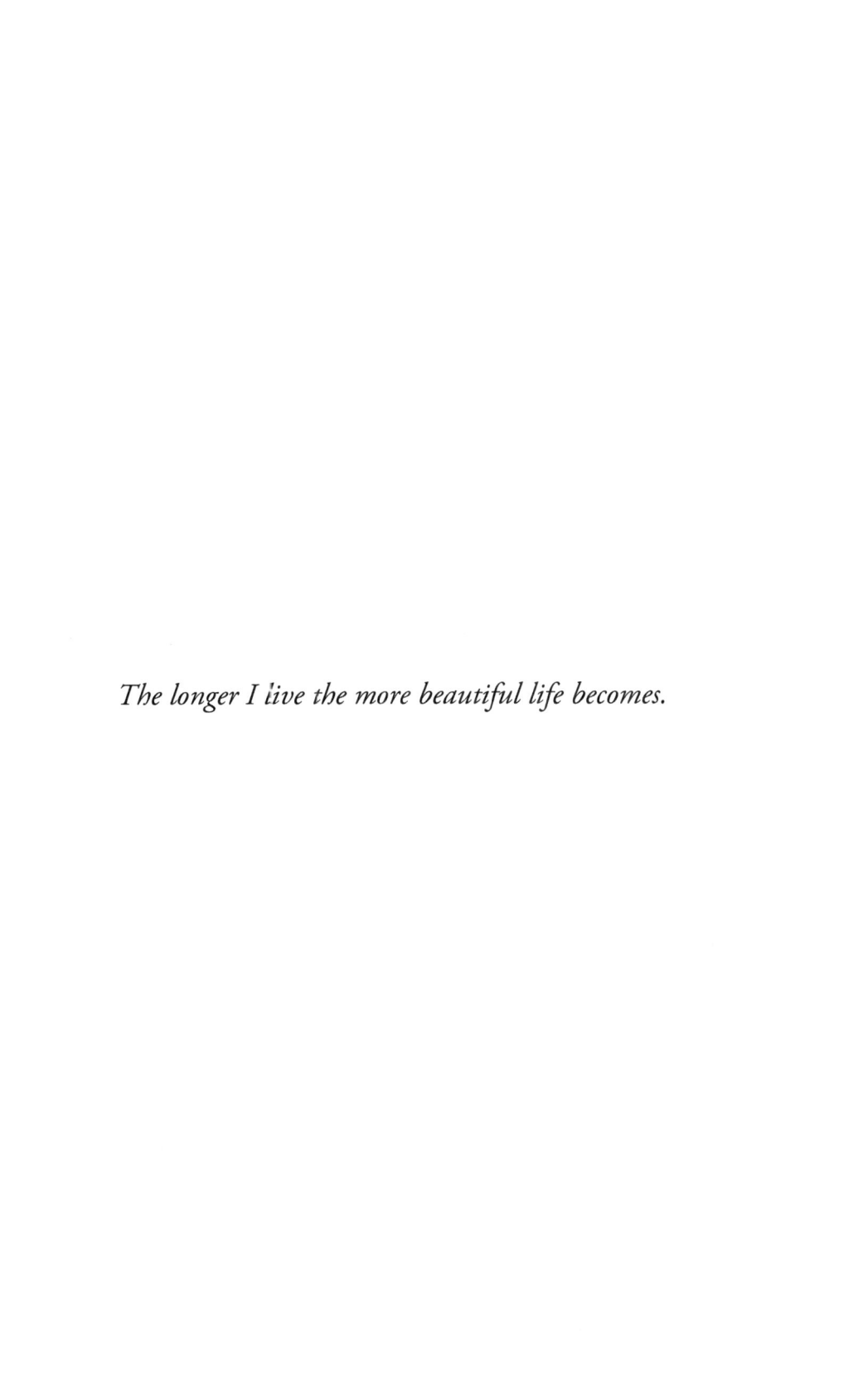

Acknowledgements

I'd like to thank some people who have made it possible for me to have the time and inspiration to write these books: First, and foremost, my wife, Susan Carter-Hope. Without her I would have been able to do nothing . . . period. She cooks and cleans and shops and washes the clothes and cuts the grass and trims the hedges and takes out the garbage and picks out my clothes and writes notes to everyone and goes on vacations with me and buys me watermelons. I have no idea how she does it all.

Kali Christine Hope, best granddaughter on the planet, prettiest girl in the world, and smartest girl in school.

Shelley Christine Hope, my daughter, whom I love now and forever.

My friends, Jerry Elkins, Dickie Nye, and Allen Simpson who, unbeknownst to them, give me great inspiration and role models for characters in my books—and in my life.

Anne Hope, best singer, guitar player, tennis player, mother, grandmother, and sister anyone could ever have.

Marky, best husband Anne Hope could ever have . . . and an excellent father, grandfather, and friend; but a poor judge of good-tasting wines.

Jon and Casey and . . . Caden. Keep on keeping on.

And,

Once again, I'd like to thank my life-long friend, Herbert Larry McRacken, Jr., for all his help in making sure the commas and semi-colons all arranged themselves in the correct places. When I write, all my punctuation marks are like illegal immigrants trying to sneak into places they shouldn't be. Larry has to be the bad guy and kick some out, arrest others, and once-in-a-while he'll even rehabilitate some of them so that they become useful and important parts of the text. He's that good!

Thanks, Lance

1

THE FUNERAL WAS SEVEN MONTHS AGO but Bill was still reliving it every day. It's hard to forget the day you buried the only woman you've ever loved your entire life. A woman you married twice, the second time knowing she only had a few months left to live. Bill and Eliza were married when they were young, then divorced for nearly a dozen years before reconnecting again. Bill never stopped loving Eliza during those long, lost years. He always wanted her back. It took Eliza a few years after the divorce to realize that she'd made a huge mistake. She wanted Bill back as well. Years of trying to conceive and failing had distorted her thinking of her role as a wife. She felt she was a failure because she knew how badly her husband wanted a child.

The self-imposed guilt drove her to leave suddenly, in the desperate, ill-conceived notion that if she left Bill, that he would find another wife and have the child he so wanted. It's true that Bill did want a child but only with Eliza—no one else. Eliza was his life, his true love, his only desire, and he was lost for twelve long years without her. He had taken a cross-country road trip with his best friend, Allen, and when he returned home he found Eliza sitting in the swing on his front porch . . . waiting for him. Of course, Allen had alerted her of their return and had been in contact with her to assure her that Bill still loved her deeply and wanted her back.

So, in Bill and Eliza's later years, they discovered true love once more in their lives. If only for a brief time. Eliza was dying. She had fought lymphoma for years and the dozens of treatments for it had irreparably damaged her liver. After fighting that dreadful cancer for half her life, it was now her liver that was killing her. There was faint hope of recovery. The doctors had told her she probably only had a couple of months left. When she was sitting in that porch swing, waiting for Bill, she almost drove away, not wanting to burden him with what she knew would be a horrible last two months.

After she explained everything to Bill, he put her in the car and drove straight to the courthouse in downtown Winston-Salem and waited in line for the justice of the peace to marry them. Then, he called his preacher and arranged a church wedding the following Saturday, just to make it official. He knew that for at least two months he would be the happiest man in the world—and he was.

After the funeral, Bill went into a long depression. He would see his friend Allen occasionally and he would go to church on Sundays but that was it. He was content to be alone and think of Eliza. He didn't have any children and no close relatives to speak of. Several of his older friends had died over the years and it was hard making new friends at his age. The times he wasn't thinking of Eliza, he was reliving the cross-country road trip he and Allen had made the previous year. They drove and camped all over the country. These two life-long friends experienced America up close and personal. They also reveled in their friendship.

Since returning from their epic journey, Bill had been so consumed with Eliza that he hadn't seen much of Allen. Just the occasional dinner together and a few phone calls—that was about it. Allen knew his friend was grieving and needed time alone. He also knew that seven months was enough. It was time to start living again and he was going to be the one to make it happen.

Since they were both retired, he waited until after 9:00 in the morning to be sure Bill was up, then he called. Bill answered, "Hello."

"Can I speak to Bill, please?"

Allen and Bill had known each other for nearly their entire lives. They went to college together and worked at RJ Reynolds Tobacco Co. together their entire professional lives. Allen knew Bill's voice, he just loved messing with him.

Bill knew Allen loved messing with him, so he didn't say anything. After a few silent moments, Allen again said, "If he's busy, just ask him to call me back."

Finally, Bill answered, "Kiss my butt. What do you want?"

"I want you to start living again, that's what I want."

"I am living."

Allen responded, "Not living like a hermit. I mean living like me!"

"I don't want to be a slut."

Allen raised his voice and said, "A slut? You think I'm a slut?"

"No, not really, you're too old to be a slut. But you'd like to be."

Allen thought about that and said, "Well, maybe for a year or two. But that's not why I called."

"Why did you call? I don't have all day to be talking to you."

"And just what are you doing all day? Eating cereal? Sipping iced tea? Washing your underwear? Tell me, old man, what else are you doing?"

Bill wanted to say something . . . but he had no response because he wasn't doing anything, except thinking about Eliza.

After a few silent moments, Allen said, "We're taking a trip. Get your stuff ready, old-timer."

Bill replied, "I don't have time to ride up to Mt. Airy with you. I'm busy."

"Busy doing what? And I ain't talking about no Mt. Airy. I don't care about seeing Barney and Goober."

Bill said, "Well, I don't want to go to Greensboro either. Call that bleached blonde old woman I saw you with a couple of weeks ago, she'll go with you."

"She wasn't old! She's younger than you, Methusleman."

"It's Methuselah, numbnuts!"

Allen thought a moment, then said, "Well, she's still younger than you, and she's not my girlfriend. Plus, I ain't talking about no Greensboro either."

When Allen said this, Bill perked up a little bit. His mind started racing and wishing and hoping that Allen was thinking about another road trip. He was almost afraid to respond, but he finally said, "Well, where are you talking about?"

"Out west, my homespun friend. Out where the prairie dogs play and the buffalo roam and the women are appreciative of real he-men, like us."

Bill almost passed out. He took so long to respond that Allen asked, "You still there?"

"Allen . . . are you serious?"

"Of course I'm serious! Unless you're too stuck in your ways to actually leave your house again."

"When?"

"Can you be ready in twenty minutes?"

Allen thought this would really shake up his friend until Bill answered, "Yes."

It took them longer than twenty minutes to arrange everything. Allen had to call the bleached blonde, as well as several other ladies he'd been seeing, to tell them he'd be unavailable for a while. Then he had to call his two grown kids to let them know he'd be gone for a while. He liked to think that they really cared if he was gone or not, but he wasn't sure. They had their own lives in different parts of the country. They'd call him on his birthday and on Father's Day and Christmas—but that was about it.

Bill only had to notify the post office and the bank of his impending absence. Then he arranged for a yard service to mow his lawn and blow off the driveway while he was gone. He also arranged for the florist to leave a fresh bouquet of flowers on Eliza's grave every week. Allen had artificial flowers on his wife's grave, which he usually changed every month. His wife, Barbara, had died nearly two years ago. Even though he put on a good act, he still missed her terribly. Nobody but Bill knew how much Allen really missed her. He could fool everyone else except his lifelong friend.

2

ON THEIR PREVIOUS TRIP ACROSS THE COUNTRY, the boys had rented a new Ford F-150 to drive and a small camper to pull behind them. They enjoyed the opportunities to camp in various scenic locations across the land. Sometimes they just needed more comfort and security than the camper could afford so they stayed in hotels and motels as well. There was no set agenda for their trip and virtually no travel plans. Even when they departed on the first day from their home in Winston-Salem, N.C., they hadn't even figured out if they were going north or south. That was the beauty of it . . . nowhere to be and nowhere to go except for where the wind blew and providence guided them.

The boys met the following day at Panera Bread to discuss the trip. Not so much to make any plans or set a time frame, but to decide where they really didn't want to go and, even more importantly, where they really did want to go. Allen said, "This here is an equal opportunity trip, buddy, but I ain't going to Texas! There ain't nothing there that I care to see. If you want to go there, I'll meet you in New Mexico when you come out."

Bill was putting some jelly on a bagel when Allen spoke and he never stopped or even looked up when he said, "Okay."

"And, I ain't going to Green Bay, Wisconsin and watch you swoon and keel over in front of Vince Lombardi's statue."

Bill took a sip from his coffee but still didn't look up at Allen as he replied, "Okay."

Allen wasn't going to stop until he elicited some type of reaction because that's who he was. So he continued, "And, I ain't going to no Lake Superior . . . "

Before he could finish that sentence, Bill interrupted. "Stop right there! You got your two vetoes and that's it. That's all you get. Now I get two vetoes and when I'm finished, it's settled. Do you understand?"

Allen leaned back against the cushion and said, "Depends on what your two vetoes are."

Bill deliberately took a bite of his bagel just to make Allen wait. When he swallowed, he said, "I don't want to go to Mount Rushmore again—it was boring. And, I don't want to go to North Dakota again. There!"

Allen didn't want to go to either of those places either, but he'd never let Bill know that. "Well, if I let you have your way on this, what do I get in return?"

Bill looked sternly at his friend and said, "I'll buy the first beer on the first night . . . maybe."

"Deal!"

And with that exclamation, they were ready to head off into the great unknown . . . sort of. The Ford F-150 they used on the last trip was great, but Allen got a better deal from the Chevrolet dealership and reserved a new Silverado for this trip. He also rented the exact type of camper they used last time—they were familiar with it and it wasn't too cumbersome in city traffic. With everything now arranged, they decided to leave Winston-Salem in two days. Allen needed some time to have last dates with two of his favorite "non-girlfriends."

Allen drove his new, rented Silverado, with the camper attached to the rear, over to S. Cross Street to pick up Bill. Bill was sitting on his porch swing thinking about Eliza and didn't even notice Allen had stopped in front of his house. Allen got out of the truck and found an acorn on the ground and threw it at Bill. He missed, mostly because he was not a good thrower and because he was not a young man anymore. Bill saw the acorn bouncing on his porch and it woke him from his dreams of Eliza. He picked up the acorn and threw it back at Allen hitting him in the leg with it, and said, "Sorry, I was aiming at your head."

Allen smiled and replied, "Just get your stuff and let's get out of here before I change my mind and take Sophie with me, instead of an old ugly man like you."

Bill turned to go into his house and asked, "Who's Sophie . . . the bleached blonde?"

Before Allen could answer, Bill went into his house. He came back out with all his stuff, plus a large cooler he was rolling along that was full of ice, Diet Pepsi and Coors Light. They packed everything in the camper and the truck and Bill opened the door to the passenger side when Allen said, "Whoa, old-timer. You're driving. I went and got this here truck and hooked up the camper and came to pick you up. You ain't done nothing but sit up there in the swing. You're driving!"

Bill didn't respond, he just walked around to the driver's side and got in the truck. He adjusted the seat, the mirror, rolled the window down a little bit, buckled his seat belt, and stared at all the controls trying to familiarize himself with the new vehicle.

Allen kept staring at him and finally said, "Are we going or not?"

"Yeah, we're going, when I'm ready." Allen kept staring at him but didn't say anything else. Then Bill asked, "Exactly where are we going first?"

"Any place but Texas, I ain't going there. Anywhere else is fine with me, just take off, I'm tired of sitting here."

So, Bill drove out to Silas Creek Parkway and soon exited onto Interstate 40-West. He glanced over at Allen who said, "Good choice."

It was a beautiful morning and they were each excited to be on the road. They made it about thirty minutes when Allen said, "There's a rest stop up here. Pull over."

Bill said, "Pull over? What are you talking about?"

"I got to pee! That's what I'm talking about. I drank too much coffee this morning, now pull over."

Bill replied, "If we stop every thirty minutes we won't get to California till we're about a hundred years old."

Allen didn't respond. He had to pee too badly. When he came back to the truck he had a map with him he'd picked up inside the rest area. He opened up the map and told Bill, "We got lots to see between here and California, my grumpy friend. You just start driving and I'll let you know when it's time for you to start having fun."

So they drove onward, toward California, each riding along with their best friend in the world. But they did indeed have lots to see before they got there.

3

THEY DROVE THROUGH THE ROLLING HILLS of western North Carolina, which soon turned into the Appalachian Mountains as they approached Asheville. Most of the drive was rather silent as the two friends reflected on the life that lay before them and the life they left behind them. As they entered the sharp turns of the mountains they both became alert but didn't discuss anything of importance. When the road straightened out a bit Allen finally asked the question he'd been dying to ask since they pulled out of Winston-Salem: "Bill, I know how you're feeling. Remember, I lost my wife too. But just how long are you going to keep moping around before you start living again?"

Bill didn't take his eyes off the road as he answered. "You know, Allen, the trouble is, you think you have time. Then before you know it, your time is gone. The last day Eliza was conscious before she passed away, we had a really good talk. She held my hand and said, 'Honey, don't you die before you're dead. Enjoy the rest of your life—that's what will make me happy. Live your life to the fullest and forget about your age. Will you promise to do that?' I promised I would . . . and I am."

Allen nodded as Bill told him this, then there was a moment of silence before Allen said, "Good thing! Because if you were going to be a boring, stick-in-the-mud on this trip, I was going to kick you out of my Ford F-150 in Asheville and find me somebody to have fun with."

Bill finally peeked over at him quickly and responded, "It's not a Ford F-150, grandpa; we're in a Silverado! And I promise you, the dark days are behind me. I'm here to have fun and enjoy life and try my best to keep you out of trouble."

Allen smiled when he heard that news, then added, "But you don't understand, hayseed, getting in trouble IS fun!" They fist-bumped and laughed, then Allen said, "Pull over up here, I got to pee again."

They decided to exit I-40 and visit downtown Asheville, mostly because Allen had forgotten to refill one of his prescriptions. He called it in and was told he could pick it up at the drugstore there in Asheville. They couldn't find a parking spot on the main street that was big enough to park the truck and camper in, so they pulled in the parking lot of a Holiday Inn. After some quick discussions, they decided not only to park here but to spend the night as well. Now they could properly explore downtown Asheville without being rushed. Both of the boys had been to Asheville over the years but had not walked the streets in quite a while. Asheville had changed.

They found a coffee shop with outside seating and decided to relax and watch all the tourists walk by. They soon discovered that there were basically two groups of people roaming the streets of Asheville: older, retired people like them and young, college-aged people. As they were drinking their coffee, Allen said, "I'll bet you five dollars we don't see a young kid come by without a tattoo."

Bill was pretty sure he'd lose this bet, but he said, "You're on." They saw tattoos on arms, legs, fingers, hands, necks, and even one young guy who had shaved his head and had a tattoo of an eagle covering his entire head.

As that one guy passed by them, Allen caught his eye and said, "I like The Eagles, too."

The young guy said, "Excuse me?"

Allen smiled at him and explained, "The Eagles . . . I've always liked their music."

The young guy turned to look down at Allen, who was still sitting at the table, and said, "This signifies strength, and power, and independence, and shows I will not be subjected to your oppressive and autocratic dictums of what life is supposed to be."

Allen frowned a little, then said, "Whatever . . . but I still like The Eagles." The young man turned and walked away in a huff. He looked over at Bill and said, "Dang, I thought we were in North Carolina, not Berkeley."

Bill laughed at his friend and said, "Let's go before you get us attacked."

They casually strolled down the street and gazed in the windows of all the art shops, gift stores, and new-age bookstores. Certainly different from the hillbilly Asheville they remembered from years ago. But they liked it. It was vibrant and fun and offered a multitude of opportunities for young people and old people—like them. They ended up at a local brewery that specialized in craft beers. They sampled several different ones in a tasting room but none that excited them—or satisfied them like their old standby, Coors Light.

One of the craft beers they tasted was some sort of raspberry blend. Allen would have spit it out on the floor if no one could have seen him. He said, "Can you believe this? A beer made from raspberries. Who in the world is going to drink some crap like that?"

Bill didn't particularly like it either but reasoned, "Remember what old Sly Stone said, 'Different strokes for different folks.'"

Allen frowned and looked over at him and replied, "What? Only thing I ever remember him saying was 'Adrianne?'"

Bill quickly understood what he meant by that and said, "Not Sylvester Stallone, professor. Sly and the Family Stone!"

Allen nodded and finally said, "Oh . . . okay."

They checked into the Appalachian Highlands Hotel next door to the Holiday Inn; it was very nice, with a restaurant and bar. They had eaten Bar-B-Que at a restaurant downtown but decided to have a nightcap at the bar in the hotel. The bar itself was on the top floor and overlooked the Blue Ridge Mountains. At night the boys couldn't see anything but they made a mental note to come up and take a look in the morning before they left. They each ordered a Coors Light and sat at a small table near a window. There were only eight other people in the bar and the background music was some type of bluegrass instrumental.

About halfway through their beer, Bill asked, "So, how serious are you with Sophie, the blonde?"

Allen smiled and replied, "As serious as I need to be."

"What does that mean?"

"You know exactly what it means."

Bill nodded and said, "Oh, right . . . you're getting her to clean your house for you?"

"If I actually told you what she was doing for me, it'd make you blush, son. So I won't put you in that awkward situation. Let's just say that . . . a man has certain needs that she understands how to fulfill, if you know what I mean."

Bill nodded, then took a sip from his beer and said, "Right . . . I get it, she's cleaning your house and cooking for you."

Allen smiled and answered, "You believe what you want to, grandpa, but I go to bed each night fully satisfied."

"Well, what about this other girl you're seeing. Does she know about Sophie?"

"Darlene? Oh, no . . . I keep those two worlds completely separate."

Bill asked, "So both of these women of yours don't mind if you're taking off across the country?"

Allen smiled and answered, "Oh, I made sure they were both well satisfied until I return, my friend."

Bill smiled and nodded at all this nonsense. Allen took the last swallow from his beer and said, "Let's go to bed, old man, before I'm tempted to head back to Winston for some dessert."

In the room, they each checked their emails on their laptops. Allen had emails from Sophie and Darlene—none from his two kids. Bill only had erectile dysfunction ads and spam. After showers were taken and the TV was turned off, they each laid in their own bed and stared into the darkness. Allen may have girlfriends back in Winston but his mind was always with his wife, Barbara, who died over two years ago. It was as if Bill was reading his mind when he asked, "Allen, how long did it take you to stop thinking about Barbara and move on with your life?"

"Who says I've stopped thinking about her?"

"I thought that since you've supposedly got all these new girlfriends that you've moved on."

Allen took a few moments to answer, then said, "I'll never move on. There was only one Barbara; she can never be replaced. Oh, I try and have fun, just so I don't shrivel up and die, but no one will ever replace her and I'll never stop thinking about her. You don't need to forget the past in order to live in the present, Bill. You can still remember Eliza and live today and tomorrow . . . and the next day."

Bill wanted to answer, but he didn't want to start crying, so he didn't say anything.

4

BEFORE CHECKING OUT THE NEXT MORNING, the boys went back to the top floor to have breakfast and take in the views of the mountains. It was spectacular. The rolling ridges and peaks of the Blue Ridge Mountains seemed to go on forever. They lingered as long as they could to enjoy the view, but eventually, Bill said, "We'd better be going, grandpa. With all the coffee you've had, we'll be stopping every thirty minutes for you to pee."

Allen nodded and added, "But it was worth it, wasn't it. We might not be Colorado or California, but that view is hard to beat."

"Yep, makes you proud to be a Tar Heel," Bill added.

"Whoa, son! I ain't never pulled for the Tar Heels and I ain't starting now. You can be a renegade, turncoat, and traitor if you want to, but don't drag me down the toilet with you."

Bill got up from the table and said, "Oh, shut up, old man, we both know that's a lie. You love Michael Jordon and don't deny it."

Allen sat there thinking, then said, "It's sorta like I love watermelons but I don't like the rinds of watermelons. Understand?"

"Yeah, I understand you're crazy. Now let's go."

After packing up the Silverado, they found their way back to I-40 West. Driving through the Appalachian Mountains was a great joy. They stopped at a rest area just across the Tennessee state line to stretch their legs, go to the bathroom, and switch drivers. They had stopped along the way at several pull-outs along the interstate so they could take in the vistas from the crest of the mountains. Just after lunch, they came upon a huge lake named Douglas Lake, which they'd never heard of. It went on for miles along the interstate. Near the end of the lake, Bill saw a sign for a campground and decided to pull over and settle there for the night.

They weren't trying to see how many miles they could cover each day, they were simply trying to see how much beauty they could uncover each day. Douglas Lake was too pretty to pass up. They checked in and set up their little camper right on the lakeshore. It was mid-afternoon by then and Allen decided it would be nice to take a short nap when everything was all set up. The short nap lasted all afternoon. Neither guy woke up until the sun was setting. They quickly set up their chairs and were able to see the sun reflecting off the lake as it dipped behind the trees. Bill started a little campfire and got the cooler out, along with a few snacks they'd brought along. A bottle of Coors Light, some barbeque potato chips, a beautiful lake, and your best friend at your side—who could ask for more?

Since they'd had a long nap today, it was easy for them to stay up late and keep the little fire going. But still, they only had two beers each. The bathrooms were only about thirty yards away but it was better to be on the safe side. They discussed religion, politics, sports, getting older, women, women, and women. Allen specifically tried to steer the conversation away from their deceased wives—and almost made it. Just after they turned the lantern off in the camper, Allen said, "Trying to figure out women is like trying to understand algebraic geometry."

Bill smiled to himself and answered, "No . . . in the arithmetic of love, one plus one equals everything, but two minus one equals nothing."

In the morning, Bill went to the campground office and brought back coffee and bagels. They sat in their chairs and stared out over the lake sipping their coffee. Then their campground neighbors woke up and started playing rap music on their radio. The boys packed up quickly and hit the road again. The road took them through Knoxville; they thought about stopping but decided against it. They drove along and discussed places they'd visited on their previous trip, places they wanted to see again, and soon the rhythm of the road had overtaken them. They drove all day, only stopping for gas, bathroom breaks, and snacks.

Tennessee was a long state to drive through. The boys drove all day and finally ended up at the Mississippi River in Memphis. Bill googled "campgrounds" and they located one, north of the city, right on the banks of the mighty river. The bad news was that the only vacant spot left was quite a distance from the bathrooms. They would have to watch their Coors Light consumption closely. At the campground office, they bought a couple of pre-wrapped sandwiches and restocked their cooler with ice and Diet Pepsi.

After the camper was set up and the chairs were put out by the little grill, Allen commented, "Dang, I don't ever want to drive across that state again. I'm pooped!"

"Me too, buddy. Hand me one of those beers." They each sipped their Coors Light very slowly and stared at the broad, flowing river, not twenty yards away from their campsite. The only noise was from the river and the crickets and the little birds.

Eventually, Allen got up and started to pick up little twigs and branches to build a fire in the grill. When he returned, he asked Bill, "What are you thinking about?" He knew Bill was thinking about Eliza and he wanted to get his thoughts and mind on something else.

He was shocked when Bill answered, "Monterey. I was just thinking that we should've made reservations at the Seven Gables Inn before we left. I bet they're booked up by now."

That statement really surprised Allen—in a good way. The Seven Gables Inn was one of their favorite places from the last road trip they made. They talked about it often and Allen made up a bunch of stories regarding their stay there—some of them were even true. He said, "Don't worry about that, grandpa, I've already taken care of it. Reservations are made, breakfast will be waiting on us, and the owner, Susan, says she can't wait to see me. She didn't mention you but maybe she'll remember you when she sees your old, ugly face."

Bill smiled when he heard that news. Both boys loved the Inn and the little town of Monterey. They each took a few moments to relive some memories of their stay there. Then Allen got up and started walking towards the river. Bill yelled out, "Where are you going, old man? Don't get too close, that river'll sweep you away."

Allen looked back over his shoulder and said, "I got to pee."

"Boy, you can't pee in that river! You'll get us both arrested."

"Well, I ain't walking a hundred yards back to the bathrooms just to take a little pee. Heck, Indians and Pilgrims have been peeing in the Mississippi for hundreds of years. It'll be fine."

"Allen, don't do it! C'mon back and I'll walk with you to the bathrooms."

Allen stopped, then picked up a rock and threw it as hard as he could into the river. "Well, I hope you don't tell on me for throwing a rock into the river!"

They walked back up the road to the bathrooms just as the sun was setting on the campground. The little campground road was lit very dimly by some low-wattage street lights. When they passed under one of the lights, on the way back, they heard someone yell out, "How you guys doing?"

They stopped and looked towards a large RV where some people were sitting around a campfire. It looked like three people were sitting there, but they couldn't really be sure. Allen answered, "We're tired, hungry, thirsty, lonely, smart, and good-looking . . . how are y'all doing?"

Bill elbowed him in the side as they heard giggling coming from the campfire. Women giggling. One of the giggling women said, "You got time to join us for a drink?"

"Sure," Allen replied. "Can my homely, ugly, uneducated friend here join us as well?"

Bill punched Allen's arm but it was too late, Allen was already walking over to the campfire. When they arrived, they found three women sitting in a half-circle, each one holding a wine glass. The woman in the middle said, "Welcome, guys. Look in the back of that RV and you'll find a couple of chairs. Would you like something to drink?"

Bill still hadn't spoken but Allen answered, "Yeah, what kind of wine are you young ladies drinking?"

The woman on the left said, "Oh, it's not wine darling. We're drinking Long Island Ice Teas. Can I pour you one?"

Bill started to say something again but Allen interrupted him and said, "Why thank you, young lady. My name is Allen and the mute old man over there is Bill. Nice to meet you."

The lady on the right-hand side said, "Is he really mute?"

Bill finally spoke and said, "Don't pay any attention to him, miss. He's already had one beer tonight and that usually puts him to sleep."

After everyone stopped giggling, the ladies introduced themselves: Ruthie, Cynthia, and Debbie. It was hard to tell exactly but the boys each thought the ladies might be somewhere in their sixties—give or take. Two of the girls were widowed and the third lady was divorced. They were from Alamogordo, New Mexico, and were on their way to New York City for a vacation. They were planning on parking their RV in a lot and staying in mid-town New York while sightseeing and going to Broadway shows.

The boys each took a Long Island Iced Tea but only sipped it . . . very slowly. They told stories and jokes all evening. The girls refilled their glasses several times but never seemed inebriated—just happy. Allen drank most of his drink but Bill poured about half of his on the ground. At any rate, they had a grand time listening to Allen tell his wild stories and watching the women laugh and giggle. When it was time to leave, Ruthie said, "Why don't you boys come over again tomorrow evening and we'll cook out something for all of us. Okay?"

Again, Bill started to answer but Allen talked over him, "We'd love to, Ruthie. What can we bring?"

"We've got plenty of food but you might want to bring yourselves some beer so you won't have to pour our drinks on the ground again." They all burst out laughing at that statement.

Allen said, "Done! We'll be here . . . and thanks. Now, you ladies sleep tight."

As the boys started to walk away, they heard Debbie say, "Shut up, Cynthia, they'll hear you."

As they walked back to their campsite, Bill asked, "Why'd you tell them we'd come back tomorrow night? We need to be on the road, old man."

Allen elbowed him and answered, "Loosen up, grandpa, you ain't too old to have a little fun. That's why we're on this here trip, to have fun . . . right?"

Bill said, "Well, maybe, but we don't want to get in any trouble either."

"Speak for yourself, Mr. Prude, speak for yourself."

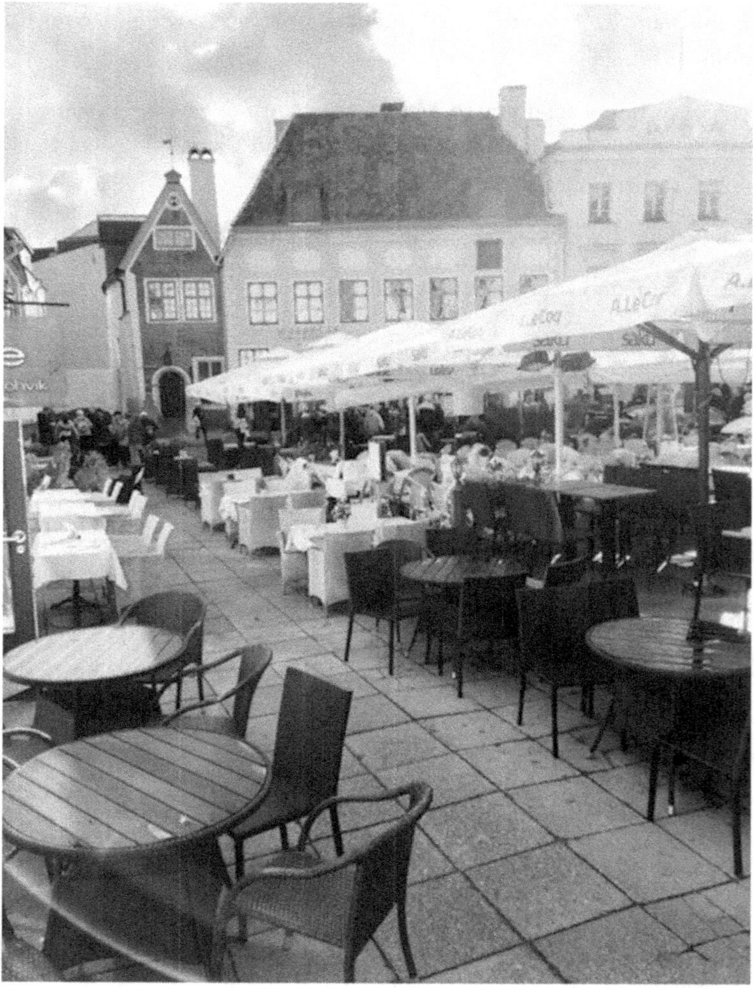

5

THE NEXT MORNING, the boys unhcoked the Silverado and left the camper at the campground. While leaving the campsite, they drove slowly by the girl's RV but didn't see any movement. They found a small diner nearby and the smell of fresh-brewed coffee and bacon cooking on the grill almost drove them crazy. Their waiter was a big heavy-set guy, with stains all over his apron and about three days worth of stubble on his face. They also noticed the sanitation rating of "B" but still, coffee and bacon? It was too hard to resist.

After two refills they discussed their plans for the day. Bill said, "I'd like to go visit Graceland since we're here."

Allen nodded and answered, "Okay, as long as we're back in time for the cookout."

"Allen, just what do you think is gonna happen tonight?"

Allen smiled and replied, "Ain't no telling, Mr. Prude. You saw how that pretty one was looking at me, didn't you?"

"Which one?"

"The pretty one, Cynthia. The other two were a little too plain and old for me—you can have them both. Might do you some good!"

They arrived at Graceland only to find the line of people waiting to get in was all the way around the block. They decided they'd visit Graceland some other time. They drove around Memphis for a bit and visited the famous Beale Street, home of the blues, then decided to go back to the campground and sit out and watch the river while waiting for the cookout. Allen said, "I'll bet old Cynthia wears something sexy and revealing tonight You saw how she was looking at me, didn't you?"

Bill ignored him, so Allen asked again, "You don't mind vacating the camper and taking a long walk by yourself tonight, do you, old man?" Bill still ignored him, so he said, "And if I leave a sock hanging on the doorknob, that means for you to sleep in the truck. You got it?" Bill continued to ignore him, so Allen starting singing

"You Got That Loving Feeling" by the Righteous Brothers. Bill turned the radio on to drown out Allen's attempt at karaoke.

It was still early afternoon when they pulled back in the campground. While driving past the girl's RV, there was still no movement they could see. They took a nap, had a snack and a Diet Pepsi, then sat under a zelcova tree and watched the Mississippi River flow powerfully by. Finally, Allen went to take a shower and get dressed for his special night. He put on his favorite Linda Ronstadt tee shirt because he thought it made his pecs look good, and then applied so much aftershave that Bill lost his breath and started coughing.

When the time came, each of the boys grabbed a six-pack of Coors Light and started walking down the drive. Allen was so excited that he almost didn't discover that the parking place where the girl's RV was located was now empty. They almost walked past it before they stopped, then turned back and forth, looking all around them. The girls from Alamogordo were gone! Allen said, "Maybe they just went out to the store or something. They'll be back."

Bill tilted his head a little and arched his eyebrows at his friend, then turned to walk back to the camper. Allen pleaded with him, "C'mon, Bill . . . they'll be back." Bill kept on walking. Allen waited by himself for about fifteen minutes, then he too walked back to the camper. They sat down and popped the top on a beer and stared, in silence, out at the mighty, mighty Mississippi.

Bill felt a little sorry for his friend, and finally asked, "What are you thinking about?"

Allen took a drink from his beer and said, "I think it would be totally inappropriate for me to even contemplate what I'm thinking about."

Bill understood.

The following morning, the boys crossed over the Mississippi River, while Allen was craning his neck in all directions looking for an RV from Alamogordo, New Mexico. They drove most of the day, only stopping for essentials. As the road took them towards Little Rock, Arkansas, they started seeing a few billboards for Hot Springs, Arkansas. On their previous trip, they had visited some hot springs in Truth or Consequences, New Mexico, which they enjoyed. Allen asked, "Do you think this Hot Springs is like the one in New Mexico?"

"Probably . . . don't know why they'd be advertising it if it wasn't. You want to check it out?"

Allen nodded and answered, "You're driving, grandpa, I'm just a passenger today."

Bill took the exit and drove through the Ouachita Mountains to find the pleasant little tourist town of Hot Springs. Towards the edge of town, they saw a nice, modern hotel with a big parking lot, which advertised "Free Hot Thermal Springs for all guests." Bill pulled in and parked. The room rates were high but the boys understood this was a tourist town. They checked in and found the hot springs pool area directly behind the hotel. Each guy had both brought their swim trunks with them, so they changed quickly and entered the pool.

Bill said, "I don't think this is as hot as the one in New Mexico. What do you think?"

Allen was smiling and answered, "The water might not be quite as hot, but she sure is." He was nodding at the other end of the pool where a young girl had just emerged from the pool wearing the skimpiest bikini either of the boys had seen in quite a while. She looked to be about nineteen or twenty years old, with long dark hair she had tied on top of her head. As both guys were gawking at her, another young lady came from the pool—they hadn't noticed her either until she walked up the steps. They weren't sure what color her hair was because she was topless. She went over to some chairs where the dark-haired girl was and both girls started toweling off. The topless girl, who had light brown hair, made no attempt to cover up or put a top on.

Both girls then sat on the pool chairs and sipped some drinks they had on a small table nearby. Bill said, "Can you believe that?" Allen didn't answer; he was still in a trance watching the topless girl. Bill flicked Allen's ear and said, "Hey, wake up!"

"I'm awake! And quit disturbing me. I'm taking in the scenic beauty of Arkansas."

Bill said, "We ought to tell the management about this; I'm sure it's not allowed."

"You shut up, old man. Ain't nothing wrong here."

"Allen, what's gonna happen if some young kids come out here and see her?"

"I wish I'd have seen her when I was a young kid . . . maybe I wouldn't be so repressed now."

Bill started to get out of the pool but Allen grabbed his arm and pulled him back. "Just come back here and sit down, old man. I didn't pee in your river, now don't you pee on my parade."

Bill sat down, but he wasn't happy about possibly seeing some rules broken. After several minutes, the two girls walked back into the pool—one in a bikini, the other one still topless. The topless one looked over at the boys and smiled. Bill looked quickly away, while Allen smiled his biggest North Carolina smile back at her. A few minutes later a waiter came walking around the pool to take any drink orders anyone may have. The two girls ordered something, then he came to Allen and Bill. Allen ordered an Iron Maiden, with plenty of ice, and Bill just ordered a glass of ice tea. As the waiter wrote the orders down on his pad, Bill said, "Young man, you might want to let the management know that one of those young ladies over there is topless."

Allen was flabbergasted! However, the young man smiled back and replied, "It's okay sir. This is the 'adults only' pool, toplessness is okay here. The family pool is on the other side of the hotel." Allen smiled again, then splashed some of the hot water on Bill. After Bill learned that the girls weren't breaking any rules, he too enjoyed the views from the hot springs, in the Ouachita Mountains, in central Arkansas.

The warm, spring water and the atmosphere was so inviting that the boys decided to stay an extra night in Hot Springs. There was a lot to see and they didn't want to miss anything . . . even Bill.

6

THEY DROVE THROUGH ARKANSAS and into Oklahoma, enjoying the comradery that old friendship delivers. At one point, Bill was driving and he glanced over at Allen, who had been unusually quiet for some time, and asked, "What's on your mind?"

Allen looked over and Bill thought he might start crying as Allen said, "I was just thinking about Barbara . . . I think about her all the time, Bill. I can't stop. I know you think because I see these other women that I've forgotten the past . . . I haven't. I can't and I don't want to."

"No, I never thought that. I know how special Barbara was . . . you can never forget that."

Allen nodded and added, "It's like when you live in a house for a long time and you get up in the middle of the night, you don't need to turn any lights on, you're so familiar with everything that you can walk around in the dark. I feel that way about Barbara. I'm so familiar with her that I don't need anything else. Some days when I wake up, I still expect her to be lying there in bed next to me. Is that weird?"

Bill answered, "No, it's not weird at all. For the last seven months, I've felt the same way about Eliza. Every morning when I open my eyes, I look over to see if she's there."

Allen wanted to stop in Oklahoma City and get something to eat but decided now was not a good time. They needed to drive and ride and think some more before they stopped. After a suitable period of time had elapsed, they saw a highway sign that indicated Amarillo was 137 miles ahead.

Allen perked up and said, "Amarillo? I told you I didn't want to go to Texas."

"It's just going through the panhandle part, not all of Texas."

"Can't we go around it?" Allen asked.

"I guess we could get off the interstate and take some back roads, go way out of the way and waste our time completely if that's what you want. Or, you could just close your eyes and I'll wake you up when we're in New Mexico."

Allen snorted and mumbled under his breath but didn't say anything. A few minutes later they saw an exit for gas and some kind of diner, so Bill steered the Silverado over. They gassed up and parked at the little restaurant, which was mostly vacant. As they walked in, Bill saw an Oklahoma pamphlet nearby and picked it up. After they ordered, he started looking through the pamphlet and said, "There's a KOA campground just before the Texas state line. We could stay here tonight or we could just keep going and drive across the panhandle at night so you wouldn't have to actually see any of Texas. What do you want to do?"

"Nah, I don't want to be driving at night. It'll be alright I guess, but you're driving while I sleep across Texas and into New Mexico."

Bill laughed and replied, "I'd forgotten how much of a weirdo you are."

"I ain't a weirdo, but a man has to have some standards in his life or he'll just turn out . . . like you."

Bill picked up a packet of sugar from the table and hit Allen in the head with it just as the waitress was bringing their food over. Allen said, "He assaulted me, young lady, you witnessed it, right?"

The waitress wasn't young and she was in no mood to mess with two old men. She set their plates down, stared at Bill, and asked, "Anything else?"

Bill was smart enough to only answer, "No, ma'am."

When they finished, Bill left an average-sized tip for the not-so-young waitress. Allen left a less-than-average-sized tip for her. As they got back in the truck and were backing out, Allen looked over at the doorway to the restaurant and saw the waitress standing there giving him the finger. He started to give her the finger back but Bill said, "Don't do it, Allen! Leave it alone."

"She gave me the finger!"

"So? You deserved it. You left her a dollar and a half tip for a fifteen dollar meal."

Allen sulked and said, "That's all she deserved! She was mean and old and ugly and she's probably from Texas."

Bill replied, "I hope she didn't see our license plate and think all people from North Carolina are as crazy and cheap as you are."

Fortunately, the drive to the campground wasn't too far. They could forget about the restaurant and concentrate on setting up the camper for the night. This part of Oklahoma was pretty flat and very treeless. The campground itself had no streams or ponds or trees or anything of significance—just flatness as far as you could see. As everything was set up and arranged, Bill sat in one of the chairs and said, "This is probably the most boring place we've ever camped. We don't even have any limbs or twigs to start a fire with."

They thought about packing up and driving across the Texas panhandle that night but made the wise decision to stay where they were and rest. Allen got them a Coors Light and some snacks while they sat there looking at nothing. Bill brought up the incident with the waitress again and told Allen, "You should've left a decent tip back there—no need to be rude."

Allen replied, "She was the one who was rude. And she was ugly!"

"What's being ugly got to do with being a decent human or being good?"

Allen took a long pull from his Coors Light and said, "It's always better to be beautiful than to be good. But it's also better to be good than to be ugly."

Allen seemed very proud of that philosophical statement while Bill was still trying to understand exactly what he meant. They discussed the weather, some friends back home, places they were looking forward to seeing again, and yes, Barbara and Eliza—they couldn't help it. Then, the sun set and everything changed. Being so far away from any cities or towns, and having no trees to obstruct their views, the stars had an opportunity to shine like the boys had never seen before. The evening sky lit up and night beamed with hundreds or thousands of stars, all blinking, trying to get the boys' attention.

They leaned back in their chairs and stared at the heavens. Allen said, "I think that's the Big Dipper over there."

Bill answered, "You wouldn't know the Big Dipper if it dropped chocolate syrup on your head."

Allen was insulted, "I graduated from college! I know stuff."

"You have an awfully high opinion of yourself, don't you?"

Allen smiled and answered, "Delusions of grandeur make me feel a lot better about myself."

Bill drove and Allen slept as they traveled across the Texas panhandle. After arriving at the New Mexico state line, Bill pulled over and woke Allen up, saying, "Go over there and stand under that New Mexico State Line sign so I can take your picture." Allen didn't even argue; he stepped out and walked underneath the large sign and spread his arms wide open as Bill took his picture. Then he reached down and picked up a rock and threw it back into Texas. Bill asked, "Why'd you do that?"

Allen smiled and said, "Just because I wanted to . . . that's why." He walked back to the truck and said, "I'm driving now, Pilgrim. Get in." Bill just shook his head and hopped in the passenger side as they took off towards Albuquerque, New Mexico.

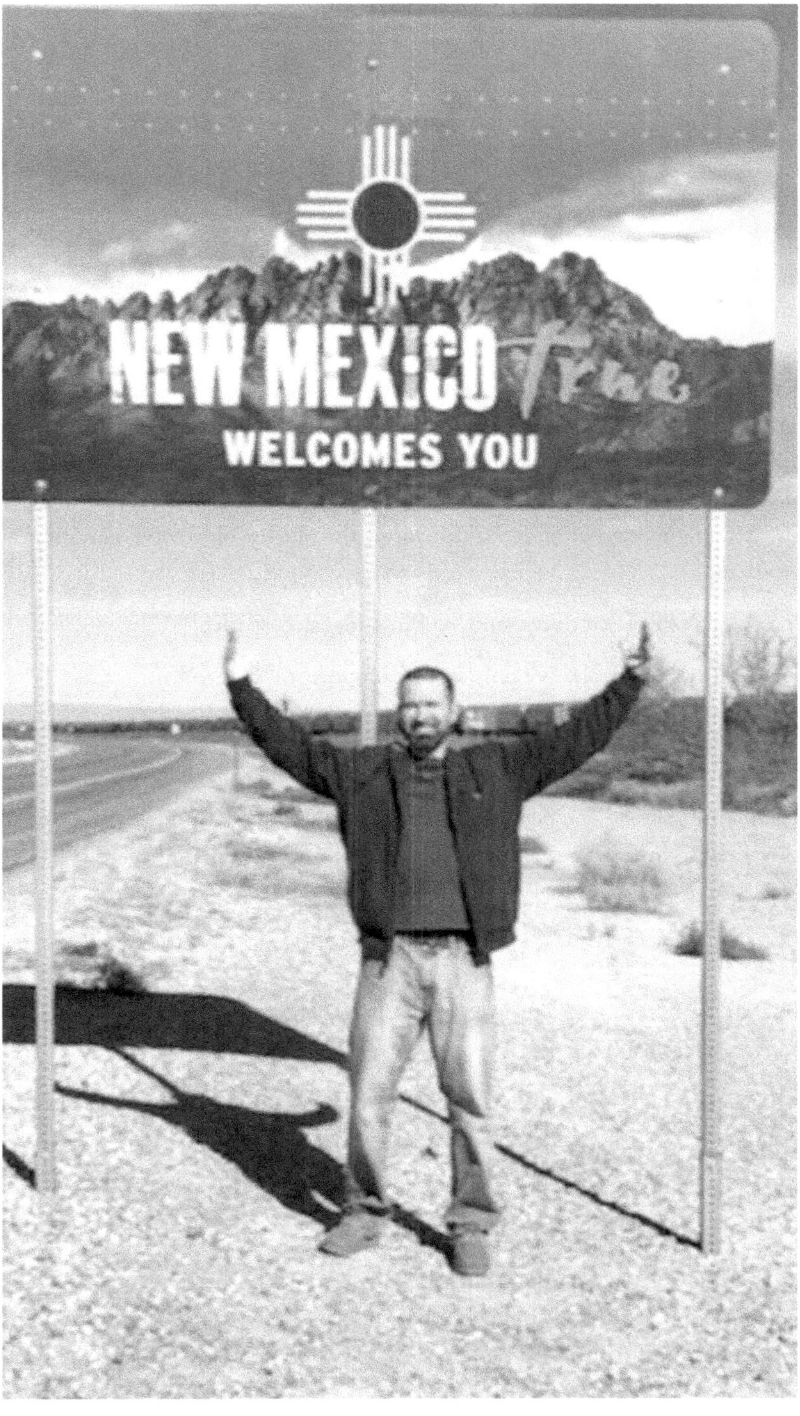
NEW MEXICO True
WELCOMES YOU

7

THEY COULD'VE DRIVEN FURTHER but they didn't want to. Albuquerque was a good place to stop and find a nice Holiday Inn for the night. The Sandia Mountain range was beautiful and Albuquerque seemed like a nice place. The parking lot at the Killarney Lodge was bigger than the Holiday Inn, so that's where they stayed. Plus, they needed a night outside the camper and a good, soft bed. After checking in, they went down to the roomy pub in the hotel. They sat at the bar, which had a nice view of the mountains across the room. Allen ordered two Coors Lights for them but the young bartender said, "Sorry, sir, but we only serve Guinness and Harp here."

Allen was too surprised to respond, so Bill said, "Excuse me?"

"This is an Irish pub, sir. We only serve Guinness and Harp."

Allen then joined in and said, "An Irish bar? Here in the middle of New Mexico? What does that mean?"

The bartender smiled and replied, "The owner moved here from Killarney, Ireland, and wanted to open an authentic Irish pub. We only serve Irish beers."

Allen asked, "Killarney? Is that anywhere near Blarney?"

"Maybe an hour or so away. Have you been there?"

"No, but that's probably all I know about Ireland. I've never tasted Guinness before; not sure if I'll like it or not."

The bartender said, "Let me give you a taste of the Guinness and the Harp and see which you like. Or, I could pour you a shot of Irish whiskey."

Bill jumped in and said, "No whiskey for him, he's hard enough to handle with beer. Just let us taste the Guinness, please."

Bill liked the taste of Guinness but Allen liked the Harp better, so that's what he ordered. As they sat there sipping their Irish beers, Allen asked the bartender how far Alamogordo was from Albuquerque. The bartender asked if that's where they were going and Allen answered, "No, probably not, but I'd like to go down there and set somebody's house on fire." The bartender didn't understand that at all but he just smiled.

Bill tried to explain Allen's statement, "He's not serious. Some old girl he met from Alamogordo stood him up the other night and he's still mad about it. Don't pay him any attention."

The young bartender replied, "I understand, sir, the closer you get to Mexico, the crazier the people get. Plus, if she lives in Alamogordo, she might be affected by all the nuclear stuff they do down there."

"You might be right," Allen said, then added, "I bet her brain was radioactive. That explains it, Bill, those old girls were nuked up!"

Bill smiled and took a drink of his Guinness, then said, "Those old girls were just trying to see how much an old, red-necked hillbilly like you would believe. And you believed it all!" The bartender laughed as Allen shook his head, still disappointed at that missed opportunity.

The boys took their beers over to a table by the window, which had a fantastic view of the Sandia Mountains in the distance. The mountains still had some snow covering at the top of each peak, which gave a startling contrast to the blues of the mountains and the yellow/reds of the setting sun. They were both quiet as they sipped their drinks and contemplated the beauty and serenity of the evening. After a few minutes, Bill said, "Remember Ellen?"

The name was a little familiar but Allen couldn't place it. He finally answered, "Was that the girl at Appalachian who was so much in love with me?" Allen and Bill had both attended Appalachian State University, where Bill had actually done very well and Allen had partied very well.

Bill looked at Allen, shook his head slowly, then answered, "No, it's the ranger we met up at Lake Superior on our trip . . . remember her?"

Allen immediately smiled and said, "Do I remember her? How could I forget her? She was hot! And, she had the hots for YOU! I thought you two were going to elope to Canada on me. Did you want to go back up there and see if she's still around?"

Bill said, "She's still around."

Allen looked intently at Bill and asked, "How do you know that?"

“We’ve emailed a few times over the last couple of months. I thought we might visit on our way back if you don’t mind.”

Allen volunteered, “We’ll go right now if you want to.”

“No, it’s nothing like that. I thought we might just drop by if we think about it.”

“Bill, this trip is great and I’m loving it but if you want to go visit this woman up at Lake Superior, we’ll go right now. I don’t mind.”

Bill was tempted, he really was, but he said, “No, it’s not like that, Allen. I was just thinking—that’s all. There are still lots of places I want to see before we even think about Lake Superior again.”

Bill was lying. For the last few months, Lake Superior had been on his mind constantly. He and Ellen had exchanged emails nearly every day for the last month, including every night on the trip from his iPad. When they met before, about two years ago, there had been instant chemistry between them that neither of them could deny. Back then, however, Bill still had Eliza on his mind. Now, things were different.

“Bill, if . . . “ Bill stopped Allen before he could say anything else.

“No more! If we have the time on the way back, we’ll talk about it. For now, let’s just enjoy this trip and see what happens. Okay?” Allen nodded, took a sip of his Irish beer and stared out at the Sandia Mountains, wishing he had someone like Ellen to think about.

After they’d showered and caught up on emails and turned the TV off, they laid in their beds with the lights off and dreamed. Each guy to his own thoughts. Each guy to his own dreams. Before sleep overtook them, Allen asked his friend, “Bill, have you ever wondered if things will change enough for the good life to find us again?”

Bill answered immediately: “The good life begins not when circumstances change, buddy, but when our attitude towards them does. We still have a life in front of us . . . don’t trip over what’s behind you.”

“Even some old, worn out, wasted, ancient men like us?”

Bill smiled in the dark and replied, “Do you remember Moses? He spent forty years in Pharaoh’s court finding out he was a somebody. Then he spent forty years in the desert finding out he was a nobody. And then he spent forty years finding out what God can do with somebody who finds out they’re a nobody.”

“So, you think we’re like Moses?”

Bill smiled again and said, "No, son, we aren't like Moses. We're like Allen and Bill; we just need to have faith like Moses."

This made Allen feel better. He had faith, yet sometimes he needed Bill to provoke him into trusting that faith again. He could sleep now.

8

THE MORNING TURNED OUT CLOUDY and overcast as they sat by the café window drinking their morning coffees. Their waitress tried to talk them into tasting the Irish morning tea instead of coffee but North Carolina was too embedded in their DNA to make that change just yet. The tops of the mountains were covered with clouds but still looked beautiful. They sat there staring out the window when a man and woman came and sat at the table next to them. They were older but not as old as Allen and Bill. Before Allen could speak, the other gentleman said, "Good morning, fellas. Where are you guys from?"

As usual, Bill left most of the conversations to Allen, who answered, "God's country, North Carolina. How about you?"

They both smiled and the woman spoke next, saying, "Fayetteville. Have you ever been there?"

"Yes, ma'am, many times. I had a good friend who was stationed there at Fort Bragg and we used to visit him."

She smiled and said, "No, not that one. Fayetteville, Arkansas. Have you ever been there?"

Allen and Bill looked at each other, unsure whether the woman was messing with them or was indeed from a place called Fayetteville, Arkansas. Before they could answer, the man said, "I'm Pastor Jeff and this is my wife, Victoria."

Allen said, "I'm Allen and this is my father, Bill." Everyone laughed . . . even Bill. Allen continued, "How long have you been a pastor, Jeff?"

"Seems like all my life, but I guess just since college. Victoria's a school teacher back home."

Bill finally joined in, saying, "We just drove through Arkansas a few days ago and stayed a couple of nights."

Pastor Jeff asked, "Where'd you guys stay?"

"In Hot Springs. " As soon as Bill volunteered this information, he knew he shouldn't have.

Victoria asked, "Hot Springs? Did you visit any of the thermal springs there?"

Bill didn't want to answer that question as twangs of guilt suddenly overcame him as he remembered watching the topless girls at the pool. But Allen jumped right in, "We sure did. We loved it!"

Pastor Jeff smiled and said, "Lived in Arkansas our entire lives and we've never been there. Glad you guys liked it."

Allen excitedly explained, "Oh, we really liked it. Very soothing and refreshing, yet exciting too. Right, Bill?" Bill only nodded, so Allen continued, "The views there were excellent as well. I don't think I've ever seen such exquisite sights as we did for those two days. Don't you agree, Bill?"

Before Bill could answer, Victoria asked, "What sights? I didn't think there was much to see there—just the thermal springs to sit in."

"Oh, no. It was very scenic and beautiful. Explain it to them, Bill."

Bill took a big drink from his coffee cup and burned his tongue a little, then said, "Where are you two headed from here?"

Fortunately for Bill, Victoria answered his question, "We're going up to Four Corners next; we haven't been there since our honeymoon years ago."

Neither guy had heard of Four Corners before, so Allen asked, "Four Corners? What is that?"

Pastor Jeff explained, "It's the point where the four states converge: New Mexico, Arizona, Colorado, and Utah. The only place in America where you can stand in four states at the same time."

"Wow, that sounds pretty cool," Allen said. "What else is there?"

Pastor Jeff said, "Well, the plaque is there. It's in the ground and you stand on it. That's how you know you're in all four states at once."

Bill asked, "Is anything else there?"

"Well . . . let's see. Do you remember what else is there, honey?"

Victoria pursed her lips and finally said, "Umm, I'm not sure."

Allen asked, "Is it near the mountains?"

"Don't really remember any mountains being around there."

Bill asked, "Any rivers or canyons?"

"I don't think so. Do you remember any rivers, Jeff?"

Jeff shook his head no and said, "I just remember it being in the middle of the desert."

Allen asked, "What do you do when you get there?"

Pastor Jeff smiled and said, "You stand on the plaque and have your picture taken."

Everyone was silent a few moments, then Pastor Jeff said, "I guess we better order some breakfast. It was nice talking to you fellows. Hope you have a great and blessed day."

The boys had a decision to make: They could take Interstate 25 north out of Albuquerque into Colorado or they could continue west on Interstate 40 into Arizona. As they were discussing it, Allen suddenly said, "Dang, Bill, we can't go to Colorado right now. I forgot about the reservations we have in Monterey at the Seven Gables Inn. If we go to Colorado we might not get there in time."

Bill immediately said, "Oh, no . . . we're not missing Seven Gables. West it is!" Will we have enough time to see the Grand Canyon again?"

"Oh, yeah, we're okay. It's just that if we detour into Colorado we might get sidetracked or something. I don't want to rush anything."

They drove most of the day as the landscape started getting more and more interesting. Their destination was Flagstaff, Arizona, where they bought gas, then took the winding road north towards the Grand Canyon. Not too far out of town was a campground they stayed at on their last trip. They were lucky to find an opening again, and not too far from the bathrooms. As the camper was up and the chairs were put out, it started getting cooler. This part of Arizona was 7,000 feet in elevation; it got cold at night.

When everything was arranged, they drove back to the campground office because they'd seen a sign for burgers and pizza. Allen ordered a large pepperoni pizza with mushrooms because they wanted to eat a healthy meal. As Bill was driving back to the camper he noticed Allen was smiling the entire way. He said, "What are you so happy about, old-timer?"

Allen looked over at his friend and replied, "There's no better feeling in the world than a warm pizza box on your lap." On this chilly night, it was nothing but the truth. They ate all they could and saved a couple of slices for breakfast. One Coors Light was all they could stand at this temperature. They wrapped up in fleece and climbed in their sleeping bags for the night. With the lantern off and darkness surrounding them, Allen asked his nightly question, "Bill, I know the Lord's coming back soon—for both of us. But I hope He lets us finish this trip. Don't you?"

Bill thought about that question, then answered, "God always keeps His appointments and He's never late. But to Him, a day is like a thousand years and a thousand years is like a day. He'll be here on His appointed time and not a second before, so there's nothing for us to worry about."

Again, Bill's words helped ease Allen's mind. But isn't that what friends are for?

The boys were ready to get going in the morning. The warm cab of the Silverado and some cold pizza slices were all they needed, except for some coffee, which they bought at the campground office on the way out. The drive up to the Grand Canyon was fairly monotonous and unexciting, but the anticipation of seeing one of the greatest wonders in the world made up for all that. They parked in one of the visitor lots and took the shuttle bus up to the south rim with all the other tourists. From what they could tell on the bus, they were the only English-speaking people there.

No matter how many times you've visited the canyon, no matter how old you are, or how jaded you may be, the first view you see will take your breath away. As it did with Allen and Bill. They didn't speak as they stared out in wonder at the incredible vistas. It was easy to lose track of reality and spatial dimensions as you gazed toward the north rim. The fact that it was eighteen miles across to the other side and a mile deep was almost incomprehensible. Without speaking, the boys shuffled along the rim, careful not to get too close to some thousand-foot drop-offs. They knew that down at the bottom of this mile-deep chasm, the Colorado River was flowing madly through on its way to a slow death in the California desert.

They went into one of the tourist shops and bought t-shirts and had another cup of coffee. They took their coffee out to a bench overlooking the canyon and sat there in splendid awe. They reminisced about their trip here before when they got in trouble with a lady park ranger who admonished them for feeding some peanuts to a squirrel. As they re-lived that story, Allen said, “I’m going to get some more nuts and find me a squirrel to give ’em to.”

Bill smiled and said, “Go ahead, old man, but I’m not bailing you out of jail if they catch you.”

Allen didn’t care; he enjoyed living dangerously. He came back from the store in a few minutes with a bag of salted peanuts. They walked down to the end of the paved area, to the last bench next to where the trees started, and sat down. Neither guy had seen a squirrel since they’d been there but they had patience. Allen threw a few of the nuts on the ground and they waited. About five minutes later, an older, stern-looking, woman park ranger walked nearby and looked over at them but didn’t say anything. There were “Don’t feed the wildlife” signs posted all along the trail.

They sat for nearly fifteen minutes and still didn’t see a squirrel; however, a couple of ravens landed in a small pinyon pine tree, waiting on the boys to leave so they could get the nuts on the ground. Finally, they gave up trying to feed the squirrels. Allen took all the peanuts from the pack and flung them on the ground in front of him. Within seconds, about six or seven squirrels appeared from the brush and started gathering the peanuts as fast as they could pack them in their jaws. It startled Allen and Bill. They were prepared to feed one squirrel, not a pack of them. Before the park ranger could look their way, they quickly got up from the bench and hustled away to safety. The guys mixed in with some other tourists and when they looked back at their bench, all the squirrels were gone; however, their stomachs were full from the generosity of an old man from North Carolina.

9

ON THEIR LAST TRIP TO THE GRAND CANYON, Allen had walked down the trail about halfway to the river. It was a tough climb back up the trail and he got sick afterward. This trip they decided to only walk along the rim and enjoy the views. Nearly every time they stopped to look, some tourist from Germany or Canada or Britain or Australia would ask them to take their picture. They didn't mind; it was a little fun interacting with everyone. By the end of the day, the boys were worn out and almost fell asleep on the shuttle ride back to the parking lot. Fortunately, Bill had made reservations at the Holiday Inn in Flagstaff for the night, so they wouldn't have to camp in the cold again.

The reservation was actually at The Lumberjack Inn, which was close to the University of Northern Arizona campus, whose nickname was the Lumberjacks. After dinner, they retired to the open bar area and listened to a young guy play James Taylor songs on his guitar. Bill got his usual Coors Light but Allen, in a salute to the Grand Canyon, got himself an Iron Maiden. They sat at a table near the rear of the bar to be away from the music. Not that they didn't like James Taylor music, but they didn't particularly enjoy it either.

After they'd been sitting for a while, a middle-aged man sat by himself at a table near them. He was well-dressed but looked a little tired and worn. When the guy looked over at them, Allen spoke, "How are you doing, sir?"

"Just fine fellas, how are you?"

Allen started to make up some yarn but the guy seemed a little distressed, so he told him the truth: "We're doing great. Is everything okay with you?"

The guy started peeling the wrapper off his beer bottle and replied, "Not really. I just visited my daughter over at the college and she really didn't want to see me, if the truth was known. My wife left me about a year ago and now it looks like my job might end—the company might close up."

Bill was sorry Allen had started this conversation. The man took a long drink from his bottle and said, "But the good news is that I've developed a new philosophy . . . I only dread one day at a time now."

Even Allen was stifled by this conversation. They both nodded to the lonely guy and Bill said, "Well, I hope things get better for you young man."

With that said, they left their drinks about half empty and decided to go up to their room. Allen went to the shower first and Bill took this opportunity to check his emails, specifically to see if he had anything from Ellen. He didn't have an email from her . . . he had four! He read them quickly and started dreaming as Allen broke the spell when he emerged from the bathroom.

Allen saw him and asked, "What are you smiling at?" Then he noticed the open iPad and put two-and-two together. "Ellen emailed you, didn't she?" Bill didn't answer, so Allen said, "Let me read it."

"Did that Iron Maiden go to your head? You're not reading my emails."

"Why not? Did she say something inappropriate? For your sake, I hope she did."

Bill said, "Oh, shut up." He then signed off his email account and closed the computer to make sure Allen couldn't access it. He started for the shower but stopped and looked back at Allen, then walked back over and picked up his laptop and took it into the bathroom with him.

As he did this, Allen asked, "You don't trust me?"

Bill said, "No!" and shut the bathroom door.

When Bill was ready for bed and the lights were turned off, Allen could hardly wait to ask his nightly question. "Bill, you know I haven't been going to church regularly since Barbara died. I know you know that. What you might not know is that I've probably done some things with these old girls that you might not approve of. The problem is that I'm sure God knows what I've been doing. He'll give me a second chance, won't He? I know He will, but I just want you to confirm that for me."

Bill smiled in the darkness of the room, then thought a moment or two before answering: "Buddy, we're all far from perfect. Even in the Bible, Abraham lied twice about Sarah being his wife because he lacked faith. Their son, Isaac, did the same thing. Their other son, Jacob, lied and connived terribly." He let those facts sink in, then continued, "Noah got drunk. Samson was a very immoral man. Rahab was a prostitute. David was an adulterer and a murderer. Jonah ran from God and Simon Peter openly denied he knew the Lord, but God gave them a second chance.

"All these people messed up, just like you, but God gave them all second chances. If we've learned anything, it's that we're all flawed people. He'll give you and me and everyone a second chance because He can use you. Your story isn't over . . . not by a long shot."

Allen didn't really know if all this stuff was true or not . . . but he trusted Bill. Bill thought about the stuff he just told Allen but couldn't stop his mind from also thinking about Ellen. When their minds settled a bit, they both slept well, there in The Lumberjack Inn, at over 7,000 feet in elevation, in Flagstaff, Arizona.

The next morning at breakfast the boys brought out a map while trying to decide which way to go next. As they were ruminating over that decision they were disturbed by a man and woman arguing about something at a table near the window. They watched but couldn't hear everything that was said until the woman suddenly got up and walked away telling the man, "I'll be in the room when you come to your senses." The poor guy sat there shaking his head; it was hard to tell if he was mad, embarrassed, or just mystified.

Allen decided to walk over and refill his coffee cup at the same time the guy decided to leave. They almost bumped into each other so Allen said, "Excuse me, sir."

The man didn't seem to notice Allen until he spoke, then he stopped and said, "I'm sorry, it's been a bad morning."

Allen, trying to make the man feel a little better, said, "We've all been there. Sometimes women are hard to understand."

The man turned to face Allen and replied, "I think we're the ones who are hard to understand. We think we're always smarter and better than women but that's not true. I think women are foolish to pretend they are equal to men. They are far superior and always have been. Whatever you give a woman, she'll make it greater. If you give her sperm, she'll give you a baby. If you give her a house, she'll give you a home. If you give her groceries, she'll give you a meal. If you give her a smile, she'll give you her heart. She multiplies and enlarges what is given to her. So, if you give her any crap, be ready to receive a ton of manure!" And with that, the man turned and walked away.

Allen filled his coffee cup and returned to the table when Bill asked him, "What did that guy say to you?"

"He just told me about his wife."

Bill was curious and asked, "What did she say to him?"

"She told him he was crazy and he told her he wanted a second opinion. So, she said, 'Okay, you're ugly too.'"

Bill picked up another packet of sugar and threw at Allen, hitting him in the stomach with it. After they finished their second cups of coffee they went back upstairs to pack their things. They'd left the television on and when they entered the room one of the morning talk shows was interviewing a celebrity psychologist, Dr. Joyce Brothers. Bill went into the bathroom first to brush his teeth, while Allen sat on the bed and watched the interview. The talk show host asked Dr. Brothers how to best relieve stress from our lives. She said, "First, go to a happy place."

Allen thought to himself, "Go to a happy place? What the devil does that mean?"

Then, Dr. Brothers added, "Then think of something bad that you can fix. Finally, look out your window and concentrate on something 'green,' and meditate on that." Allen stared at the television like it was from Mars. Bill came out of the bathroom and asked what he was watching. Allen reviewed the conversation he'd heard from Dr. Brothers and asked Bill what he thought of it.

Bill picked up the remote control and turned the television off, then said, "That's what I think of it. Go brush your teeth, do your morning constitutional and let's get moving."

They never did decide exactly where to go to next, so they just got on I-40 West and continued driving towards California. This high desert country was scenic, in a desert sort of way. When they crossed into California they saw a sign advertising Joshua Tree National Park. Bill quickly googled it and found that it wasn't too far out of their way. It sounded interesting so they decided that would be their next overnight stop. They stopped twice for gas, then stopped for bathroom breaks and snacks twice more before finally coming to the national park very late in the day.

The campground for the park was near the entrance and had plenty of open spaces. Apparently, Joshua Tree was not on the "to do" list of most vacationers. At the campground office, they asked about having a campfire and the attendant told them it was okay but they'd probably need to buy some wood for the fire since there would be very little wood in the park. They bought two bundles of wood and some sandwiches to take with them.

They finished setting up the camper just at dusk and quickly started a fire to sit around. The sandwiches weren't that tasty but the Coors Light and the company were terrific. They supplemented the meal with some Doritos and chocolate chip cookies. There was complete silence in the desert, only the crackling sound of the fire. The boys enjoyed the silence and didn't feel the urge to break it with conversation. They'd known each other long enough to simply enjoy the company without words.

During their second, and last, beer of the evening, they suddenly heard a loud screeching noise, then a howl. It startled them and Allen said, "What in the world was that?"

Bill answered, "Something out there just caught dinner."

"What do you think it was?"

Bill said, "I refuse to answer that question on the grounds that I don't know the answer."

Allen kept feeding the fire until the wood was all burned up, then they went to bed and made sure the lock on the door was securely fastened . . . just in case. Before they fell asleep, Allen asked Bill if he prayed every night at bedtime. Bill said, "Of course I do, don't you?"

Allen answered, "Well, I don't know the Bible as good as you do."

"You don't have to know the Bible to say a prayer, numbnuts. Just ask the Lord for advice or guidance."

Allen, being Allen, said, "Oh, okay. Lord, lead us not into temptation. Just tell us where it is; we'll find it."

Bill started to pick up his shoe and throw it at his friend, but giggling along with him seemed a little more appropriate as they laid in their beds, in the dark, in Joshua Tree National Park.

10

ALLEN AND BILL STARTED THEIR NEXT DAY at the campground headquarters with some fresh coffee. Since they knew very little about the park itself, they asked a ranger to tell them about it. They learned it was about 800,000 acres of rugged mountains and hostile desert, full of desert wildlife as well. The boys told of the screeching sounds they heard last night and the ranger said it was probably a coyote catching a jackrabbit or possibly a bighorn sheep.

They drove down a lonely road in the park and decided to take a trail into some low mountains. Neither one of them remembered to bring any water as they started walking. The trail was initially fairly flat, then it started rising towards a flat rock promontory ahead of them. About halfway there Allen asked, "Did you bring any water?"

Bill held out his bare hand and replied, "Yeah, here, have some."

Allen said, "How can two college-educated, intelligent human beings go off on a hike in the desert with no water?"

By the time they reached the small summit on the trail, they were parched. The desert air made it seem worse. They enjoyed the view but didn't stay long because they were so thirsty. They each picked up a rock and threw it as far as they could but Bill's went considerably farther. Allen said, "I wasn't trying."

Bill said, "Well, get you another rock and try harder."

Allen frowned and replied, "Dang, I'm thirsty. Let's get back to the truck."

Upon returning to the camper, they opened and drank a bottle of water each. Then they opened a can of Diet Pepsi as they watched a scorpion scuttle across some rocks. After they quenched their thirst, they drove around the park and loved the sheer beauty of it. Joshua trees were starkly magnificent and very striking. There were just enough rocks and low mountains to make it tantalizingly beautiful. At one stop, Bill found a fist-sized rock embedded in the trunk of a Joshua tree. It took him about five minutes of hard work to free the rock, while Allen drank another bottle of water. When he finished, he expected his shirt to be wet with perspiration but it wasn't; it was just too dry out there.

Bill brought his rock back to the truck and set it on the dash, very proud of it. Allen didn't comment. At the park headquarters, Allen bought a t-shirt with a picture of a Joshua tree on the front and Bill bought a book about the history of the park. As they drove out of the park they passed the entrance station, where they had to stop and let the automatic arm raise up. A lady ranger was standing there greeting those coming and going. She looked at them and noticed the rock on the dashboard. She put her hand up and said to the boys, "You know you're not supposed to take anything out of the park, don't you?"
Allen quickly said, "It's his, ma'am. I told him not to take it."

She just smiled and said, "You boys come back soon."

After they drove out, Bill said, "You just beat all, don't you?"

"Well, you broke the law, son."

Bill said, "Some friend you are!"

Allen replied, "A friend is someone who has the same enemies as you have, not someone who helps you break the law."

Bill answered, "Oh, shut up and hand me a bottle of water. And don't touch my rock either."

They pulled over at a rest stop to look at the map and decide which way to go. Bill said, "Look here, the Salton Sea isn't too far away. You want to see that?"

"What is it?"

"I'm not really sure, but we've got plenty of time don't we?"

Allen nodded and said, "Yeah, let's go, but first let's get something to eat. I'm hungry."

The Salton Sea was actually farther away than it seemed on the map. By the time they arrived, they were ready to sit and relax. The man in the campground office was very friendly and answered their questions. The actual campground itself was combination campground and semi-permanent residential area. It seemed as though many of the RVs were more permanent in nature than on vacation. There were plants and shrubs growing around some of them, and clotheslines with clothes hung out to dry at others. The boys were assigned an open lot, about half a mile from the office, right on the shores of the Salton Sea. The briny smell was especially strong near the water where the guys parked for the night.

On each side of them were larger RVs that seemed as though had been there a while. When they set up their little camper and got the chairs out, their neighbors on each side came over to greet them. Hazel and Johnny came over first. They were somewhere in their sixties and had obviously taken up the relaxed, bohemian lifestyle that was apparent around the shore. Johnny had a long, gray ponytail as well as a sizeable beer gut. Hazel also had long, gray hair that flowed loosely around her shoulders, except for the bit that she had tied behind one ear with some sort of yellow flower.

As they walked over, Johnny said, "Good afternoon, fellas. Welcome to the Sea."

Allen and Bill both smiled and Allen answered, "Thank you, sir, it's good to be here. We've been driving most of the day and we're pretty tired."

As he answered, the neighbors from the other side walked up, each one holding a beer in their hand. It was two men, also in their sixties, also with longish hair, and each one with a scruffy white beard as well. They both seemed to be in good shape and happy as one of the men said, "I see you've already met the welcoming committee. I'm Tom and this is Dennis."

Bill smiled and answered, "Nice to meet you guys. It sure is pretty out here."

Allen jumped in and said, "Let me get us a couple of beers from the cooler. Can I offer you guys anything?"

Hazel went back and brought back beers for Johnny and her, and everyone stood making small talk while gazing out into the blue waters of the Salton Sea. It seemed odd to Allen and Bill that on such a gorgeous day that they didn't see anyone in the water or on the shore. Bill asked, "How deep is the water out there?

"Oh, you can probably walk out a hundred yards and it won't be up to your waist," Dennis said. "And it's so salty that nothing lives out there. Nothing to fish for, no waves, and a rocky shore are about all you'll get here . . . but it is nice to look at."

Everyone nodded in agreement and Tom asked the boys what brought them out here and how long they were staying. Allen said, "We were just studying the map and thought it looked interesting. We haven't made any plans at all; we just go where the road takes us." Again, everyone nodded as if they totally understood that concept.

Allen and Bill both expected one of the four to ask them where they were from, but no one did. Neither did any of the four volunteer any information about themselves, other than their first names. Silently, Allen was wondering if Hazel and Johnny were married, but neither of them had on any rings at all. Bill was wondering about Dennis and Tom: Why were two men in their sixties living together in an RV on the shores of the Salton Sea? Plus, he was wondering if any of the other four were curious about them. Why two men were traveling around the country together in a small camper? If any of them did wonder about that, the subject never came up.

As the sun started setting, both sets of neighbors meandered back to their own homes. Johnny said, "We usually sit out in our chairs at night and talk. Be glad to have you guys join us if you want to "

Allen answered, "Sounds great, thanks. We'll see you later, then."

The boys changed their clothes and put on shorts because they wanted to walk down to the water before total darkness set in. With each step they took towards the water, the briny smell grew stronger and stronger. Allen asked, "So, is the entire sea salt water?"

"I guess that's why they call it the Salton Sea. Hard to understand how it could be so salty this far inland." Bill added.

Even though they could smell the salt in the air and in their minds they knew it was salt water, they still had to taste it to be sure. They each took a small handful of the water and tasted it, then quickly spit it out. It was worse than any ocean water they'd ever tasted.

Later that evening, as Allen and Bill were sitting out in their chairs, their neighbors also came out and brought their lawn chairs over so all six could sit together and talk. A few jokes were told, then Dennis appeared to light a cigarette—except it wasn't a cigarette. Allen and Bill both worked at RJ Reynolds Tobacco Co. their entire professional lives; they knew what tobacco smelled like. This wasn't tobacco.

Dennis took a long pull, then passed the "cigarette" to Hazel, who inhaled deeply, then passed it to Tom and Johnny. When Johnny finished, he passed the "cigarette" to Bill, who never moved. Johnny said, "It's good stuff, straight from Mexico."

Bill replied, "I think I'll pass." Johnny then tried to hand it to Allen, who started to reach across Bill to accept it, but Bill pushed his arm back and said, "He'll pass, too."

“Suit yourselves.” Johnny said, “It’s good stuff, takes all your cares away.”

Allen looked over at Bill, who answered, “I’m sure it will but we’ll stick to our Coors Lights for now.”

As the night progressed, the other four passed “cigarettes” between themselves all evening. At one point, Hazel got up and went over to her RV and started playing a CD of The Grateful Dead. She danced by herself for a few minutes, but since she was in her mid-sixties, a few minutes was all she could dance. Allen and Bill enjoyed their company and the comradery of people from their generation. Allen was secretly thinking he wished he could somehow just take one toke without Bill seeing him; Bill was wondering if he’d ever get the “cigarette” smell out of his clothes.

The boys rose early the next morning, before any of their neighbors even thought of stirring, and discussed whether to stay another night. Allen thought it might be fun but Bill said, “You can’t fish here, you really can’t go swimming, the water stinks pretty bad, and you know they’re doing something illegal, don’t you?”

Allen smiled at him and said, “Okay, grandpa. Pack up and we’ll head out before the devil inside you talks you into doing something that might turn out to be fun.” Bill didn’t respond . . . he wanted to, but he didn’t.

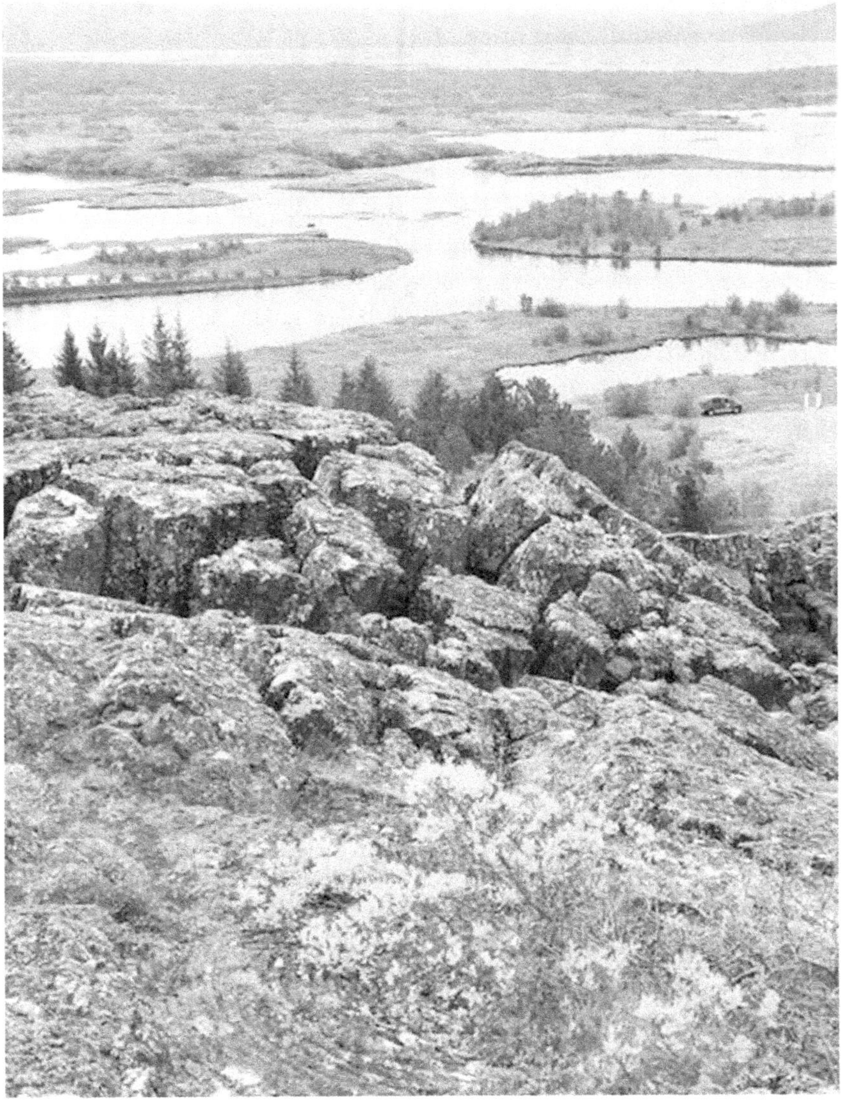

11

NEITHER OF THEM WANTED TO GO into Los Angeles, so they decided they'd bypass the city and continue up north. They stopped at a roadside diner for breakfast and to formulate their plans for the day. Bill ordered coffee, with eggs, bacon, and toast. Allen ordered the large stack of pancakes and a side order of bacon with his coffee. Their waitress was a young lady, maybe in her mid-twenties, with a completely bald head. When she took their order, Bill said, "Maybe she had cancer and she's taking chemo."

Allen shook his head and added, "That ain't from chemo. You can see a little stubble around the edges; she shaved it off."

"Why would a young girl shave all her hair off? That's crazy!"

Allen answered, "I guess she just doesn't want to be boring." The young lady came back to refill their coffee cups and Allen simply couldn't help himself, so he asked, "Young lady, we're curious, would you mind telling us why you have no hair?"

She smiled and replied, "I had mousy brown hair that I didn't like and I wanted to be a blonde. The problem is that I'm stuck between 'I need to save money' and 'you only live once.' So, here I am." Allen nodded, whereas Bill was too dumbfounded to make any response. She smiled again and said, "My name's Teri, one 'r' and one 'i.' Your food will be right out."

Bill looked at Allen and said, "Well, I guess that makes sense. We are, after all, in California."

Teri brought their food and refilled their coffee cups again while the guys discussed their plans. When they finished eating, Bill excused himself to visit the restroom. When he returned from the bathroom, he found Allen eating a large piece of blueberry pie with ice cream . . . after he'd already eaten breakfast. He stared at his friend and asked, "What in the world are you doing?"

Allen finished swallowing, then said, "I'm eating this in case I get hungry later."

Bill reached down and picked up another packet of sugar from the table and hit Allen in the arm with it and said, "I'm going to pay the bill. Make sure you visit the bathroom before you leave."

Allen looked back at him and said, "Is it safe for me to go in there yet?"

There were two options on their drive northward: inland, through the lower Central Valley and visit Death Valley National Park and King's Canyon National Park, both of which they missed on their last trip, or go back to the coast and drive up the Coast Highway to Monterey. Even though they had never seen the two national parks, which were inland, and they had been on the coast highway before, it was still an easy choice: the coast was incredibly beautiful and simply too alluring to pass up. They decided to bypass all the congestion around Los Angeles and make their way over to the coast, north of the city, at Santa Barbara.

The drive was easy and exciting. Each guy remembered their last time on the California coast and they were both looking forward to it again. During the drive, Bill asked Allen about his two grown kids and how he was getting along with them. Allen answered, "We get along pretty good . . . I leave them alone and they leave me alone. It's not really that bad, it's just that they live so far away it's hard for us to be close. Plus, they were always closer to their mother anyway. They call and send cards but we only see each other about twice a year. The sad thing is that twice a year is probably all we could handle. I know they love me and I love them, we just have nothing in common, except their mom." Allen started to say something else but changed his mind, then asked Bill, who had no children: "What about you? Anybody but the ranger thinking about you while you're gone?"

Bill smiled at the mention of the ranger. He hoped she was thinking about him. She hadn't emailed him in a couple of days and he was a little worried about that. He glanced over at Allen and answered, "You know, when you're twenty-five, you really care what everybody thinks. When you're fifty you stop caring what everyone thinks, and when you're seventy you finally realize no one was ever thinking about you in the first place." Bill was certain Allen would enjoy this little bit of humorous wisdom . . . but Allen didn't comment, he only frowned a little and then nodded.

Along the drive to the coast, Bill wanted to stop at one place and see the site where the old television show Wagon Train was filmed. They stopped and walked around, got bored, and to Allen's credit, he kept his mouth shut, which was hard for him to do. Then, a few miles later Allen wanted to stop at a homemade Ice cream stand on the side of the road. Allen got a big cup of peach ice cream and Bill got a small cup of vanilla. They sat on a bench eating their ice cream and watching the traffic pass by. A mutt of a dog soon came up to them and sat down at their feet, looking up at them. Bill said, "I wonder what he wants?"

Allen answered, "I guarantee you he doesn't want any vanilla ice cream." Bill turned to look at Allen, who continued, "He'd probably rather go eat some grass or smell where some other dog just peed."

"What's wrong with vanilla ice cream?"

Allen shook his head and said, "Ain't nothing wrong with it, grandpa. There just ain't nothing right with it either. It lacks excitement and flavor and taste . . . sort of like you."

Bill said, "Okay, Mr. Know-it-all, let's just see about that." He still had about a quarter cup of the ice cream left, so he sat the cup down on the ground in front of the dog. The old dog sniffed the cup, then looked up at Bill, who said, "Go ahead, boy, it's okay." He first licked it a little, then he quickly lapped it up and started chewing the cup it came in. Bill was proud. He looked at Allen and said, "See, I guess you'll have to change your opinion of vanilla ice cream now, won't you, old man?"

Allen ate a spoon full of his peach ice cream and replied, "My opinion may have changed, but not the fact that I am right." He took the last spoon full of ice cream he had and held it for the dog to lick. Then said, "Let's hit the road."

Bill smiled and said, "Well, I guess I win then don't I?"

Allen stopped walking and looked over at his friend and replied, "Let me teach you something that may come in handy during your life: It does not matter whether you win or lose, what matters is whether I win or lose!" Before Bill could think of a response, Allen hopped in the passenger side of the Silverado and shut the door.

They made it to the coast of California and picked up US 1 North, which would take them all the way up to Monterey. It was getting late in the day and they found a roadside diner with a great view of the ocean. They sat down and looked at the menu while taking in the vast panorama of the Pacific Ocean. Their waitress, an unassuming middle-aged woman, soon came over and took their order. Bill ordered a vegetable plate and Allen ordered a hamburger steak with fries. They sipped their Diet Pepsi and gazed out the window, just relaxing after a long day. Soon, their food came and the waitress had Bill's plate of vegetables and then sat down another plate of vegetables in front of Allen.

Bill looked at Allen, who was expecting the hamburger steak he'd ordered, and Allen said, "I don't think this is what I ordered young lady."

The waitress, whose nametag read Andra, frowned deeply and said, "Correct me if I'm wrong, but didn't you two order the same thing?"

Bill started to say something, but Allen jumped in and answered, "Yes, you are correct, Andra. I'm good . . . thank you."

When Andra strutted away, Bill said, "You ordered the hamburger steak, not the vegetables."

Allen nodded and replied, saying, "Let me teach you a valuable lesson, son. When a woman says, 'Correct me if I'm wrong,' do not under any, I mean any circumstances, do it." They both nodded and ate their vegetables like the good old boys they were. Andra even got a nice tip at the end of the meal.

Bill googled "campgrounds" and they finally found one with a view of the ocean, which is what they wanted. There were others closer and less expensive but closer and less expensive is not what they were looking for. They were looking for beauty, scenery, eminence, and magnificence. There were no fires allowed here in southern California because the threat of wildfires was too great, but that was alright. Their camp was located on a small bluff about seventy-five yards from the ocean. It appeared that the campground itself was only about half full. As they drove in they noticed the license plates on all the vehicles and only saw one from outside of California. Apparently, most tourists are not camping. Bill and Allen were happy they were camping. Although their little cots were not as comfortable as the beds in a Holiday Inn, the scenery was incomparable.

A sailboat floated by as the sun set, turning the entire western world into shades of golden red. There were absolutely no clouds as the guys watched in pleasure as the sun slowly dipped down into the ocean. After the edge of the sun actually touched the horizon, it seemed as though it took no time whatsoever to disappear out of view. No words were exchanged during this period; their visionary senses were on overload and any supplemental communications were unnecessary.

As they started on their second Coors Light of the evening, Bill lit the little lantern they had when their conversation began. It wasn't long before Allen got around to asking his serious question of the evening. Bill knew it was coming; he always let Allen work his way into it. Allen asked, "Bill, you know I've been having fun with those two old girls back home, and I know that you know what I mean by 'having fun.' And, it is fun! Why does God say that sex isn't good? I don't understand that."

Bill wasn't expecting that question. He wished he'd had a little campfire so he could stir the ashes a bit as he thought. Finally, he said, "Buddy, God doesn't disapprove of sex . . . that's ridiculous. God created sex. One of the ways that husbands and wives express their love is through the sexual union. It doesn't have to be a dirty word. It doesn't have to be a taboo subject. It's something that can be enjoyable and pleasurable. But the only place that God will bless it is within the boundaries and safety of a marriage relationship. Outside of marriage, sex can be an extremely destructive thing. We need to keep sex in its proper place."

Allen listened and then said, "But Bill . . . is it really that bad a thing?"

Bill said, "Hold on a minute." He grabbed his iPad and started googling something, then said, "Listen to this: Fatherless sons are 300 percent more likely to be incarcerated in state juvenile institutions. Sixty-three percent of teenagers who attempt to commit suicide live in fatherless homes. Seventy-one percent of high school dropouts are from fatherless homes. Ninety percent of all runaways and homeless children are from fatherless homes. Eighty-five percent of all youths sitting in prison grew up in a fatherless home. Sex outside of marriage leads to these types of things, son. I know this is not what you wanted to hear, but it is what it is."

Allen said, "You're right, it isn't what I wanted to hear. But I ain't gonna be having no fatherless children. Besides, I know what you're thinking when you see that ranger up at Lake Superior . . . and don't tell me you're not!"

"You got it all wrong, buddy. I'm not telling you anything. I'm only repeating what the Bible says. You're a grown man and able to make your own decisions."

Allen took his last drink of Coors Light and answered, "Yeah, well . . . I don't want to end up down there just because I had a little fun with old Sophie."

Bill smiled and said, "Well, why don't you try having a different kind of fun with old Sophie?"

Allen crushed his beer can and replied, "A different kind of fun? Have you seen her bazoongas?"

Bill picked up a twig and threw at Allen, and they both laughed. Then, they both thought. One thinking about big bazoongas and the other one thinking about a lady ranger up at Lake Superior.

12

THE NEXT DAY THEY DROVE ALONG THE COAST HIGHWAY, which gave them continuous panoramic views of the ocean to one side and the coastal range mountains on the other. It was hard for them to imagine a more scenic or fun drive. Just before they came to San Luis Obispo, the road climbed up towards some rolling hills and eventually they passed through some low-hanging clouds for a short period. Allen was driving at the time and remarked, "I hope we don't hit a hailstorm up here."

"A hailstorm?" Bill exclaimed, "Why in the world would you think that?"

"Hailstorms can come up anytime and be dangerous if you're not prepared."

Bill looked over at him and said, "Sometimes I think you've completely lost your mind."

Allen shot back, "Hailstorms can be dangerous! There was one that killed over a thousand people one time."

"One hailstorm killed over a thousand people? Allen, there is no way in the world I'm believing that."

Allen huffed, "Look it up. It's true."

Bill got out his iPad and googled "weather disasters of the twentieth century." He knew he hadn't heard of anything weird like that during this century. There were all sorts of strange weather occurrences but none involving large numbers of deaths caused by hailstorms. Bill closed his iPad and said, "I didn't see anything. You're dreaming again, grandpa."

Allen said, "It happened! I remember it from college." Allen majored in history at Appalachian State, he sounded sure of himself.

Bill said, "I looked at every weather disaster for the last century and a half . . . nothing!"

"Century and a half? No, numbnuts . . . this happened back around the 1300's. Look it up."

Bill opened the iPad again and googled back to that time frame. Sure enough, during the Hundred Year War between France and England, English forces were stranded in the open when trying to fight the French when a big storm with huge hailstones came up and killed over a thousand men. It was hard to imagine that. It was even harder for Bill to imagine that Allen had remembered it. He closed the iPad again and Allen said, "Well?"

"I found it. You were right."

Allen beamed a big, bright smile as they emerged from the clouds back into the sunlight, just outside of San Luis Obispo, California.

North of San Luis Obispo they started looking for an interesting place to stop and eat. The highway had been alternating between sea level and rising up into the low mountains. As it leveled off again at the ocean, they saw an old, red, double-decker bus that had been converted into a small restaurant. It was named The Bus Stop and there were several cars in the lot. Allen pulled in a safe spot and asked, "You sure you want to try this place?"

"Sure, you only live once."

"No," Allen replied, "you only die once . . . you live every day."

Bill didn't particularly like that analogy but he didn't say anything. Inside the bus were a few small tables with people sitting and eating. There was one table open next to the bathroom and that's where they sat. A middle-aged man walked over, handed them a menu, and said, "Welcome to my bus, gents. My name's Maury. Can I bring you something to drink?"

Allen said, "Diet Pepsi for me, Maury. Looks like a great place you have here."

Maury smiled and replied, "Yeah, it's pretty cool. Keeps me out of trouble most of the time." He looked at Bill who also ordered a Diet Pepsi, then added, "Special today is the chicken skewers. Best tasting chicken in California. My wife's secret recipe."

Allen asked, "Your wife does the cooking?"

"Oh, no . . . it's just her recipe; my daughter does all the cooking. She's back in the kitchen. My wife is an organic farmer, mostly grows high-end mushrooms." Neither guy had ever heard of high-end mushroom farming, so they didn't ask any questions.

Maury went to the kitchen and his daughter brought the drinks out to the table. She was a light-skinned black girl with a very curvy body and a beautiful smile. She set the drinks down and asked the guys if they were ready to order.

Allen said, "I am, young lady. I'll have those chicken fingers your dad told us about."

She smiled and corrected Allen, saying, "They're actually chicken skewers, not chicken fingers, sir."

Allen nodded and Bill added, "We'll both have the chicken skewers, miss. Thanks."

When she walked away, Allen asked Bill, "You think her mother is black?"

"Of course her mother's black. What sort of dumb question is that?"

Allen said, "Well, she could be adopted."

"So what? Her mother would still be black."

Allen took a few seconds to comprehend that, then said, "I don't understand, but I also don't care . . . so it works out."

The chicken skewers were, indeed, very good. Bill complimented Maury and his daughter as they left to pay the bill. Maury told them of a secluded campground several miles up the coast that sounded interesting. Bill wrote the name down on a napkin and they started on their way. Maury was right; if they hadn't been looking for the campground, they'd have never seen the sign for the entrance. They drove in and found the headquarters building hidden in the trees. A man was sitting on the porch smoking something and listening to some sort of psychedelic music. He signed them in and gave them directions to their spot but didn't say much.

The ocean was visible through the trees as the guys found their location, which was fairly close to the bathrooms. It was still daylight, which made setting up the camper pretty easy. Their campsite had a path through the trees that ended up with an unobstructed view of the Pacific. After everything was set up, they took their chairs and cans of Coors Light down the path to the clearing. As they sat down to relax and watch the sunset, Bill said, "Look over there." He was pointing off to his left at some people walking down the beach.

Allen sat up and asked, "Are they naked?"

"They sure look naked but I don't have my glasses with me." Bill was straining and squinting to see more clearly.

Allen quickly added, "Oh, they're naked alright and they're walking this way."

It seemed to be a group of about six or seven people coming towards them. Since neither guy knew what to do, they did nothing. It soon became evident that all seven people were naked and old. There were four women and three men, all over sixty, and all wearing nothing but sandals and grins. They came up to the guys and one lady said, "Hello, boys Care to join us for a walk?" Neither guy responded so the lady asked, "You guys okay?"

Allen was too busy staring, so Bill answered, "Yes, ma'am, we're fine. We're just a little surprised, that's all."

One of the men spoke next, saying, "Surprised at what?"

Allen looked at Bill, who looked back at the woman who spoke first, then Bill said, "I guess by your appearance. We weren't expecting that."

The woman said, "Why not? This is a nude beach, boys, for seniors only. Or didn't you know that?"

Allen quickly stood up and held out his hand, saying, "Nice to meet you, ma'am My name's Allen and that's Bill. We didn't know about the beach but we do now and we love it."

She said, "Well, come and join us. You'll have to take your clothes off though . . . that's the rules."

Bill said, "I appreciate the offer, ma'am, but we've had a long day and we'd just like to sit and relax for a while."

She said, "Okay, boys, but you can't sit out here on the beach like that. If you sit out here, you have to be nude . . . it's the rules."

"Sorry, ma'am, we didn't know. We'll move on back to our camper."

The lady said, "Okay, but if you change your mind, come and join us." They picked up their chairs and Coors Lights and walked back up the path to the camper. As they sat down next to the Silverado, Bill shook his head and said, "California . . . "

Allen smiled and added, "You gotta love it."

After their second beer and trips to the bathroom, they retired to the camper and looked forward to the darkness, where they could talk more freely with each other. Eventually, Allen said, "You know, ever since Barbara died, I feel like I've been shipwrecked."

Bill answered, "Well, we all hope for clear sailing in the sea of life. But we also know that there will be shipwrecks—things that just don't make sense. Don't lose your faith, brother, your faith should be stronger because of it."

Allen asked, "How do you figure that, Bill?"

"Look, there's going to be days when everything is good and it's easy to accept those days. But you know the next shipwreck is just around the corner. It might be a week, or a month, or a year . . . but you know it's coming. You just have to have faith that God is in control and will take you through every storm that comes your way. Have faith, buddy. You'll be fine."

Allen thought for a moment, then said, "Thanks, Bill. I appreciate that." Then thought to himself, "Will I be fine? Will I ever be fine?"

13

THE FOLLOWING MORNING THE GUYS WOKE UP early and walked down the path towards the ocean again. They looked both ways and didn't see any nude people in either direction so they started walking towards the shore. When they got to the point where the waves and sand met, they stopped and stared out across the horizon. It was a quiet and introspective moment or two before Bill asked, "Remember the last time we stood on the Pacific shore and I threw a rock way out into the ocean past your rock?" They had previously had a rock-throwing competition on the last trip in which Bill won every contest.

Allen huffed up and said, "Find you a good one, old man, and let's see how you do now." They both took a few seconds to find a suitable rock, then Allen said, "Go ahead. I need to see how far I have to throw to beat you."

Bill's rock flew through the sea breeze like a shot and landed out past the breakers. He smiled and looked at Allen but didn't say anything. Allen tossed the rock up and down in his hands a few times then turned sideways to throw and suddenly yelled out, "Here come the naked people—let's go!" With that, he turned and started walking quickly up the path towards the camper.

Bill looked up and down the beach but didn't see anything. When he finally caught up with Allen at the camp, he said, "I didn't see any naked people out there. In fact, I didn't see any people at all out there."

"Did you have your glasses on?"

"No."

Allen smiled and said, "See? Saved you again from getting in trouble. Now pack up your stuff and let's hit the road, old-timer."

The road wound through the Santa Lucia Mountain Range with wide-open vistas of the ocean in the distance. There were several spots wide enough for the Silverado to pull off the road so the scenery could be enjoyed as it was meant to be. At one hairpin turn, there was a nice wide area with a couple of picnic tables available. Bill pulled off the road and they took the cooler over to the picnic table and sat down. Each guy had a Diet Pepsi and a pack of Doritos as they stared out at a distant ship moving up the coast. After several minutes, a new BMW pulled off the road and parked next to them. A well-dressed man got out and went around to open the door for a well-dressed woman. They both seemed to be in their forties and were each very attractive—almost like models.

The man and woman stared out at the ocean, then walked over to the vacant picnic table. They looked down at the bench and spoke to each other but didn't sit down. When they looked over, Allen spoke, "Beautiful day isn't it?"

The man replied, "It sure is. I hope you two are enjoying it."

Bill nodded as Allen answered, "Yes, sir, we are. By the way, that's a beautiful car you have there."

The man didn't respond and the woman never even looked their way. Allen and Bill continued drinking their soda and let the couple be alone. After a minute or two, the woman got back in their car and the man continued to stand there and stare into the ocean. Then he looked over at the guys and asked, "What do you do for a living?"

Allen looked down at his Diet Pepsi, then answered, "I breathe in and out."

The man had a quizzical look on his face, then nodded towards Allen, and got in his car. When they drove away, Bill said, "Well, that was weird. I wonder what else the future has in store for us."

Allen smiled and crunched up his Diet Pepsi can, and said, "Bill, the best thing about the future is that it only comes one day at a time now . . . and we can handle that."

They continued sitting on the picnic table long enough to drink a bottle of water and have some cookies as they gazed out beyond the horizon. A few cars and trucks passed them but no others stopped. Bill picked up a rock and threw it down the hill as far as he could, away from the road. He didn't say anything but he did turn and look at Allen, who ignored him. Then Allen asked, "You met Sophie, that old girl that I've been seeing back home. What do you think of her?"

"I'm glad you found someone to spend time with."

"That's not what I asked. What do you think of her?"

Bill didn't really want to answer that question because he thought Sophie was a floozy who was just using Allen because Allen had money. He took so long to answer that Allen said, "Well?"

Bill picked up another rock and threw it down the hill again, then said, "If she wasn't the way she is, you'd be perfect for each other."

As Allen was trying to comprehend the meaning of that statement, a black cat emerged from the roadside and slowly walked across the street, completely ignoring them. Allen said, "I wonder what the significance of that is?"

Bill walked over and sat next to him and replied, "A black cat crossing your path signifies that the cat is going somewhere. That's all."

Allen spit on the ground, then said, "I just don't want to make a mistake with a woman at my age."

Bill answered, "Well, what have you learned from all your history with women?"

"I've learned from all my experience that I've never learned anything from my experience." Then he stood up from the bench and picked up a rock and threw it as hard as he could, up the hill. Neither guy commented.

Then Bill added, "Buddy, the best advice I can give you is to simply 'be yourself.'"

Allen kicked another rock lying on the ground, then said, "'Be yourself' is about the worst advice you can give some people."

The afternoon got away from them before they realized it. After sitting on the picnic bench up in the hills, they drove down to the coast and found an outdoor restaurant where they could eat fish sandwiches, drink a cold Coors Light, watch the ocean, and observe some young people surfing and sunbathing. Less than a hundred yards away was a campground right on the ocean, so they signed up for the night and made sure they could sit out on the beach fully clothed.

The afternoon was spent lounging on the beach, napping, and looking at girls—not necessarily in that order. A man about their age was walking down the beach and walked over to them holding a handful of seashells. He said, "Nice to see some people from my generation out here. Most of the people around here are young."

Allen responded, "It's nice to be here. Do you live here, sir?"

"Yeah, a couple of miles inland."

Bill asked, “Are you retired?”

The man said, “Yeah, I’m retired. I was tired yesterday and I’m tired again today.” It took the guys a few seconds to catch that, but they did. “Okay, fellas . . . have a good day and enjoy this weather.”

He shuffled away looking for more shells and the guys opened up a fresh can of Coors Light. Allen fell asleep first and spilled his beer into his lap, whereas Bill’s beer spilled into the sand. They didn’t care. Napping on the beach in California with your best friend in the world—what could be better

14

AFTER A LEISURELY MORNING OF SITTING in their chairs and sipping coffee while staring into the ocean, it was time to get moving. If it weren't for the reservations at the Seven Gables Inn in Monterey, they would have probably stayed longer. As they were finishing their coffee and lost in their own thoughts, Allen said, "Bill, you know I like being around old Sophie and a few other girls, but I don't ever think I'll feel the love I had with Barbara with any of them. I'm pretty sure that feeling was a once-in-a-lifetime thing. I just don't see that type of love happening again. It gets confusing, Bill. What does the Bible say love is?"

Allen had always relied on Bill's knowledge of scriptures. Allen would go to church and try his best at times, whereas Bill taught Sunday school and several small groups during the week. Allen knew Bill studied the Bible and he often relied on him for understanding and confirmation. Bill poured out the last few drops of his coffee and explained, "The Bible doesn't give us a definition of love, buddy; it tells us what love does. Love is patient. Love is kind. Love is longsuffering. Love doesn't remember the faults of others. It's what love does. So just do loving things."

Allen smiled and answered, "Oh, I'm doing loving things alright. That's not the problem."

Bill smiled back at him and said, "You know, the more I learn about you, the more I like my dog."

"You don't have a dog."

Bill stared over at him and said, "Yes, you're right, but if I did . . . now let's get going."

Allen rose from his chair and said, "Whenever people agree with me I often feel I must be wrong."

They still had one more night before checking in at the Seven Gables Inn so they were in no hurry. They stopped for a late breakfast and pulled off the road at every opportunity to gaze out over the cliffs into the ocean. Around mid-afternoon they arrived in Big Sur, which is a small eclectic town of hippies, ex-hippies, rich people, a few celebrities, and a collection of other strange people. They had visited Big Sur on their last trip but didn't spend much time there. Allen didn't really want to spend another night in the camper; he wanted a nice soft bed with some amenities. Bill was driving and spotted a small hotel back off the road, with a sign that advertised ocean views. He pulled in the dirt parking lot and they went inside and found a room available. Their room did not have an ocean view but the small patio area out back did.

There was no bar and no grill or restaurant at the little hotel, so after several minutes of sitting outside by themselves, they decided to walk towards the little town of Big Sur. One of the first places they came to was a place called The Grateful Dead. They weren't sure what kind of establishment it was but Allen's curiosity caused him to open the door and look in—it was a bar. They entered to find no one else inside except a young, long-haired bartender. Allen ordered them two Coors Lights and they each took a seat at the bar.

The bartender brought the beers over and said, "Anything else?"

Allen answered, "What else do you have?"

"Nothing. Just beer."

Allen looked at Bill, who shrugged his shoulders, and said, "No, we're good."

The young bartender went to the other side of the bar and continued watching FOX news. Allen and Bill reminisced about their earlier trip to the Seven Gables Inn and were hoping they wouldn't be disappointed during this trip. As they were re-telling a story about a woman they'd met at the Inn, the young bartender slammed his fist down on the bar startling them. He was mumbling something they couldn't hear and Allen asked him if he was okay.

He never took his eyes off the television screen and answered, "It's the freaking government! Always trying to run our lives. I wish they'd leave us alone!"

Bill wished Allen could just leave it alone . . . but he was Allen. He couldn't leave it alone. "What's the government done now?"

The young man suddenly turned towards them and said, "The Lord's Prayer is 66 words long. The Gettysburg Address is 286 words long, and there are 1,322 words in the Declaration of Independence. Yet, the government regulations on the sale of cabbage total 26,911 words." Then he slammed his fist down on the counter again and looked back at the television.

Allen looked at Bill who shook his head back and forth very quickly. He understood. After they drank their Coors Lights, a little quicker than they wanted to, they quietly eased out the door as the young bartender never took his eyes off the television screen. Safely outside the bar, Allen commented, "I hope that young man is gonna be okay."

Bill said, "Everyone has a purpose in life. Perhaps his is watching TV."

They walked down the street a couple of blocks and found a nice, family type diner. It was a little early but they decided to go ahead and eat now, then sit out at the hotel patio and watch the ocean later. A pretty young waitress brought them menus and Bill immediately started checking it out. Allen, however, was checking out the young waitress and didn't look at the menu initially.

After a few moments, Bill said, "We need to leave."

Allen finally stopped gazing at the young waitress and looked at Bill, "Why? I like it here."

"Take your eyes off that young girl and look at the menu, numbnuts." Allen opened his menu and saw the various listings of kale, asparagus, cauliflower, chickpeas, spinach, tofu, zucchini, and onion soup. No burgers, no pizza, no chicken, no nothing that they could fathom eating. As they were trying to understand the futility of their predicament, the young waitress came back to take their drink orders.

Allen didn't especially want to leave, because of the waitress, but Bill came to the rescue and said, "Our wives just texted us and they want us to meet them down the street. I'm sorry, young lady, maybe we'll come back later." She smiled and wished them well and both guys watched her walk away—which was the only good thing about this little restaurant.

After walking the streets of Big Sur, the chairs on the patio, plus their cooler full of Diet Pepsi and Coors Light, was a welcome retreat. On the way back to the hotel they picked up a pizza to bring back with them. In honor of the pretty waitress at the vegetarian restaurant, they bought one without meat. When Allen ordered the meatless pizza, Bill asked him, "Are you sure that's what you want?"

"Yeah, I might start being a vegetarian now."

Bill shook his head and asked, "Why? Because of that pretty girl or you just suddenly love animals now?"

"I'm not gonna be a vegetarian because I love animals—that's crazy. I'll be a vegetarian because I hate plants!"

Their vegetarian pizza was delicious. As was the Diet Pepsi they had with dinner and the Coors Light they had after dinner. By then, the sun was setting and once again the entire western world was lit up with yellows and ambers and reds as the sun kissed the ocean and slowly sank down. The beauty of that scene over the ocean never ceased to amaze each guy.

As they were nearly finished with their beers, a woman came out and sat on the patio near them. She wasn't beautiful, but she wasn't ugly either. Bill guessed she was around fifty or so. She kept looking over and eventually Allen said hello to her. It seemed as though that was the invitation she was looking for. She started talking and didn't want to stop. She told them about her life, her ex-husband, her two children, her job, her political preferences, and anything else she could think of. Even Allen couldn't get a word in. She took a small sip of her wine, then continued on again about what a sorry, pathetic man her ex-husband was.

When she stopped to take another small sip of her wine, Allen commented, "I guess you didn't notice all those things about him before you married him, huh?"

She set her glass down and said, "No! I thought that I had finally met Mr. Right. But I had no idea that his first name was Always!" She said she was going up to her room to refill her wine glass, so the boys took that opportunity to make an easy getaway. Allen went to the showers first and Bill checked his email, hoping for something good. It was very good. Ellen had emailed him twice. Bill read each one at least three times and then started typing his response. He was so consumed with thoughts of Ellen that he didn't notice Allen come out of the shower.

Allen took one look at him and saw that big wide grin and Bill typing furiously on his iPad and knew what was happening. He said, "Tell Ellen I said hi."

Bill kept typing and answered, "Okay, I . . . " Then he suddenly realized what had happened and said, "Why do you think I'm emailing Ellen?"

"I don't think it, old man, I know it! Look at that silly grin on your face. That says it all!" Bill's face flushed a little as he stumbled for something to say, but Allen rescued him when he continued, "It's alright. In fact, I'm a little jealous. I wish I had someone who made me smile like that. Keep on typing and tell her I said hello."

Bill did keep on typing, but not saying as much as he wanted to say. He finally closed the iPad and started for the shower, but stopped before he closed the door. He looked back at the iPad lying on the bed, then looked over at Allen, who said, "Go on and take your shower. I'm not gonna read your emails!" Bill nodded and started to close the door when Allen teased him by reaching toward the iPad with his hand. Allen said, "Go on . . . you can trust me." Bill nodded again and shut the door. Four seconds later, he came out, walked over to the bed, picked up the iPad, and went back into the shower.

After their showers, Allen turned on the television but couldn't find anything except soccer to watch, so he turned it off. When the lights were off and things settled down, Allen said, "Bill, if you want us to go up to Lake Superior to see Ellen right now, it's okay with me."

Bill was quiet for a few moments, then answered, "No . . . I want us to keep going. I'm loving this trip, I hope you are. Ellen is . . . important, but not like you might think. She might be more important later but only time will tell. I don't want you to worry about her. Things are fine and we'll see what happens."

Allen was happy to hear that; he was loving the trip as well and didn't want to stop. So, he added, "Well, it's good to hear that but I guess I always knew I was Number 1 with you, anyway."

Bill smiled and replied, "Aren't you a little strange to be Number 1?"

Allen laughed and added, "You have to be odd to be Number 1."

Drowsiness soon overcame them both as thoughts of friendship, Lake Superior, pretty waitresses, and Ellen lulled them off to sleep in a small hotel room on the seaside cliffs of Big Sur, California.

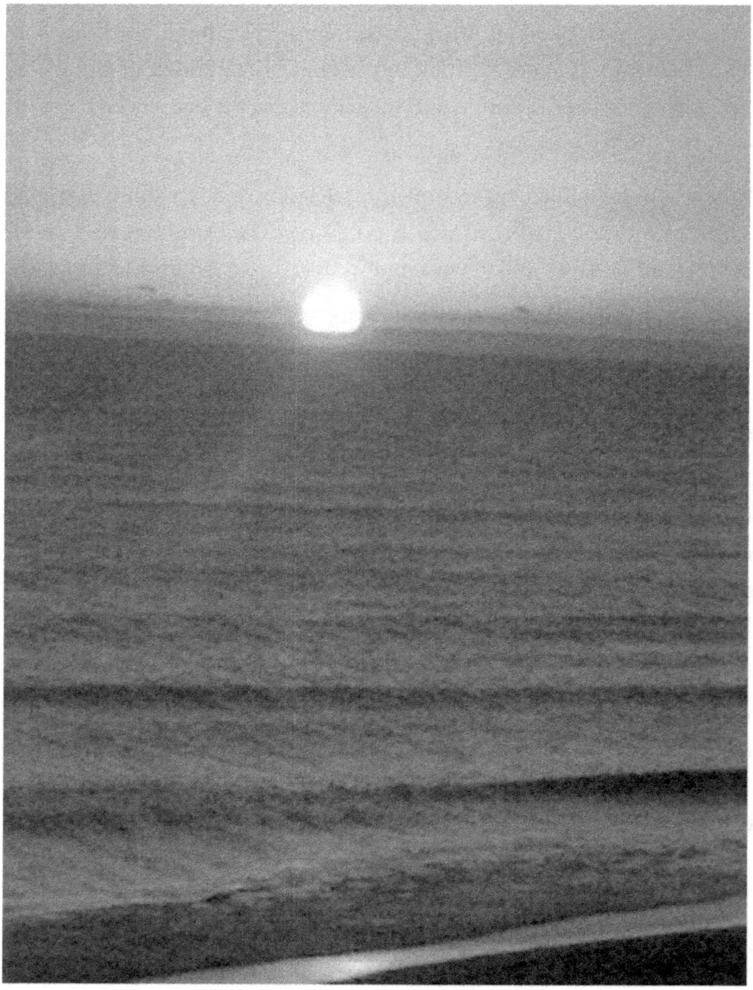

15

THE DAY HAD FINALLY ARRIVED when they could check in at The Seven Gables Inn. However, check-in time wasn't until 2:00 p.m., so they had all morning to make the leisurely drive to Monterey. They stayed on US 1 and made a short stop at Andrew Molera State Park because it looked interesting. It had a few old cabins and several waterfalls with views of the ocean at all times. Bill was driving along the curvy road in the park when they came upon two girl hitchhikers. He didn't apply the brakes but he did take his foot off the gas pedal as he asked Allen, "You want to give them a ride?"

"What if they're serial killers?"

"You think those two young ladies are serial killers?"

Allen said, "Could be. This is California and the way reality is nowadays, you just can't afford to take chances."

Bill stepped back on the gas pedal and replied, "Reality is always controlled by the people who are the most insane."

The highway roughly followed the Big Sur River down towards the ocean and then wound northward where they soon came into the sprawling outer limits of Carmel. They decided to stop there and take a coffee break and walk around the scenic little village for a bit. There was a small café on the beachfront that had outside seating, which appealed to them both. They sat and ordered coffee and a small pastry while watching all the other tourists file by. Bill observed, "I don't remember it being this busy the last time we were here."

Allen only nodded and sipped his coffee. He enjoyed watching the diverse group of people walking the streets. After a few minutes, their young waitress came back to see if they wanted anything else and Allen tried to make conversation with her. "Sure is beautiful. Do you live here, young lady?"

"Unfortunately, yes." She pouted

Allen asked, "You don't like it here?

"Nothing to do . . . it's boring."

"You mean you can't have fun with the beaches, the mountains, the scenery, and all? Surely you have some fun."

She curled her upper lip a bit and replied, "Most of the time I don't have much fun. The rest of the time I don't have any fun at all. You want anything else?"

Allen didn't know how to respond to that, so Bill answered, "No, ma'am, we're good." She sauntered away to bring joy to another table across the patio and the boys continued their people watching. Bill didn't want a second cup of coffee so they wandered on down the side streets of Carmel and passed the Hog's Breath Inn, where they almost enjoyed a drink on their last visit. Allen wanted to walk down to the beach area but when they started walking, the sand was so fluffy and deep that it was coming over and into their shoes, so they stopped and went back to the truck.

After emptying the sand from their shoes, Allen took the wheel and started the journey around the bay to Monterey. Once he was on the highway, he looked quickly over at Bill and noticed he was smiling and looking out the window, at nothing in particular. He started to ask him what he was looking at that was making him smile . . . but he knew.

The streets of Monterey brought back great memories. The bookstore full of Steinbeck novels, the t-shirt store across the street, the world-famous aquarium, and of course, Cannery Row—the setting of one of their favorite books. Neither guy spoke as Allen drove slowly through the winding streets. When he turned the corner and arrived at The Seven Gables Inn, it was like a fairy tale come true for them. Allen stopped the truck and they each consciously counted all the gables at the big house, simply to assure themselves that, yes, this was indeed the place with seven gables.

Allen parked the Silverado and they each got out and stared alternately at the big house then out into Carmel Bay. The inn was on the bay and the sound made by the waves as they lapped onto the big rocks at the shoreline was almost like a sedative to the guys. It took a few moments for them to actually move away from the truck. Bill finally said, "Let's go." Allen followed him up the steps and into the great house. At the registration desk was a big plate of oatmeal raisin cookies. Susan, one of the owners, remembered how much the guys from North Carolina had enjoyed the cookies from their last trip, and she was expecting them.

As Allen took a bite from his cookie, Susan came from the back and greeted them. She hugged them both and they all laughed together. She said, "I've got your room all ready for you. You wanted the room facing the bay with a king-sized bed, right?"

Bill stopped chewing momentarily, but Allen understood the joke Susan was playing on them and elbowed Bill, saying, "She's messing with you, you old prude." Susan and the boys then all laughed together. As each guy was carrying their suitcases up the stairs to the room, Allen asked Bill, "So, you really don't want to share a king-sized bed with me?"

Bill kept climbing the stairs as he answered, "Once upon a midnight dreary, while I pondered weak and weary, over many a quaint and curious volume of forgotten lore. While I nodded, nearly napping, suddenly there came a rapping . . . and the answer is no. Never. Not in your wildest dreams!"

As they came to the door of their room, Allen said, "Since when did you start quoting John David Crow?"

Bill opened the door and kicked over Allen's suitcase as he ignored that question and entered the room. Bill took the queen-sized bed on the right and Allen took the bed on the left. There was a large window between them that was open with a light breeze blowing the curtains as they sat their luggage down. Near the corner was the door that led out to a small balcony overlooking Monterey Bay. Susan had already arranged for two rocking chairs to be placed out there facing the water with a small table between them. On the table was a tin full of raisin oatmeal cookies. She had thought of everything.

Bill lost the coin flip, so it was his job to go out and bring dinner back. There was no better place to go than to sit out on the balcony, sipping a cold Coors Light, eating a good meal, with cookies, and watching the sun set over Monterey Bay. Bill found a small diner near the bookstore and got them chicken dinners to bring back. When he walked in the room, Allen said, "Look at this, you won't believe it."

Allen was sitting at the small desk in the room, with his iPad opened, pointing to the screen. Bill set the food down and walked over to see a full screen-shot of Allen's friend, Sophie, completely topless. The caption at the bottom of the page read, "We're missing you."

After both fellows had stared at the screen for several moments, Bill said, "Quite a surreptitious, cynosure you have there, my friend."

Allen looked over his shoulder at Bill and replied, "Them ain't sins, old man, them's boobs!" They both stared a few seconds longer, then Allen quickly shut the screen down, saying, "You won't let me read your emails, I'm not letting you see mine."

Bill smiled and replied, "I hope you keep that promise."

After things had settled down from the effects of Sophie's email, they took their chicken dinners out to the balcony and started with a Diet Pepsi, leaving the Coors Light for dessert, along with the cookies. The lower the sun dipped into the sky, the larger it seemed to get. Several sailboats made their way into the cove and the temperature seemed to drop a few degrees as they finished their dinner. Not much was said as they enjoyed this reflective time together. Allen still had Sophie's picture on his mind and Bill was hoping he might have an email or two from Ellen waiting on him.

After they had each opened a Coors Light, Allen asked, "Remember old Ed Leigh?"

"Yeah, he was a good guy. Whatever happened with him?"

Allen took a small drink and answered, "His wife died of cancer a few years ago and he moved to Hilton Head. I hear from him occasionally and he says he's 'living the life' down there."

Bill asked, "What does that mean?"

"It means he's lonely, sad, and missing his wife . . . same as us."

Even though they had thoughts of Sophie and Ellen, those words were true beyond comprehension. They each picked up an oatmeal raisin cookie from the table but neither guy took a bite. Neither guy was able to take a bite. So, they sat there and looked at the sun kiss the ocean, on the balcony at the Seven Gables Inn, in Monterey, California.

16

AS USUAL, BREAKFAST AT THE INN was overwhelming. Susan remembered how much the boys enjoyed thick-cut bacon with their eggs and hash browns. When they were finishing their meal, Susan came out and spoke with them. "Good morning, fellas, did you enjoy the breakfast?"

Allen answered, "Susan, how could we not enjoy it? The only thing that would have made it better is if you'd have cooked up a big bowl of grits."

Susan knew what grits were; she just couldn't understand why anyone would want to eat them. So, she ignored that comment and asked them what their plans were for today.

Again, Allen answered. "We're not really sure. On our last trip we visited the aquarium and the museum and walked along Cannery Row. We also drove over to Pebble Beach and took the 17 Mile Drive." When he said this, he looked over at Bill. They had previously had a discussion on the actual length of the 17 Mile Drive, which was, in fact, only thirteen miles long.

Then Bill asked, "Do you have any suggestions for us?"

Susan quickly volunteered, "Why don't you go on the whale-watching boat this afternoon. The whales are migrating and they guarantee that you'll see them."

Allen asked, "How can they guarantee that?"

"Because the whales are migrating up the coast. They come to the same spots every year. If you don't see any whales, they reimburse your money and it costs you nothing."

Bill looked at Allen and he nodded, so it was decided over their third cups of coffee that they would go whale watching. After breakfast, they went back to the room and sat out on the balcony watching the waves crash into the rocks on the shore. They could have done that all day. The rocking chairs on the deck were very comfortable and the temperature was perfect, as it almost always is in northern California. It was a couple of hours before they had to leave for the whale watching, so they relaxed and rocked and talked. The conversation eventually got around to sin and if God would forgive Allen of all his past dalliances. He was having trouble with this. Again, Bill tried to reassure him,

"Look, remember when God kicked Adam and Eve out of the Garden of Eden because Adam sinned?"

Allen remembered that, but not exactly WHY they were kicked out, so he answered, "Yeah, I remember that. Old Adam must've really messed up big-time."

Bill stopped rocking and looked over at his friend and said, "Well, he didn't murder anyone. There were no other people on Earth to murder. He didn't commit adultery, because there were no other women on Earth. He didn't steal anything, because everything was already his. He didn't cheat anyone out of anything and he didn't rob anyone. So, why did he get kicked out of the Garden of Eden?"

Allen had never thought of any of that before, so he truthfully answered, "I have no idea."

"He got kicked out because he disobeyed the direct word from God. God told him not to eat the fruit from the forbidden tree, but he did it anyway. He thought his way was better than God's way—and that, my friend, has been the story of mankind ever since. Whenever men disobey the direct word of God, they always get themselves in trouble. Then, to make matters worse, Adam tried to blame it all on God."

Allen said, "What? What do you mean?"

"When God asked him why he ate the forbidden fruit, Adam said, 'The woman YOU gave me made me do it.' Then God asked Eve why she ate the fruit and she said, 'The serpent YOU put here made me do it.' Then God asked the serpent why he led them both astray but the serpent didn't have a leg to stand on."

Bill waited for Allen to laugh at that little joke, but instead, Allen sat there nodding and staring intently back at Bill. So Bill continued, "So . . . lying, cheating, murder, adultery, none of that stuff got them in trouble—-God would have forgiven any of that. What got them in trouble was not believing His word and ignoring Him."

They both leaned back and started rocking again in silence. Bill may have told Allen a little more than he wanted to hear. After a few silent minutes Allen said, "At least I know now why God made Adam first." Bill looked over but didn't say anything, so Allen continued, "He made Adam first because He didn't want any advice from Eve on how to make Adam." Bill didn't want to laugh but he couldn't help himself.

Then Allen said, "You know what else I learned, buddy? Heels and lipstick will put the fear of God into people." He was on a roll now and continued, "You know, one big difference between men and women is that if a woman says 'smell this,' it usually smells nice."

As they both laughed, Allen held his fist up for Bill to fist-bump him; but Bill punched him in the arm instead. Then they continued their rocking in silence. The kind of silence that isn't awkward. The sort of silence that is comfortable between two life-long friends.

The whale-watching boat held about twenty people, of which Allen and Bill were the oldest by a considerable margin. Allen bought some Dramamine at the ticket office and they both took a pill, just in case. As the boat left the pier, all the passengers lined up on the sides of the boat to see the coast clearly. A man and woman stood next to Allen and told him they were there on their honeymoon. Second marriages for both of them. The man looked to be in his late thirties but the woman seemed quite younger than him. When Allen told the man they were from North Carolina, the woman answered, "Oh, we've been to Myrtle Beach before, haven't we darling?"

Allen started to correct her but Bill elbowed him and whispered, "Shut up."

Her husband then added, "Oh, yeah, we sailed up the coast from Georgia to Washington, D.C., then sailed up the Potomac River. We love the water."

Allen asked where they were from and he answered, "Kissimmee, Florida. Been on the water my entire life."

Again, Allen started to question the man about that statement, since Kissimmee wasn't actually on the water. But, Bill leaned in close to him and said, "Let it go." So he did let it go. He didn't want to but he did.

The man had the strong scent of beer on his breath and bragged about owning a dry-cleaning business and offered to give the boys a discount if they ever got to Kissimmee. Bill knew if he didn't get Allen away from this man pretty quickly that Allen would say something they'd both regret. Bill tugged Allen's arm and said, "Hey, buddy, let's check out the other side and see what view is like over there."

The boat was about halfway out of the bay itself by this point and the waves were picking up. Each guy had to hold onto the railing for stability as they walked. And, they were each very glad they'd taken a Dramamine.

Then, the boat stopped before actually clearing the bay, still within sight of most of the buildings on shore. Bill hoped nothing was wrong with the motor. As everyone was wondering what happened, the captain of the boat came on the loudspeaker to calm all the passengers and assure them this is where they'd spot the whales. No one on board believed him. They weren't far enough from shore for whales to be swimming by; however, the guarantee was made that if they didn't see any whales that their one-hundred-dollar ticket would be fully refunded.

Bill had picked up a brochure in the ticket office about the company and the whales. He looked at it to learn that Monterey Bay dropped from the shoreline to suddenly over six hundred fifty feet. Then only a short distance out in the ocean it dropped again to over a mile deep. Certainly deep enough for any whales. Before he could tell Allen this information, everyone suddenly looked towards the front of the boat to see a massive whale rise a little from the water and blow a stream of mist from its blowhole. Then another whale, then another one, and another one . . . they were appearing all around the little boat. Not menacingly, just curious or probably just passing through.

For about twenty to twenty-five minutes this pod of whales amazed and mesmerized the people on the boat. All the iPhones on board were snapping pictures furiously. One younger couple asked Bill if he would take their picture with a whale in the background. He only had to wait about ninety seconds before he was able to do just that. None of the whales actually rose completely out of the water, like they do on TV commercials, but they did rise enough to clearly see them. Then, just as suddenly as they came . . . they were gone. The engine started up again and the boat headed back to shore.

Everyone was still buzzing over what they'd seen when the man from Kissimmee and his wife came back over. The boat was still rocking a little but not too bad. The man was holding his iPhone out to ask Allen to take their picture, but just as he started to ask, he bent slightly over and puked all over Allen's shoes. The man's wife held him and asked, "Are you alright?" He nodded and they both staggered over to the seats. Neither one of them said "I'm sorry," or made any attempt at an apology. Bill wanted to laugh, he really did, but it was so disgusting that he just couldn't bring himself to make it any worse.

When the boat docked, the man from Kissimmee and his bride stumbled off, still with no apology to either the captain or Allen. The captain quickly hosed down the deck while Allen got some rags from the captain and took his shoes and socks off. He threw them all in a trash can and stayed barefoot while the captain hosed off his legs and feet. A perfectly fine afternoon and beautiful memories all ruined by a man from Kissimmee, Florida.

Back on shore, Bill spotted a small tourist shop and they went in and bought Allen a pair of flip-flops to wear back to the Inn. Fortunately, it was only a few blocks back to their room. When they walked in the door, the smell of oatmeal raisin cookies suddenly lifted their spirits. Allen's scowl turned suddenly into a bright smile. Susan had once again saved the day. They loaded up with cookies and went upstairs. Allen took a long, hot shower. Bill sat outside and ate a cookie . . . and dreamed. He first thought of his wife, "I wish Eliza could've seen that." He opened a Coors Light from their cooler and ate another cookie. Then, unconsciously, he also thought, "I hope Ellen can see that one day."

17

SUSAN HAD TOLD THE GUYS about a food delivery service that would bring food to their room if they didn't want to go out. Bill ordered a country-style steak dinner and Allen ordered the flounder. Each guy was perfectly content to sit out on the balcony in their rocking chairs and watch the waves. They were also anxiously anticipating sundown again. The colors of the sunsets over the ocean were always awe-inspiring. Bill had opened a Diet Pepsi but Allen didn't want anything yet—he was content to rock and look and talk.

Bill asked if Allen had received any more emails from Sophie. Allen smiled and replied, "Yeah, no more pictures though. She told me that she ended up liking me more than she had originally planned."

"Well, do you like her back?"

"I like her back and her front; her other parts are good too . . . if you know what I mean."

Bill turned and stared at him, which meant "Answer the question, numbnuts."

So, Allen said, "I like her alright, but just to have fun with. Nothing serious. I like lots of women. That's the problem . . . I like a bunch of them, but I don't 'love' any of them. I think Barbara ruined me, Bill. I keep comparing them all to her, and of course, none of them can measure up to my Barbara. She was a once-in-a-lifetime woman.

"So now I meet some old gal and have some laughs and other stuff, or until she starts to get serious, then I move on to the next one. You know, at our age, there's a lot more women left than men. A lot of the men have died off and these women are searching for companionship. So, I feel like it's my duty to provide a civic service and make myself available." Allen felt good about his creative justification for womanizing. He was hoping his explanations would help convince Bill that he was not all that bad.

Bill didn't respond. He drank his Diet Pepsi and continued rocking and gazing out at the ocean. Finally, Allen needed to hear something, so he asked, "Well?"

"Well, what?"

"You don't have anything to say after I just spilled my guts out to you?"

Bill set his empty can down on the table and answered, "Yes, two things: If you know you can do better, then do better."

He was silent for a moment and Allen couldn't take the silence, so he asked, "And what's the second thing?"

"Go get us a beer." Allen did as ordered. He went to the cooler and got two ice-cold Coors Lights as he thought to himself, "I knew he was gonna say that."

Allen and Bill usually rose early for breakfast, before most other guests had even awoken; however, when they came down this morning they found two couples sitting at a table near the window. It was hard to tell how old they were . . . anywhere from forty to fifty, and they all had on wedding rings. They were friendly and said hello, then told the guys they were also life-long friends, all the way since middle school. Interestingly enough, each of the couples had started dating their spouses in high school and had never stopped dating all the way through college. One of the women nodded towards her husband and said, "He's the only guy I've ever kissed."

The woman from the other couple said, "Not me. We broke up once in high school and I kissed his friend, Philip, underneath the stands at a football game. He smoked, though, and had terrible breath. I guess I was a real floozy back then." They all laughed at that story, which she'd probably told a thousand times before. When she finished, both couples held hands and looked into each other's eyes. It made Bill a little sentimental and nostalgic . . . Allen wanted to throw up.

One of the men asked, "Where do you two live?"

Bill immediately answered, "Oh, we're not together! I mean . . . we're traveling together, but we're not together—like, you know, together." Before he could stumble any further, Allen came to the rescue,

"He means, we're not gay. Our wives passed away and we're just out seeing the country. Two old friends trying not to get in too much trouble."

The two couples laughed and told the guys they were from San Diego and just loved traveling up into northern California. They were on their way to the wine country for several days before going back home. Allen told them a little about the trip and a lot about their previous trip. He had them all begging for more stories about the adventures they'd been on across the country. One of the men asked Allen to join them for dinner tonight at a restaurant in town so they could hear more stories. Of course, Allen jumped at that opportunity, then looked over at Bill who nodded okay.

The two couples soon took off for the day while the guys enjoyed another one of the delicious breakfasts at the Inn. Susan always had fresh fruit on the table, which the guys loved. The problem was that Bill and Allen both loved the watermelon best. It was always a race to see who could eat the watermelon first. Unfortunately for Bill, Allen usually won that contest and was never remorseful in the least about eating most of the melon. Today, as usual, they both started on the watermelon before they ordered. Allen was seated with his back to the window and Bill was directly across from him, facing the window. They were each filling their faces with the fresh, sweet melon and there was one, rather large chunk left in the bowl. Suddenly, Bill pointed out the window, behind Allen, and said, "Dang, there's a girl out there in a thong."

Allen almost fell out of his chair trying to turn and look out the window. When he did, Bill scooped up the last chunk of the watermelon. When Allen didn't see the phantom girl in the thong, he turned back around to question Bill, only to see his best friend in the world nibbling on the last piece of watermelon from the bowl. Allen's face drooped into a frown as he figured out what had happened to him. Bill put the last little chunk into his mouth and said, "Here . . . wanna lick my fingers?"

It may have been the best breakfast Bill ever had in his entire life. Allen's mind was racing a hundred miles an hour . . . but the watermelon was gone. After they finished eating, Allen got up and went to the juice bar and brought back two glasses of orange juice to the table and said, "Alright, a chugging contest. Let's go."

Bill wiped his mouth with his napkin and got up from the table, then walked away. He didn't win often, except at rock-throwing, and he wanted to savor every minute of it.

The day was filled with window shopping and buying an odd souvenir or two. Allen bought Sophie a John Steinbeck novel called *Sweet Thursday* and Bill bought a small painting of a sunset over the bay. They visited the aquarium again and, as before, were stunned by its size and variety of marine wildlife. A couple of hours of walking around town wore them out. They sat outside a small café and watched sailboats coming in and out of the harbor. Finally, they decided to go back to the room and take a short nap before meeting their new-found friends for dinner later. With a gentle breeze blowing through the window, it took them about two-and-a-half minutes to fall asleep.

They were meeting the two couples at a local Italian restaurant called Vincenzo's. It was right on the bay with large glass windows facing seaward so everyone could sip wine and watch the sun set over the Pacific. The woman who had kissed Philip underneath the stands back in high school insisted they all share a bottle of red wine. Neither Allen nor Bill liked red wine but they were trying to be polite. Oddly enough, none of these four people, except one of the men, had ever been out of the state of California. And he had only been to Phoenix once for business.

Bill found this fact hard to comprehend, so he asked again, "You've really never been out of California?"

The other woman replied, "Why should we? California has everything. Beaches, mountains, deserts, large cities, wine country, wilderness, national parks . . . why should we go anywhere else?"

The other four all drank red wine as Allen started his commentary to make them understand. He described the Grand Canyon, as best as a human being could. He told them about fishing for salmon in Oregon, the stunning views of Mt. Rainier, and the Space Needle in Seattle. He chronicled the drive across Washington and Idaho and illustrated and narrated Yellowstone National Park. He told of the mountains, the geysers, the buffalo, and the views of the Grand Teton Mountains. He became reverent in his description of the battlefield at the Little Big Horn. He told of the Great Lakes and the vastness of Lake Superior, without mentioning Ellen.

Then he described Niagara Falls so that it seemed alive. He told of the little town of Mystic, Connecticut, and of visiting Mount Vernon and hearing stories of George Washington. By the time he finished his storytelling, the wine bottle was empty and there was complete silence at the table. Bill was very proud of his friend. He secretly wished he could've taped the entire speech. The waiter came and asked if they wanted more wine, and not until then was the spell broken. One of the men said, "Wow! That was really something, right honey?"

The other woman, who had never kissed anyone in her life but her husband, said, "I guess so . . . but I'll stay in California."

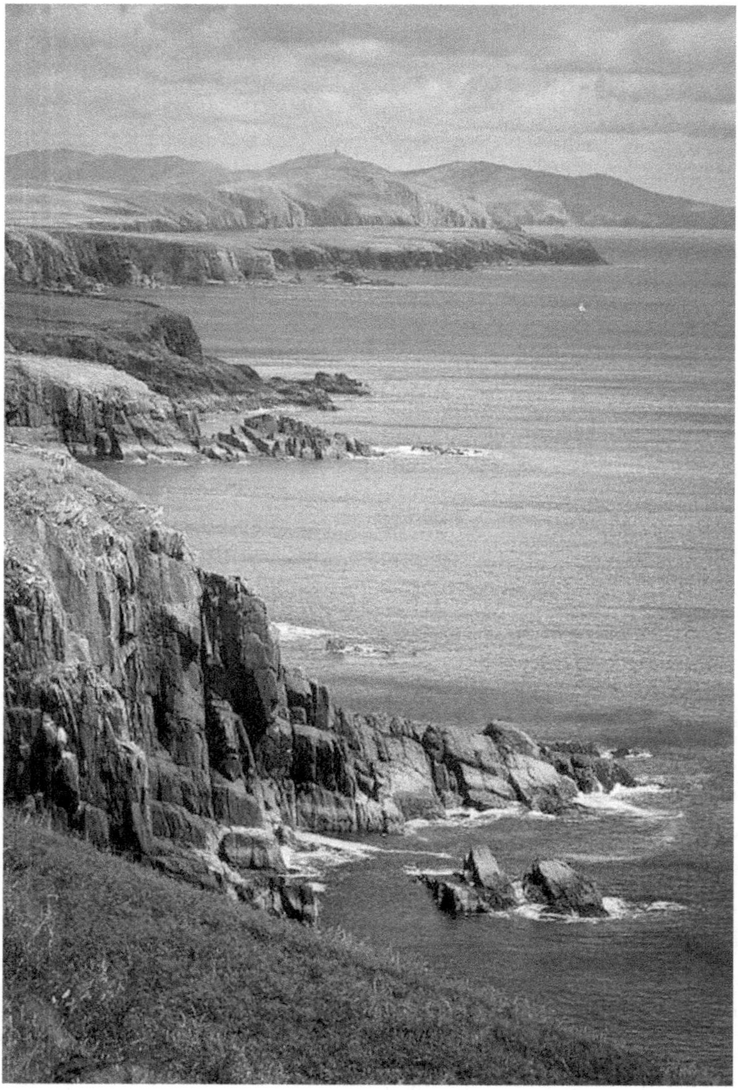

18

BACK IN THE ROOM, each guy checked his emails. Allen had an email from Sophie, with no pictures, that promised him a "good time" when he returned. Bill had two more emails from Ellen. She told him of a storm on Lake Superior that had caused some damage. Then she asked him if he remembered their "nature walk" they took on a small deserted island off the coast of Lake Superior. This nature walk was supposed to only take an hour and a half. They were gone for nearly four hours. Bill never explained the time lapse to Allen, even though Allen asked him about it nearly a hundred times. Each time he was asked what he and Ellen did, his answer was always the same, "We went on a nature walk." That's all he would say.

As the lights were turned off, Allen thought of Sophie and Cynthia and Pam, but his mind always came back to his deceased wife, Barbara. He could never stop thinking about her. Ever. Bill thought of Ellen and what might happen when they met again. Would they feel the same as they did before? Could he feel the same as before? What could possibly happen if the spark was still there? Ellen had told him before that she would never leave her home in Lake Superior. He didn't think he could ever leave Winston-Salem. How could this relationship ever work out? Did he want it to work out? Could he ever stop thinking about Eliza?

At breakfast, Susan told them that the two couples had checked out and were on their way to the wine country. That got them to thinking . . . they'd always heard of the wine country but had never been there. So, it was decided, while eating pancakes and watermelon, that they would visit the wine country next. When Susan came back to check on them, Bill asked her about the wine country, she replied, "Do you guys like to drink wine?"

"Not really. We mostly just like beer."

"If you don't like wine, why do you want to go there?"

Allen said, "If it's sweet and tastes good, I'll drink it."

Susan said, "Honey, none of it is sweet. This isn't North Carolina. You're talking about high-class snobbery at its best. The wine up there is dry, dry, and drier.

Unless you like that stuff or you just like looking at grapevines mile after mile, why would you want to go?"

Over an apple tart dessert and a cup of coffee, they altered their plans. No wine country. They would spend their last day in Monterey walking around town, sitting out by the ocean having a drink, and dining at a seaside restaurant. It was only a two-block walk to the middle of Cannery Row, which made it very accessible for two guys with troublesome knees. They bought some chocolate from a specialty store, then had homemade doughnuts from another place, and finally settled in after lunch at a bar with outdoor, seaside tables.

They were seated next to a man wearing a bow tie and coat, sitting with his wife, who was wearing blue jeans and sandals. Usually, it was Allen who started conversations with strangers but as soon as the guys sat down, the man said, "Good afternoon, gentlemen. How are you today?"

Allen spoke right up, "We're doing great, sir. I hope you are."

The woman was reading a magazine and never looked up from the pages but the well-dressed man replied, "Yes, we are. What are you two statesmen doing to keep your minds fully invested these days? Certainly, you're not just reading magazines wasting your time away, are you?"

Bill immediately thought, "Allen, don't get involved in this!" But it was too late.

"Well, sir, I enjoy a good magazine from time to time, but I also enjoy the simple pleasures of life, like figuring out the algorithms of the stock market and which IPO's may have the best ROI."

The man was slightly taken aback, but not for long. He introduced himself, "My name is Dr. Dennis O'Bryant and I'm a doctor of international studies at the University of Santa Cruz. This is my wife, Mrs. O'Bryant."

She then looked up from her magazine and said, "My name is Pansy but my friends call me Punk."

The Doctor quickly corrected her, saying, "Her name is Mrs. O'Bryant."

Bill said, "Nice to meet you Mrs. O'Bryant."

Allen added, "Good afternoon, Punk."

Dr. O'Bryant did not appreciate this latitude Allen had taken.

Bill quickly changed the subject to ask, "Exactly what is international studies, Dr. O'Bryant?"

"I try to teach the younger generation the importance of international financial implications and how each country's economy, directly and indirectly, affects its neighbors and all other countries around the world. It's a challenge if I must say so myself." He smiled at his self-righteous remark.

Allen nodded and looked very serious as he asked, "The University of Santa Cruz . . . is that an online university?"

"It most certainly is not! It is, in fact, one of the most prestigious and distinguished schools in the entire University of California system."

Allen said, "Oh . . . I'm not familiar with them. What's their nickname?" Allen knew exactly what their nickname was, he just trying to get under the skin of the renowned doctor.

He replied, "Sports names are not the issue here. We are a school who has produced Rhodes Scholars, senators, and congressmen, as well as prominent and respected graduates around the world."

Allen couldn't stop, "That's great, but what's your nickname . . . I can't seem to remember?"

Before the good doctor could continue his argument, Punk spoke up and said, "It's the Banana Slugs."

Allen acted very surprised and repeated, "Banana Slugs? Really?"

The doctor suddenly stood up and grabbed the magazine from Punk and said, "We have to go. Good day, sirs."

He stormed away as Punk looked at the boys and smiled while whispering, "Thank you."

When they were alone, Bill said, "Sometimes, I just want to smack you, and other times I want to shake your hand." When he said that, he reached his hand over and Allen shook it as they both giggled at the entire affair.

In honor of their last day in Monterey, they ordered Iron Maidens to toast the evening's sunset with. As they started on their second Iron Maiden, they added an order of nachos as well. It was so relaxing on the oceanfront, they didn't need to talk. They just observed: A table with two college kids holding hands; another table with a couple their age whispering to each other; and all sorts of various

Californicators strolling down the boardwalk, trying to figure life out, here on the left coast.

They finally made it back to the Inn to find that Susan had once again spoiled them with cookies. Allen took two Coors Lights out on the balcony and waited for Bill to join him. When Bill didn't come out after a few minutes, Allen looked inside the room to see Bill smiling and typing on his iPad. Allen would let him finish, as he wished he had someone special to type a message to.

The sun had set and it was a little cool as Bill came out and brought them both a jacket to put on. Allen didn't mention Ellen and Bill didn't either. They ate cookies and talked about their boyhood, then college high jinks, and finally their deceased wives . . . it always got around to that. It had to get around to that.

After the required silence, Allen asked Bill if he had regrets about the way things worked out with his wife. Of course, everyone has some regrets; so did Bill. He didn't exactly answer that question when he said, "Nobody who has ever given their best has regretted it." Allen didn't really know what that meant, so he left it alone. Then Bill asked him, "Have you had the chance to learn from your mistakes?"

Allen set his Coors Light bottle down and thoughtfully replied, "Yes, I've learned a great deal from my mistakes, and I'm sure that I can repeat them exactly."

They both smiled and Bill reached over with his Coors Light bottle and clanked it against Allen's, as they watched the waves crashing on the shore, while they sat on the balcony of the Seven Gables Inn, in Monterey, California.

19

BILL AND ALLEN BROUGHT THE INN'S OWNER, Susan, a gift from North Carolina to give her when they left. It was a nice sweatshirt that had the state outline of North Carolina on the front, with the word "Home" written on it. As they were finishing their last breakfast, she came to check on them and refill their coffee cups, when they gave her the present. She started crying and hugged their necks, then went into the restroom and put the sweatshirt on. She insisted on having her picture taken with each guy as she was wearing the shirt.

She had a large tin full of cookies for them as they were checking out and made them promise to come back soon. They made that promise, each one secretly hoping he would be able to fulfill it. They loaded up the Silverado with their luggage and the souvenirs they had bought and put the cookies on the console up front between them. Bill took one long last look up at the balcony where they loved sitting, while Allen stared across at the waves splashing against the rocks before he got in the truck. Susan started crying again as the boys pulled away from the Inn. Neither one of them spoke as they left, to avoid crying in front of each other.

When they finally were away from Monterey, Bill looked at his friend and asked, "You alright?"

Allen looked back at him and answered, "I've got nothing to do today but smile."

Since they ruled out visiting the wine country, Bill had suggested they visit Yosemite National Park. It wasn't too far away, just east of them in central California. Susan's breakfast, and the cookies, still had them full around lunchtime, but they did stop for gas and to stretch their legs in the little town of Modesto, California. It seemed to be a quiet little town in the middle of California's central valley, near the Tuolumne River. Just entering town was a large arch welcoming visitors to the city.

Bill pulled the Silverado into a large gas station/restaurant type place for them to refuel and go to the bathroom. Allen went inside to get them a couple of Diet Pepsis for the road and started talking to the lady cashier. Allen said, "Nice little town you have here."

She huffed a little and replied, "I wouldn't call two hundred thousand people so little. Would you?"

Allen could tell he may have unintentionally insulted her, so he tried to make up for it. "No, I meant that it's very pretty and has a nice feel to it. And I really liked the arch as we drove in. It makes it feel like a hometown."

She eased up a bit and said, "Yeah, the arch is nice. My name's Gail. Where are you from?"

Allen pointed out to Bill, who was standing beside the truck and said, "We're from North Carolina, just traveling around the country. Thought we might ride over to Yosemite."

Gail nodded and replied, "I've never been east but my sister, Linda, used to live in Georgia . . . she loved it there."

Allen smiled and said, "Well, we love it here in California. You have a beautiful state."

"It used to be," Gail remarked, "until the government started ruining everything."

"What do you mean, 'ruining everything'?"

"You know, hiking up taxes and taking away our freedoms. It's awful what they're doing."

Allen wasn't sure what he could say without offending Gail, so he just nodded and kept silent. But she didn't; she continued, "Giving money and power to the government is like giving whiskey and car keys to teenage boys. It's never gonna end up good."

Allen kept nodding and slowly shuffled towards the door. He waved and hurried over to the truck and hopped in the passenger side, saying, "Let's go, old man." Bill took one final deep breath of the fresh air and they continued down the road towards Yosemite.

They arrived at the entrance about mid-afternoon, early enough to secure one of the sought-after camping sites for the night. The drive to the campground was awe-inspiring. The view of the famous "half dome" was visible for miles. It wasn't as crowded as the Grand Canyon, but it was close. The little two-lane road was packed with cars, trucks, campers, bicycles, and walkers. But it was beautiful. The road followed the river with views of the many waterfalls, high cliffs, deep valleys, and ancient giant sequoias. It was more than either guy had imagined.

The campground was located next to the Merced River, which ran through the park. It was a fairly shallow, clear, swift-moving river which reminded the guys of the small stream in Washington where they went salmon fishing on their last trip. There was plenty of daylight left but they wanted to be out of the truck. After the camp was set up, Allen took the two camp chairs and Bill brought some drinks and snacks down to the banks of the river. Flowing water always seemed to rest the soul and soothe the inner spirit.

It was fun doing nothing. After several minutes they started reliving the days just spent at the Seven Gables Inn. Then, eventually, the conversation got back around to women—just like it always does. Bill didn't volunteer much, except to say that he and Ellen were in constant email contact. Allen admitted he'd been having a few rather nefarious conversations with Sophie and one other unnamed lady back home. Bill asked, "Don't you feel bad leading those girls on like that? What if they're expecting more than you're willing to give right now?"

"Oh, I'll give 'em everything I can . . . you can rest assured of that."

"You can joke about it, Allen, but you know what I mean. Don't you ever think about it?"

That comment made Allen reflect on just exactly what he was doing. Was it wrong? Should he stop leading these girls on? Then his introspective thoughts became more serious. He was silent for a little too long, so Bill said, "Don't agonize over it. I was just wondering what you thought about all that stuff."

After a couple of minutes, Allen answered, "Sometimes I lie awake at night and ask myself, 'Where have I gone wrong?' Then a voice says to me, 'This is going to take more than one night.'"

Bill reached down and picked up a small pebble from the ground and threw it in Allen's lap, and said, "Boy, you ain't no good at all, you know that?"

"Yeah, Bill, I do . . . I sure do."

After a few minutes, Allen went back to the truck and brought the rest of Susan's cookies back with him. Sitting on the river bank, sipping Coors Light, and eating cookies was an afternoon that would be hard to beat. Several other campers settled in but none came down to where they were sitting. They had almost fallen asleep in their chairs when they heard a noise. They looked downstream to see a man and woman wading down the river—in the water, not on the banks. They looked to be in their early twenties and the girl seemed to be very pretty.

When they came to where the guys were, they stopped and waved, and the young man asked, "Is this the campground?"

Allen still seemed a little groggy, so Bill answered, "Yes, it is. Are you staying here?"

The guy replied, "No, sir, we're not. We're just traveling through the park and checking to see exactly where we are."

Allen then came to life and asked, "You're walking through the park in the river?"

The girl answered, "Not exactly. We just took it as a short cut to cut off a few miles. We're headed over to El Capitan where we're meeting some friends." El Capitan was a vertical rock formation over three thousand feet tall in the northern part of the park. Then, the girl asked, "Do they sell any food here?"

"No, not here in the campground, but we'll be glad to share some cookies with you if you're hungry."

The man and woman looked at each other, then the girl said, "Really?"

"Yeah," Allen replied, "come on over." So, they climbed out of the water and sat on the grass near the guys. Bill passed the tin full of cookies over to them and they each took one. Allen said, "Take more than one; we're stuffed with 'em anyway." So they did.

The young guy introduced them as Caden and Sophie.

Allen quickly said, "Sophie? I've got a girl . . . I mean, I've got a friend named Sophie."

Bill jumped in and said, "That's right, tell them about your friend, Sophie. She's an interesting woman. I'm sure they'd like to hear about her."

The girl said, "Yeah, what's she like?"

Allen was temporarily at a loss for words. But not for long. "She's a real beauty and very hard-working, too. She's actually a trial lawyer who handles corporate lawsuits for the tobacco industry. She has sued big tobacco and made many, many people a bunch of money."

Bill looked at his friend and just shook his head.

The young girl, Sophie, said, "I wish I could be like that but I don't know if I'm smart enough."

Then Bill spoke and added, "Sophie, don't let what you can't do interfere with what you can do."

Sophie seemed to reflect on those words, then said, "Maybe I could do something like that. What do you think, Caden?"

Caden kept eating his cookie and didn't answer, so Bill answered for him, "Sophie, the world is full of magical things patiently waiting for our senses to grow sharper."

Then Caden chose to speak, "Aww, you couldn't ever do anything like that, Sophie. You flunked out of school and you're too old to start now." Sophie looked like she might start crying.

Bill looked fiercely at Caden and said, "Young man, you never look good trying to make someone else look bad."

With that said, Caden got to his feet and ordered, "Let's go. We need to be moving."

Sophie got up, looking at Bill the entire time. As they walked into the river, Sophie looked back over at Bill and started to say something . . . but she didn't.

When they had gone out of sight, Allen commented, "I thought you were gonna hit that boy."

Bill was still gazing downstream, where they had gone, and replied, "The only reason he's still conscious right now is because I didn't want to carry him to a doctor."

They sat there in silence, looking at the river, Allen waiting for Bill to calm down. After several minutes, Bill spoke again, saying, "Trial lawyer?"

20

THE NIGHT WAS A LITTLE CHILLY as the guys got ready for bed. There was no internet service here in the depths of Yosemite so they just got in bed and talked. During a lull in the conversation, Allen asked, "Bill, have you ever seen an angel? I mean a real angel?"

"Why are you asking that? Has something happened?"

"No . . . I was just wondering, that's all. You're a lot more religious than I am and I thought if anybody ever saw one, it would be you."

Bill thought a moment before he answered, then said, "The Bible tells us that men have often entertained strangers that were actually angels—we just didn't know it. Billy Graham described them as God's 'secret agents.' I like that because they really are undercover. God promised us we'd never be alone, that He would always be there, and He promised us that His angels are there for us."

"But have you ever seen one?"

"I don't know. Maybe I have. Maybe you have. I doubt an angel would come down to Earth disguised as a human and announce to you that he's an angel. Most likely, they just come down here and do God's will, helping us out, then go back to heaven. You may never even know that he helped you."

Allen thought about that, then asked, "So, it's possible that I have seen an angel?"

Bill smiled and answered, "Yes, I'd say with all the trouble that you've been in, it's extremely likely angels have been helping you for years and you didn't even know it."

All Allen could say was, "Hmm." After a few minutes of silence and just before Bill was able to drift off to sleep, Allen asked another question, "Bill, why do bad things happen to good people?"

Bill was unsure if he wanted to open that can of worms this late at night, but he did. "Allen, God always has a plan. 'Oops' is never in His vocabulary. Many, many times we don't understand His plans. His ways are above our ways. He sees the 'big picture' where all we see is the immediate picture. I don't know if we'll ever know the complete answer to things—we only have to trust that He does. Why does a young twenty-seven-year-old mother die of cancer? I don't know. Why does a gunman burst in a church and shoot people? I don't know. Why are good people living in poverty? I don't know. Why was I the only person to get a ticket for driving seventy miles per hour on the interstate, when everyone else was also driving seventy miles per hour? I don't know."

Bill stopped to let this moment of levity catch up with Allen, but all he said was, "Hmm."

Bill waited, but the next sound he heard was some gentle snoring sounds from his friend. So, he stared at the ceiling of their little camper and wondered about all those things himself. Why did God take Eliza from him so suddenly? Why did He take Barbara from Allen? Why, why, why? He finally drifted off to sleep with many unanswered questions, but one ultimate answer.

Early the next morning a coffee and pastry food truck pulled into the campground. Since Bill and Allen were early risers, they didn't have to wait in line. Bill got the coffees and a couple of scones while Allen took the chairs back down to the river. They went to a different spot on the river this time and they could see a large waterfall off in the distance. Not large in the amount of water coming over the edge, but large in how far the water fell from the top to the bottom. Bill wondered if the two hikers from last night made it to their campground okay. Allen added, "Well, I hope she did."

The coffee wasn't that good but it was hot and that meant a lot on this chilly morning. As they were finishing up the scones they saw a man come from the woods just upstream. He was zipping up his pants when they first noticed him. They knew he had gone into the woods to pee instead of walking down to the toilets. He casually strolled by and said, "Good morning."

Bill nodded and Allen added, "Good morning to you, sir. Are you feeling good today?"

The man smiled and said, "I am now. Hope you guys are." He took a few steps towards Allen and reached his hand out to shake Allen's hand and said, "My name's Jody. Nice to meet you."

If nothing else, Allen was a quick thinker. And when someone who just finished peeing wants to shake your hand, you have to think quick. He said, "Jody, I've been fighting a cold all week; I don't want to give you my germs." Then he pointed over to Bill and said, "That's my friend Bill over there. He doesn't have a cold."

Jody took four steps over to Bill and stuck his hand out. Bill didn't think as fast as Allen but he did have more courtesy and politeness, so he shook Jody's hand and said, "Nice to meet you, Jody." Jody told them a few places of interest to see, then he shook Bill's hand again and said goodbye.

As soon as Jody was out of sight, Bill rushed down to the riverbank and scrubbed his hands with water from the Merced River. He scrubbed until his hands were almost numb from the cold water. Then he walked back to the chairs and flicked the water from his fingers onto Allen, who yelled, "Whoa! What are you doing?"

"I thought the cold water might help fight your cold." Allen deserved it . . . and he knew it. Bill walked back towards the camper, leaving Allen to bring both chairs by himself. They spent the rest of the day touring Yosemite and even going on a couple of short hikes. Bill wanted to spend another night but when they got back to the campground, it was full. The ranger called two other campgrounds and everything was already booked. So, they reluctantly headed back west, out of Yosemite, and ended up in a small town called Oakdale.

The reason they stopped in Oakdale was because Bill saw a Starbucks as they entered town and he pulled the Silverado into the parking lot. Allen asked, "You want a five-dollar cup of coffee?"

Bill switched the ignition off and replied, "No, but I do want to use their free wifi for a few minutes."

It took Allen about twenty seconds to figure that out . . . Bill wanted to check his email. Allen ordered the cheapest thing on the menu as Bill logged in. Soon, he was smiling and typing furiously. Allen left him alone and bought a blueberry muffin to munch on as his friend was catching up. He walked outside and sat at a table watching the cars pass by, eating his muffin. Lots of pickup trucks in Oakdale; it reminded him a little of North Carolina. Bill finished up and came outside to get him and suggested they stay in Oakdale for the night. He'd seen a sign advertising the McKinley Arms Hotel as they drove in and it wasn't far away.

The hotel was rather small, but well equipped with a restaurant and bar. The girl behind the desk welcomed them, saying, "Good evening. My name's Andrea. How many nights will you be staying with us?"

Bill answered, "Just one night, Andrea."

Andrea smiled and asked, "One king-sized bed?"

Before Bill could get too insulted, Allen answered, "Let's get two beds, honey, in case I want to stay up late watching a movie. I don't want to disturb you."

Andrea quickly said, "Two beds it is, but if you change your mind, the beds are sort of big so you can both fit in one bed comfortably."

Bill started to correct this entire mess, but then just smiled and said, "Okay, dear, lead the way."

The hotel restaurant had a good selection for dinner and the boys stuffed themselves. Then they retired to the bar to have a nightcap and reflect on the day's events. Allen said, "I'd like to come back to Yosemite again and stay for a few days." He looked at Bill, who seemed as though he didn't hear him. So, Allen repeated, "I'd like to come back here and stay a few days, how about you?"

"I heard you the first time, grandpa." Bill hung his head and said, "I was thinking about one of the emails I got from Ellen."

"What did she say?"

"She said she really missed me and couldn't wait to see me again."

Allen asked, "And that made you sad?"

"I'm not sad . . . I'm just . . . I don't know what to do."

Allen looked flabbergasted! "You don't know what to do? Look, Bill . . . every minute you're not dead should be a minute you're enjoying the heck out of life. Let's go there right now! We'll leave in the morning."

"No, we're not leaving in the morning."

"Why not?"

"Cause she's not there. She's visiting her sister in Florida."

Allen took a drink of his Coors Light and asked, "Well how long do I have to carry your mopey, love-sick self around with me? You're dragging me down."

Bill smiled and said, "Shut up. We're going to see and do everything we want to before I even think about going to Lake Superior."

"Bill, the function of a man is to live, by God, not to exist!"

"Look, Allen, she's in Florida and she won't be back at Lake Superior any time soon. We're good. Stop worrying about it."

"You sure?"

Bill smiled at his friend and assured him, "Yeah, I'm sure."

Breakfast was spent discussing where to go next. The choices were to stay in California and go back over to the coast or to hit I-80 and go east towards Reno, Nevada. On their previous trip, they traveled up the California coast and loved the scenery; however, they had never been to Reno and that entire section of the country. It was a difficult decision. As the waitress poured their third cups of coffee, she overheard part of the discussion and asked them where they were going later. Allen answered, "We're not sure yet. We can't decide if we want to stay in California for a while or head east over to Reno. What do you think, young lady?"

She kept holding the coffee pot, put her other arm on her expansive hip, and then said, "If it were me, I'd go to Reno."

Allen was a little surprised at her answer and asked why. "Well, I'm not from California and I'm not all smitten with it like most people are." Then she set the coffee pot down on the table and continued, "You know, gentlemen, there is science, logic, and reason. There is also thought verified by experience. And then there is California."

Bill and Allen both laughed at her statement but she never broke a smile; she just kept staring into space. Since she wasn't from California, Bill asked her where she was from. She replied, "I'm from Oklahoma. You know, back during the dust bowl when all the Oakies left Oklahoma and moved to California, it raised the I.Q. of both states." Then she looked down at them and asked, "Anything else?"

21

AFTER LOOKING AT THE MAP and eventually flipping a coin, they resumed their journey towards Reno and through the Sierra Nevada mountains. As soon as they started east on Interstate-80 the Sierras came into view. These mountains weren't like the Appalachians, which rose gradually through a series of rolling hills. The Sierras rose dramatically from the central valley. The boys could see the snow-covered peaks a long time before they actually got there. As Allen was driving, Bill got out his iPad and googled these mountains, specifically the area they would be passing through.

He said, "Hey, I-80 goes right through the Donner Pass."

That location triggered some memories of Allen's days at Appalachian State University, where he majored in history. Allen stated, "That's where those people in the wagon train got stuck one winter and they all ate each other." Bill was too busy reading to respond, so Allen continued, "It got down to the last two alive and one of them looked at the other one and said, 'You should've brought a compass.' Then the other one said, 'I hope you taste a lot better than you look.'" Bill kept reading and still didn't respond to Allen's comments, so Allen finally asked, "Do you have any other questions you want answered?"

Only then did Bill look up and reply, "Life is full of questions. Idiots are full of answers."

Allen opened his mouth to respond but then thought better of it. After stopping for gas and snacks and restroom breaks, they finally arrived at the area known as Donner Pass. They pulled off at one of the several areas available to stretch their legs and gaze out at Donner Lake. At a little over 7,000 feet, the wind was quite chilly, which required them both to get a jacket from the truck.

Bill retold the story he'd read on the computer earlier: Back in 1846 the Donner party was trying to get to California and misjudged how long it would take. The route through the pass in the mountains was blocked by snow and they were forced to stop in November and spend the winter at this spot. They were not prepared for the winter temperatures and the heavy snow. Of the eighty-one settlers, only forty-five survived to reach California. Some of them had to resort to cannibalism to survive.

Allen bought them a cup a coffee to sip on as they sat on a bench near the railing and thought about those awful facts. With the lake below them and mountains all around them, they could've sat for quite a while and enjoyed the scenery—except for the wind. The cold gusts soon drove them back inside the Silverado to continue the journey towards Reno.

The east slopes of the mountains were a lot steeper than the west side, which they just came from. Bill had started driving this section and the twists and turns, plus hauling a camper behind them, were hard. They soon saw a sign for Lake Tahoe and decided to check it out. Plus, Bill was worn out from all the turns on the interstate. They took the little side road over the state line into Nevada and saw several nice hotels and casinos. Neither guy cared much for gambling but they did want to get out of the truck and find a nice place to sit and relax.

The Lakeside Beach House restaurant had easy access and a great view of Lake Tahoe. The bar had outside seating that extended on a pier out over the lake. Mountains ringed Lake Tahoe making it one of the most scenic lakes in the world. The guys were mesmerized at the view and the setting. Bill decided they would have a drink or two there, then have dinner there, then have another drink or two. He didn't ask for Allen's approval. In fact, Allen was fairly quiet as they were walking down and as they sat and ordered their first Coors Light. When the beers came, Bill asked him, "Okay, what's wrong? You don't like this place?"

"No, this place is great."

"Well, what then?"

"I've sent Sophie a few emails and she hasn't answered any of them."

Bill nodded and asked, "I thought you didn't really care that much about getting involved with her. Right?"

"Well, I don't. But I don't want to be ignored either. I gave her some good nights, so she could at least answer my emails."

Bill took a healthy drink and said, "Buddy, with women, for every mile of road there are two miles of ditches."

Allen picked up his bottle of beer, clanked it against Bill's, and said, "Truth."

Bill had a mountain lake fish plate and Allen ordered the filet mignon. They each had an Iron Maiden with dinner as they soaked in the mountain scenery. Bill could tell Allen was still a little depressed about Sophie ignoring his emails and he couldn't seem to cheer him up. Their waiter was taking an order from the table next to them and Allen thought he heard the waiter say something about someone killing themselves. He listened a little closer and heard the name of a minor Hollywood actor. When the waiter came back to their table, Allen asked him about it and the waiter confirmed that the young actor had left a suicide note and overdosed on something.

Bill and Allen had heard the name of the actor before but really knew nothing about him. When the waiter left, Allen asked, "Bill, why in the world would a young successful person like that kill themselves? I just don't understand."

Bill started to eat a piece of his key lime pie but instead he put his fork down and said, "Listen, there are four things you should know about every person on this earth. No matter how successful or unsuccessful they are, or how beautiful or ugly they are, or how famous they are, everyone shares these four traits.

"One, everyone is essentially empty. No matter how much money or prestige someone has, unless they've found Christ, that person has to deal with emptiness. We're all born with a hole in our hearts that only He can fill.

"Two, people are lonely. There is a sense of loneliness in every individual.

"Three, people have a sense of guilt. They may try to mask it with alcohol or drugs or have psychiatrists tell them it's not there. But they have to deal with their guilt over the things they have done wrong. I remember reading something from the head of a mental institution who said, 'I could release half of my patients if I could find a way to relieve them of their sense of guilt.'

"Four, people are afraid to die. Some may strut around and say, 'Not me. I'm not afraid to die.' But they are.

"Remember, you used to be one of those people. I used to be one of those people. Fortunately for us, we responded to the Gospel. Let's hope they all do."

This was way, way more than Allen wanted to hear, but he knew Bill was probably right. After a few silent moments, Bill asked him, "Well, what do you think?"

"Heck, I don't know, Bill. I just wanted old Sophie to send me some more naked pictures."

Bill reached over and picked up two packets of sugar and threw them both at Allen. Then they both thought about loneliness, emptiness, guilt, fear, and naked pictures of Sophie.

22

BILL ENJOYED LAKE TAHOE SO MUCH he made the decision that they'd stay another day and enjoy the lake. Allen was still feeling a little depressed because Sophie was ignoring him. They sat out at a lakeside restaurant for breakfast and Bill tried his best to cheer up his friend. "Quit worrying about her so much; you've got other girls, don't you?"

"Yeah, but I've trained her just like I wanted her."

"You trained her?"

Allen looked out at the lake and replied, "Of course I did. She knows exactly what I like and how I want things done."

Bill said, "Are we talking about cooking dinner or something else?"

"You know what we're talking about . . . she knows exactly how I like things."

Bill took a moment, then said, "Well maybe that's why she's not answering you back. Maybe she's found someone who does things like SHE wants them done. Have you ever thought about that?"

Allen quickly answered, "Nah . . . ain't possible." But he didn't say anything else either. He quietly sipped his coffee and stared out over the lake.

After several minutes, a swarthy-looking, middle-aged man sat at the table next to them. He had a copy of the Wall Street Journal and ordered an espresso. He had on sunglasses and was dressed in a pale-looking linen suit with no tie and also wearing no socks. Usually, Allen would start up an immediate conversation with the guy, but today, he just ignored him.

As the man ordered his second expresso, he caught Bill's attention and said, "Beautiful morning, isn't it?" He didn't seem to have any type of accent but he looked foreign.

Being polite, Bill answered, "Yes sir, it's truly beautiful out here."

The man asked, "Do you gentlemen live around here?"

"No, we're just passing through and enjoying the scenery."

The man folded up his paper, then took a sip of his expresso and asked, "Would you be interested in some female companionship?"

Bill wasn't entirely sure he comprehended exactly what the man asked so he didn't answer right away. But Allen did. He said, "What type of female companionship?"

The man took his sunglasses off and said, "Any kind you desire."

Bill perked up and immediately exclaimed, "No, we would not!"

The man leaned a little closer to their table and said in a low voice, "Male companionship?"

Bill stood up from the table and looked down at the swarthy-looking man and said, "You need to leave. Right now!"

The man put his folded paper underneath his arm and took one last sip from his expresso, then took a business card out and said, "If you change your mind." He put the card on the edge of their table and walked away.

Bill said, "Can you believe that?"

Allen picked up the card and read it, then replied, "Wow." Then he put the card in his shirt pocket when he thought Bill wasn't looking.

But Bill was looking. "What do you think you're doing?"

"I ain't doing nothing."

"You take that card out of your pocket and throw it away right now." Allen started to argue with him, then he frowned a little bit, but Bill wasn't playing. He said again, "Right now!"

Allen took the card out and read it again, then laid it on the other table. Bill reached over and grabbed the card, tore it in little pieces and dropped all the pieces into his coffee cup.

Bill drove them around Lake Tahoe and stopped many times to enjoy the views. He even pulled over at one place and convinced Allen to take a short boat trip with him over to a small island with a castle on it. The boat ride to the island brought back vivid memories for Bill of a similar boat ride to an island in Lake Superior with Ellen. Allen was just hoping he didn't get sick from the way the small boat was rocking.

When that was finished, they gassed up the Silverado and set off down the mountain for Reno, or as the billboards say when you enter town, "The Biggest Little City in the World." As they drove into town, there were many other billboards advertising the casinos and all the other various shows that were available. Suddenly Allen pointed out the front window and screamed, "Dusty Springfield!" Bill just glanced at the sign before passing it. Allen said, "She's at the Stardust tonight. We've got to go!"

Bill didn't argue; he loved Dusty Springfield too. Bill always thought she had one of the sexiest voices he'd ever heard.

The Stardust was easy to find because it rose high above Reno's skyline and was visible for miles. When Bill pulled in the parking lot, he almost hit an old woman in a walker who was scurrying back to her car, holding a bag of nickels she just won in a slot machine. It shook him up but Allen said, "Hurry up, let's go."

"I almost hit that old woman! I'm not going to hurry up." Bill eventually found an open space for the Silverado and the camper down at the end of the lot. Allen wasn't happy about being so far away from the casino. As soon as Bill turned the motor off, he jumped out and said, "Let's go!" He started walking very fast, occasionally looking over his shoulder to make sure Bill was following. By the time Bill actually walked in the casino, Allen was already at the ticket window buying their tickets for the night's show.

Bill asked, "How much?"

"Don't worry about it. You buy us a drink later."

Bill looked sternly at Allen and asked again, "How much?"

"You don't want to know."

"Allen, you didn't do something stupid, did you?"

"Bill . . . they had some front row seats. Front row! How many times will we ever have the chance to see Dusty Springfield again in our lives? Huh?"

Bill nodded, then asked again, "How much?" When Allen finally admitted how much he paid for the tickets, Bill just turned around and walked away. Allen followed him to the bar area where Bill sat at the bar and ordered an Iron Maiden. Allen was a little apprehensive about saying anything, so he also ordered an Iron

Maiden and sat there . . . and waited. Eventually, after Bill drank most of his Iron Maiden, he turned to Allen and asked, "Front row?" Allen looked at him and nodded. Bill then asked again, "For sure?"

"Yep." With that affirmation, Bill held out his fist and Allen fist-bumped him . . . and they were good again. They ordered a second drink and watched all the slot machines whirring in the background, thinking about sitting in the front row and watching Dusty Springfield sing to them in a few hours. Soon, a lonely-looking older man sat two seats down from them and ordered a scotch on the rocks. When the man looked over, Allen said, "How're you doing, sir?"

"I thought it'd take me a couple of hours to lose my money today but I guess I'm improving . . . it only took me thirty minutes." He asked where the guys were from and Allen told him, North Carolina. The man then asked, "Are you boys Baptists? I'm from Oregon and I've always wondered about Southern Baptists . . . what they're like."

Bill just knew Allen was going to make up something good to confound the man but instead, he told this story: "Not long ago, a passing ship rescued a man from a desert island. He'd been stranded on that island for over twenty years. When they came ashore to get him, they saw three huts he had built on the island. The captain of the ship asked him what the three huts were for. The man said, 'The first one is where I eat and sleep. The second one is where I go to church. And the third one is where I used to go to church.' And that, my friend, is what a Baptist is." Bill immediately burst out laughing, then Allen joined him, but the other man only stared at them with a quizzical look on his face. Before the guys could stop laughing, he got up from the bar and walked away.

Since Allen bought the Dusty Springfield tickets, Bill paid for their room at the Stardust. They each put a dollar in the slot machines and didn't win anything, so they went to the room to take a nap before the concert. Bill couldn't sleep because he had two more emails from Ellen, which he had to memorize and then write her back. Allen had no emails, except for erectile dysfunction ads, so he fell asleep quickly. But Bill only closed his eyes and daydreamed.

They got to the auditorium early and Allen bought a Dusty Springfield t-shirt. There was a comedian as an opening act, but neither guy laughed at anything he said. Then, Dusty came on stage. They knew she wasn't twenty-five any longer. They knew she wasn't even forty-five any longer. It didn't matter. They loved her. When she sang the following lyrics, Allen knew, he absolutely knew, she was singing those words to him . . . and him alone:

"I don't know what it is that makes me love you so, I only know I never want to let you go
'Cause you've started something, oh, can't you see? That ever since we met you've had a hold on me
It happens to be true, I only want to be with you."
Oh, look what has happened with just one kiss, I never knew that I could be in love this this
It's crazy but it's true, I only want to be with you."

Then she sang:

"The only one who could ever reach me was the son of a preacher man
The only boy who could ever teach me was the son of a preacher man
Yes he was, He was, ooh, yes he was
Being' good isn't always easy, no matter how hard I try
When he started sweet-talkin' to me, He'd come 'n tell me 'Everything is all right'
He'd kiss and tell me 'Everything is all right'
Can I get away again tonight?"

Bill knew, he knew for sure that she was singing those words only to him . . . and nobody else.

They clapped and yelled and cheered like they were seventeen again. Dusty made them feel that way. And it was a good night . . . there in the Stardust Hotel and Casino, in Reno, Nevada.

23

AFTER THE DUSTY SPRINGFIELD CONCERT, the boys found it hard to sleep. They relived each song well into the night. Before leaving Reno the next day, they decided they would take a side trip down south a little to the state capital of Carson City. When Bill asked Allen why he wanted to go there, Allen answered, "Cause that's where they filmed Bonanza and I always loved Little Joe, Hoss, and Pa." The movie set was now a tourist attraction where fans could walk in the house and see all sorts of memorabilia of the show and the Ponderosa. Bill found it interesting, whereas Allen found it fascinating. Before he left, Allen bought a Bonanza t-shirt and a framed picture of Lorne Greene, Michael Landon, and Dan Blocker.

Even though there was still plenty of daylight left, they decided to camp at the Ponderosa campground—because Allen wanted to. Since they were still high in the Sierra Nevada mountain range, it got cold pretty quick. They put on their coats and built a nice fire to sit around that night. There was no Wi-Fi out in the wilderness so they couldn't check their emails, which left them both a little disappointed. But, having a magnificent view of the mountains, a cold Coors Light, and your best friend sitting next to you, made up for any Wi-Fi disappointments.

Bill added a few more twigs and small pieces of wood to the fire, which didn't so much keep them warm as it added to the warmth of the conversation. Allen said, "You know that during the entire concert last night, Dusty kept looking down at me and smiling, don't you?"

Bill turned to him and asked, "Really? You think she was smiling at you?"

"Of course, she was! We were on the front row, not ten feet away from her. I should've gone backstage after the show."

Bill shook his head and replied, "You think they'd let some red-necked hillbilly like you go backstage?"

"The way she was giving me the eye? She'd have been ecstatic to have me back there."

Bill said, "And just what do you think you'd have done back there with her?"

"I'll tell you this, grandpa, after I finished my visit with her, she wouldn't be Dusty anymore!"

All Bill could do was pick up a small pebble and throw it at Allen's legs, as they both laughed at what might have been with Dusty Springfield. The cold eventually drove them both inside the camper to the warmth of their sleeping bags. After they'd settled in and turned the lantern off for the night, Allen usually got serious with his questions, like tonight: "Bill, do you ever worry about the future? What's going to happen to us? Is our health going to go downhill? Will we ever be happy again? You ever think about stuff like that?"

Bill wished that Allen would give him some sort of "heads-up" about the nightly question, so he could prepare his answers better. But the fact was that these questions were not something Allen ever prepared; they just came from his mind as events happened. Bill thought for a moment, then replied, "Sometimes it's good that we don't know what's coming. We don't know what kind of threats are aimed at us or what the Devil is trying to do to us. All kinds of things are happening that we have no clue about. But God's at work. He reveals to us exactly how much we need to know, when we need to know it—not necessarily more and certainly not less. If you need to know something, God will tell you. If you don't, then He won't. He knows your troubles before they come to you. He's been there. You just have to trust him, buddy. Okay?"

Bill waited for a response . . . but instead, he heard the unmistakable sound of Allen gently snoring in his sleep. So, Bill thought about his response. What did the Lord know about his intentions with Ellen? What did Ellen want from him? And what exactly did he want from her? Sometimes, it was harder to convince himself than it was to convince Allen of what he was trying to tell his friend. Sometimes, he was more confused than his friend . . . if that was possible.

The next morning was cold! As quickly as they could, they packed up and heated up the Silverado. As Bill drove back towards Reno and I-80, he spotted a diner that served breakfast and pulled in an open spot off to the side. The waiter asked if they wanted coffee, which of course they did. He then asked, "Regular or decaf?"

Bill was too stunned to answer, so Allen blurted out, "Death before decaf!"

The waiter said, "Huh?"

Bill then assured the young man that regular coffee was fine. He then asked him if the diner had Wi-Fi—he wanted to check his email from Ellen. The young man stopped and stared down at Bill and replied, "Computers are useless. They can only give you answers." Neither Allen nor Bill could argue with that. Plus, they dearly wanted coffee, so they let the young man leave without any further questions.

Breakfast was wonderful and filling. The young waiter seemed aloof, however, and wouldn't joke around with Allen or respond to his silly questions. When he brought the bill back to the table, he initially handed them the wrong one. He quickly caught his mistake and said, "I hope he didn't see that."

Bill answered, "Who?"

"My dad. He's back there watching everything I do. I'll never be what he wants me to be."

Bill started to reach for the correct bill from the young man, but instead he looked up at him and said, "Young man, be what you want to be, not what others see you as." The young waiter stared at Bill, like he wanted to say something but couldn't find the words. Then Bill added, "There is nothing that cannot happen today."

Bill left the young man a nice tip and they went out to the Silverado. When Bill started the engine, Allen said, "I hope you didn't get that kid killed."

Bill started pulling out of the driveway, then looked over at his friend and replied, "Everybody dies but not everybody lives." Nothing else was said until they exited onto I-80 East, then Bill ordered, "Get the map out so we won't get lost."

Allen never moved a muscle until he looked over at his friend and replied, "To get lost is to learn the way." Bill had no idea what that meant or what Allen was trying to tell him, but it sounded profound. So they left the map in the glove compartment and starting driving, then smiling, then laughing . . . right out there on Interstate 80, in northern Nevada, in the middle of nowhere.

Allen had taken over the driving chores as Bill was napping on the drive through the high desert. Bill woke as he noticed the Silverado slowing down, then he asked, "Where are we?"

"We're not anywhere . . . but we're fairly close to Winnemucca."

"Why are you stopping?"

Allen didn't answer until he had safely pulled off the road. Then he replied, "Look at all this."

Bill didn't see anything but desert scrubland. No trees, no mountains, no water, no nothing. "What am I supposed to look at?"

"This! Look at it . . . it's completely barren. Not even any fences anywhere. This is about as remote an area as I've ever seen." After saying that Allen got out of the truck and started walking into the barren void. Bill quickly got out and followed him, not saying anything or asking any questions. Allen walked about two hundred yards into the desert, then stopped and stared off into the vastness. There was nothing to see in any direction. Bill followed him but never said anything. When Allen had stopped, Bill waited a few seconds, then picked up a rock and threw it as far as he could into the void. Allen followed the rock's path until it hit the ground causing a small dust tail. Then he turned around and walked back towards the truck.

When they were both seated, Allen started the engine and put it in gear, then said, "It takes considerable knowledge just to realize the extent of your own ignorance." That being said, he pulled back onto the highway and continued down the interstate towards Winnemucca, Nevada. Even though it was only 165 miles from Reno to Winnemucca, it felt like they'd been driving all day. The barrenness left them drained and exhausted—exhausted from nothing to see or focus on. On the edge of town, they saw a sort of hotel/casino/rest-stop type of place, so Allen pulled in the lot.

Even though it wasn't yet noon, both guys went to the bar and ordered Iron Maidens. They needed a drink. The bartender was a lady of unknown age. From the looks of her skin, she had spent way too much time in the sun. She reminded Allen of the desert itself . . . dry, dusty, barren, and worn. Bill thought she could be anywhere from forty-five to sixty-five. Allen said, "I'll find out how old she is."

"Don't be asking her how old she is, Allen. She won't like that. It's not polite."

Allen was affronted. "I know what I'm doing, old man." He motioned for the bartender lady to come over and said, "Hello young lady. My friend and I graduated high school a few years apart. Can you tell which of us is older?"

She looked closely at them both, then said, "No. Do you want another drink?"

"Not right now. We were just talking about age and how irrelevant it is to us. I mean, we do whatever we like and eat what we want. We don't let age determine how we live. Don't you agree?"

She nodded and answered, "Sure . . . let me know if you want another drink."

Bill elbowed Allen and said, "She's not going to tell you how old she is, numbnuts, women don't do that."

Allen said, "Watch and learn. Hey miss, can you settle an argument for us? I think people in their forties are smarter than people in their fifties . . . what do you think?"

She walked over to them and flipped her towel over her shoulder and replied, "If you want to know how old I am, why don't you just ask?" Then she turned and walked to the other end of the bar.

The boys sat there staring at each other, a little embarrassed, and a little guilty. Finally, Bill said, "Let's go down to the restaurant and get something to eat."

They finished their drinks and walked past the end of the bar where the lady bartender was standing and Allen stopped, looked over at her, and asked, "Okay then . . . how old are you?"

She smiled and replied, "None of your business."

24

THE PLAN WAS TO TRY AND MAKE IT TO ELKO, Nevada, by evening, which they did rather easily. The scenery started changing the closer they came to Elko. Mountains could be seen in the distance and they followed the Humboldt River for several miles and it led them directly into town. Just short of the city limits, the river widened and there was a small campground directly on the banks of the small river. They decided to camp there and enjoy the views of the mountains in the distance. Since there was no one else camping here, they could pick their spot . . . next to the bathrooms.

Once the camper was set up Bill unhooked it from the Silverado and they decided to ride into Elko and explore the little town. Elko was in the middle of its annual Basque Festival and the entire town was closed to traffic. Bill parked in a general lot and they started walking the streets. They found strongman competitions, bull-riding events, food and wine tasting, Basque dancing, and a traditional running of the bulls scheduled for later in the day. They also found several legal brothels all open and doing a brisk business, from what they could see.

Allen wanted to walk into one of the brothels just to see what it looked like. Bill elected to stay out on the streets. When he walked in the door a well-dressed woman, about forty years old, greeted him and asked if she could help him. Allen answered, "What do you have to offer?"

"Honey, we can offer anything your little heart desires." Allen wasn't prepared for that particular answer and he stuttered a little so the woman continued, "What age range are you interested in?"

Allen then smiled and asked, "What age ranges do you have . . . I can be pretty particular."

The madam smiled and told him, "Anything from twenty-one to half-past heaven." Allen blushed a little and she said, "Hold on." She walked over to a phone sitting on a table and spoke a few words, then came back over to Allen. Almost immediately, five women came from a back room . . . all of them provocatively dressed, or undressed, as the case may be. Two were very young looking, two were fairly middle-aged, and one was rather mature-looking. All of them were smiling seductively at Allen as he was admiring the eye candy. The madam asked, "Anything catch your eye?"

Allen didn't hear her because one of two middle-aged women had shimmied a little and one of her boobs was exposed. The madam noticed Allen's excitement and asked him, "I see you like Nancy. Nancy, come over here and meet . . . what's your name, honey?"

Allen's eyes were about to explode from their sockets as Nancy bounced over. She said, "Nice to meet you . . . "

Allen said, "Bill, my name's Bill. A great pleasure to meet you, Nancy." She put her hand out for Allen to shake it but he didn't notice her hand . . . not at all. Then he said, "Let me go outside and get my friend. He'd probably like to come inside as well. I'll be right back." When Allen went out the door, he grabbed Bill's arm and said, "Let's get out of here before I get us both arrested." They scurried on down the street and eventually stopped at a wine-tasting truck. Allen told Bill of what he'd seen in the brothel but left out the part of using Bill's name . . . no use in getting him all upset.

The wine was a little too dry for their tastes but the ham sandwiches and cheese trays from the next food truck were delicious. They watched some weightlifting contests and a little dancing before retiring to a saloon for a cold Coors Light. They learned that the running of the bulls would be starting in about an hour and couldn't decide whether to stay and watch it or not. The bartender was trying to convince them to stay and watch the entire "Basquo Fiasco." He said, "There'll be fights, naked women running around, drinking, and even some bull goring—if we're lucky."

It was quite a temptation but after their one Coors Light, they decided to quietly make it back to the Silverado before things got too rowdy. It was a good decision. As they brought the camp chairs out next to the little river, they could hear the music and noise from the parties in town. They were able to see the sun set almost directly downstream and watch the little birds dive around the water looking for dinner. The Coors Light was cold, the sky was flaming red, and the conversation was as comfortable as an old pair of blue jeans. It was nice to be in Elko, Nevada . . . but it was even nicer to be out of Elko, Nevada.

They sat out and listened to the water flowing in the Humboldt River well after dark. They had one more Coors Light each, then because they were camped next to the bathrooms, they split a Diet Pepsi. Allen retold the story of walking in the brothel, this time he added to it substantially and hysterically, as only Allen could. Then he talked about his wife, Barbara, for a bit . . . then he became silent. Eventually, he told his friend, "You know Bill, I probably need to change. If you hadn't been there today, I might have 'visited' one of those old girls in that place."

Bill thought for a moment then said, "We all like the idea of change, of starting over, of becoming someone different than what we are. Move to a new place, escape our problems, get some new friends, or maybe even get married . . . hoping that any of that will make life better. Some people even think a change in their appearance will do it. I read once that 80% of women are dissatisfied with their appearance. They all want to look like someone in a magazine, like that would make them feel better. They want change and they want it instantly. From Botox or liposuction . . . anything to reinvent themselves. But, can we really reinvent ourselves? Can we really change? Here is the answer, Allen: No. You cannot change who you are on the inside. You can change your appearance, or your location, or your relationships, but you can't change yourself any more than a drowning person can save himself. Some people say 'the answer is within.' But in reality, it's the problem that is within. Within our hearts. And you know what that problem is. There is only one person who can change the human heart, Allen, and you know who that is . . . don't you?"

Both guys were silent for a minute or two, then Allen said, "Bill . . . "

"Yep."

"Let's go to bed."

The entire little town of Elko had a collective hangover in the morning. The boys finally found a diner that was open for breakfast only because the people running it were Mormons. Everyone else was taking the morning off and recovering from the festivities of last night. A young woman in her early twenties was serving them. She had on a long dress all the way down to her ankles and had her hair tied on top of her head in a bun. Allen was mesmerized by her. She was very pretty and extremely polite and respectful. However, they didn't serve coffee or Diet Pepsi or anything with caffeine in the diner. Allen and Bill needed caffeine!

They ordered a couple of breakfast sandwiches to go and left the young lady to serve the other good and faithful Mormons of Elko. Bill spotted a 7-Eleven and they stopped there to get their coffee. Not as good as restaurant coffee, but better than nothing. Back in the Silverado, Allen finally pulled the map out and they discussed their options, which were very limited. They could either go east to Salt Lake City or turn around and go back to Reno. Allen remembered reading about the Dead Sea in Israel and how people could float in the water there while reading a newspaper. He wanted to see if he could do that in the Great Salt Lake as well. So, with a Mormon-made biscuit, a 7-Eleven coffee, and dreams of floating in the Great Salt Lake, they headed east once again.

25

THE FIRST PART OF THE MORNING, driving into the rising sun, was blinding and uncomfortable. Bill would pull over at every chance just to get off the road. At one crossroads there was a small casino at the intersection. From what Bill could see, there were no other businesses around at all, not even a gas station. There were a few cars parked out front and the sign on top of the building was lit up. Bill pulled into a parking space but didn't turn the engine off. Allen asked, "Are we going in?"

"I don't know. What do you think?"

"Might as well; it beats staring into the sun all morning. At least we can go to the bathroom and get something to drink."

They locked the doors on the Silverado and started walking to the front door. Before they got there, a man and woman walked out of the door and said hello to them. Allen replied, "Good morning to you as well. This is the casino isn't it?"

The man answered, "Yeah, it's not very fancy but they'll be glad to take your money."

Bill asked, "Why's it out here in the middle of nowhere?"

The woman told him, "It's the last exit before you get to Utah. All the Mormons come over here to gamble and drink. They can't do that in Utah."

Bill looked around and quickly counted five other cars besides theirs. Then noted, "There must not be many Mormons up here."

The woman said, "Tour buses. They drop off a load of people, go back to Utah to buy gas, pick up more people, then come back and pick them up late in the day."

Both guys thought: "Tour buses?" And neither one of them grasped that idea until they walked in the casino. It was booming. It was also bigger than it looked because it had a downstairs section that was below ground level and was actually larger than the upstairs section. Allen and Bill walked around and were amazed at all the people playing slot machines, blackjack, and various card games. It must have taken eight or ten tour buses to transport all these people. They eventually found an open area that served drinks and snacks so they took a seat to watch all the action.

Soon, a young lady in a very short skirt came to them and asked if they wanted to order anything. Bill ordered a Diet Pepsi and Allen got a coffee. They both ordered BLT's to munch on as well. The place was full of all sorts of people, from all age groups, all pretty well dressed. When the waitress came back Allen asked her about the casino being located so far out in the desert. She answered, "It's not that bad. We all live in Utah and bus over here or carpool. It's a pretty good job and most of the Mormons are good tippers as well."

Allen asked, "Not all of them?"

"Well, not the women so much, but the men are. And the shorter your skirt is, the better your tip will be." She smiled as she shared this information.

After she walked away and they had finished eating, a well-dressed, older man came by and spoke to them, "Everything okay, gentlemen?"

"Yes it is. We're just taking in the scenery." Allen said. Then he asked, "Are you here with the group?"

The man smiled and replied, "No, sir. I work here, I'm the food manager. Can't afford to retire just yet." He looked to be in his mid-sixties and a little worn from all those years of living out here in the desert. He asked, "Are you fellas from Salt Lake City?"

"No, we're just traveling through and thought we'd stop and rest a bit." As Allen said this, the man winced a little and grabbed the back of a chair to steady himself. Allen asked, "Are you okay?"

"Yeah, my back catches sometimes and gives me a fit. I need to get it checked out soon I guess." Both guys understood and nodded. Then the man said, "It was a lot more fun living in the sixties than it is being in your sixties." All three of them smiled and nodded at that pearl of wisdom. Then he knocked twice on the table and said, "Hope you guys have a great day. Let me know if I can do anything for you." He limped away to a back room as the guys were thinking about him and what his life must be like.

After a moment or two, Allen said, "I wonder what people say about us, Bill?"

Bill stood up and replied, "It isn't what they say about us, it's what they whisper."

By the time they climbed back in the Silverado, the sun was a little higher in the sky which made driving eastward more comfortable. The countryside was wide open scrubland, with mountains in the distance but a long way away. Bill knew a little about this area because of a course he took in college. He knew the Mormons came here in the 1800s to settle the region. Each guy wondered why anyone would ever decide to stop here in an area with no forests, no rivers, no rangeland, and basically nothing but desert. They couldn't figure it out.

When they crossed over into Utah the speed limit changed to 80 mph and Allen decided to push the Silverado about 5 mph over the limit. Even when cruising along at 85, they were the slowest vehicle on the interstate and were actually holding up traffic in the right-hand lane. For over an hour they only passed one vehicle, which was an old, worn Ford pickup truck hauling a trailer full of pigs; however, Allen got a great deal of satisfaction from finally overtaking another vehicle. When he finally got around the trailer of pigs, he shouted out, "Yes!"

Bill, who was dozing at the time, said, "What?"

"Nothing. Go back to sleep and keep dreaming, old-timer." Bill did go back to sleep and Allen kept on driving, while his mind was constantly switching thoughts from his wife, Barbara, to Sophie, to sin and redemption, and even to Bill and what would happen when they finally went to Lake Superior and met Ellen again. He wanted Bill to be happy but he also didn't want to lose his friend. He was lonely and had been lonely ever since his wife died. Women like Sophie only filled a temporary void in his life. He knew that. What concerned him most was if this feeling of loneliness would haunt him for the remainder of his life. So, he drove along and wondered what the future held in store for him, while Bill slept and dreamed and hoped what the future might hold in store for him on the shores of Lake Superior.

They made it to the Great Salt Lake without any additional stops. Bill googled camping and found campgrounds near them. The first one was not located on the lake so they followed the road south where the next campground was very close to the lakeshore. It was a rather large camping site but it seemed to be almost deserted. They checked in and received a spot near the restrooms that was within thirty yards of the water. When Allen pulled into their camping spot, they didn't see any other campers within eyesight of theirs. After the camper was set up, Allen quickly changed into his bathing suit. He grabbed a magazine he was saving for his experiment of floating and reading in the Great Salt Lake.

Bill finished setting everything up while Allen started for the water. Allen could smell the briny water well before he walked in. It was warm, which was good, and there were no waves, which was also good. He walked in about fifteen feet and the water was only up to just past his ankles. He walked another thirty feet in and the water hadn't reached his knees yet. He kept walking and walking and walking. He was at least a hundred yards from the shore and the water just barely reached his waist; however, this was deep enough to float in. He bent his knees a little and tilted back, then went completely under the water. It happened so fast that he didn't close his mouth in time and got a mouthful of briny, warm water. He jumped up quickly and started coughing so hard that Bill heard him on the shore a hundred yards away. Bill yelled out, "You okay?"

Allen tried to stop coughing so he could answer, finally yelling back, "I can't float!"

Bill yelled back, "You need a boat?"

"No! I can't float in this crap." Bill was walking in as fast as he could and was within forty yards of Allen, and he heard Allen say again, "You can't float in this crap, it's awful."

Bill got within ten yards of his friend and laid back into the water, floating like a raft. Allen was shocked that his friend was floating like a duck right in front of him. He laid back into the water again and again went straight to the bottom. He did close his mouth this time but came up for air saying some words unworthy of any ears in this Mormon lake. Bill continued to float and smile, saying, "Wow, this is great!" Allen tried twice more and each time went straight to the bottom. Bill rose from the water and stood up, pointing down the shoreline and said, "Why don't you try over there."

Allen took two steps, realized Bill was messing with him, then said, "I'm outta here." He started walking back to the shore while Bill laid back into the water and started whistling while he was floating. Allen stepped on a small pebble in the water, so he stopped and picked it up and threw it near Bill. Bill heard it splash but that only made him whistle louder.

That evening, before sunset, they were sitting in the shade of the camper, drinking a cold beer when they heard the sound of a truck on the highway. They stood up to look and noticed it was a food truck. They each waved their arms and the truck slowed down, then pulled off the road as they walked over to it. The driver said he usually stops if he sees several cars but was glad he saw them in time. He had various sandwiches in a warmer and all sorts of snacks and fruit as well. They took their dinner back to the camper and watched as the sun set to their backs and cast a shining glow across the lake. Way down the shoreline they saw another RV set up for the night. Just before it was totally dark, they noticed two people wade into the water for a few minutes before coming back onshore. They couldn't tell if the people were old or young, male or female. They were too far away and it was too dark to tell.

Since there was no wood to build a fire, Bill brought the lantern out of the camper and set it between them for comfort. Allen reviewed their casino visit and seemed especially concerned about the older guy who was the food manager there. He said, "Bill, I wonder why that guy still has to be out there in the middle of nowhere suffering from his health at that dead-end job?" Bill had no answer, so he didn't say anything. Allen continued his thoughts: "Maybe he gambled away all his savings. Or maybe he never saved anything to begin with. He might be a drunk. Or, maybe an ex-wife took it all from him. What do you think?"

"Buddy, we'll never know why people suffer or why God allows them to suffer."

Allen nodded thoughtfully, then asked, "But why do YOU think He allows it?"

Bill threw his empty Coors Light can in the trash and said, "Probably to humble our exalted opinions of ourselves and to teach us to depend on Him instead of ourselves." Allen thought about that statement but didn't respond, so Bill added, "Maybe even to produce in us a mercy and compassion for others going through the same things we are." Allen still didn't say anything but he did nod his head at those comments. Bill closed his thoughts by saying, "You know, Allen, Jesus is all we need. But a lot of times we never understand that until Jesus is all we've got."

26

BY THE NEXT MORNING, the saline smell from the Great Salt Lake was beginning to overpower them. They now understood why there were not many people out here camping. They packed up quickly and found a service station that sold biscuits and coffee to start their day with. Bill was pumping the gas and Allen was munching on his biscuit when he asked, "Bill, you wanna go see the Mormon Tabernacle Church? It's right up here in Salt Lake City, not too far away."

"Sounds fine to me."

Allen finished his biscuit and said, "Great, let me go get another bacon biscuit first before we get there. I don't think Mormons eat bacon, do they?"

Bill wasn't exactly sure if they ate bacon or not but reasoned, "They're not Muslims, they probably eat bacon. I know they don't drink caffeine but I think that's all they don't do."

Allen said, "Well, I ain't taking no chances. I'm getting me another bacon biscuit just in case."

He ate his biscuit and Bill drove them to downtown Salt Lake where the famous Tabernacle was located. He parked the Silverado and they paid their admission fee and stepped inside the large church. It was huge. The tour guide explained the history and building of the temple and told them that the entire facility was built of wood. Allen didn't believe that the entire building was wood; certainly there had to be some steel or concrete somewhere . . . so he started looking.

Two stops later, during the tour, Allen pointed towards a far wall with a balcony and said proudly, "There! That's a steel plate connecting those beams."

He stated that fact loudly enough so that the tour director could obviously hear it. All eight members of the little tour group turned to look where Allen was pointing, then they looked back at the tour director who answered, "It's wood, painted to look like steel. They did that a lot so that the state inspection people would feel better about the construction and let it pass the building codes of the day. Trust me . . . it's wood." Allen didn't believe a word of that but he kept his mouth shut, only after Bill elbowed him in the side. Near the end of the tour, the group was brought to the very back of the huge church, which was two hundred fifty feet long. The tour director told them to stay there while he walked to the front of the church where the pulpit was.

As he walked up front, Allen noticed a steel brace holding two large doors together. He elbowed Bill and said, "Look. More steel." Bill nodded but didn't say anything so Allen walked over to the brace and knocked on it with his knuckles, then tapped it with his finger.

When he walked back to the group, one of the other men looked at him and asked, "Well?"

Allen answered, "It's wood painted to look like steel. Didn't you hear the tour guide earlier?"

Just then, they heard a voice say, "It's wood. I told you so." But there was no human with the voice. Everyone in the group was looking around when the voice spoke again, "Up here." The entire group looked up towards the ceiling thinking God was speaking to them. Then, "No. Up at the front of the church." The tour director was standing in the choir loft and waving to them nearly two hundred feet away. He said, "They built this church with such fantastic acoustics that people can hear normal conversations, like this, over two hundred feet away."

One of the ladies spoke quietly and said, "Can he hear us?"

"Yes, ma'am, I can. I can hear all of you just like you can hear me." Everyone in the group spoke to the tour director to prove to themselves that it was indeed true.

As they finally started to leave the tour and walk out the door, Allen said, "Dang, that was pretty cool. I can't believe those crazy Mormons could build something like that."

Then a voice came from nowhere, "I heard that."

They rode around Salt Lake City for a couple of hours then decided to take the interstate south into the lower sections of Utah. When they left the urban area, they stopped at a nice hotel off the interstate to stay for the night. It had a nice restaurant and bar with fantastic views of the Wasatch Mountains off to the east. It also had a rooftop bar that had a little shady area and a large open area as well. Neither guy was totally certain of the protocol of alcohol being served here so close to the Mormon epicenter. As they were checking in, Allen asked the clerk, "You have a bar here in the restaurant, don't you?"

"Yes, sir, and one on the roof as well. Great views of the mountains up there."

Allen smiled and stuttered a little with his reply, saying, "And, umm, there's . . . "

The clerk saved him: "Yes, sir, we do serve alcoholic drinks here."

After checking in the room and using the bathroom they went up to the rooftop bar and sat under a large umbrella facing the mountains. A young lady in Daisy Duke shorts came to take their order. They each ordered a Coors Light and Bill also ordered some chips and salsa to munch on. A couple of buzzards floated by on some thermals about a thousand feet above them and few puffy clouds floated past. Bill had his iPad with him and connected to the hotel's Wi-Fi to check his emails. Soon, he was smiling and typing back email replies to Ellen. After a few minutes of furious typing and smiling, Allen looked over at him and said, "Shut up!"

Bill stopped typing momentarily and replied, "I didn't say anything."

"But you wanted to."

Bill smiled and answered, "Yeah, but not to you."

As if he didn't already know, Allen asked, "Who are you typing to?"

"You know who I'm typing to."

"What does she want?"

Bill smiled again and answered, "She wants to know if I'm missing her and thinking about her."

"Well, are you?" Bill didn't answer that question. Instead, he closed his computer and waved for the waitress to come back over. After he ordered a second beer, Allen asked again, "Well are you thinking about her?"

"When I'm writing to her I think about her. Not all day long, though, like you think I am. I've told you before, I'm having a blast on this trip and don't want it to end anytime soon. I'll see Ellen when the time is right." He wanted to assure his friend that everything was good.

After a few silent moments, Allen looked over at his friend and asked, "You know how the Mormon church started, don't you?"

Bill didn't know and he was also pretty certain that Allen didn't know either, but instead of saying that, he answered, "No. How did it start?"

"Well, old Brigham Young was living in Ohio at the time and he was a handsome dude. All the girls wanted to marry him and he didn't know what to do. He couldn't make his mind up because he liked all the girls. He was a real ladies' man." He looked over at Bill who said nothing, so he continued: "Old Brigham would date a different girl every night of the week, trying his best to keep them all happy. But one day his daddy, who was a Baptist, by the way, told him he needed to settle down and quit being such a playboy—it wasn't the Baptist way.

"Brigham thought about that for a long time: settle down and be a good Baptist or find a way to have all the girls. Well, you know what he did next. He got him a couple of wagons and about twelve of his favorite girls and headed out west. When he would pass through towns on the way out west, other guys would see what he was doing and they joined him. By the time he finally made it into Utah, there were about two hundred wagons full of girls and only three wagons of guys.

"They came upon the Great Salt Lake and Brigham said that this was where they would stop. But one of the other guys, a big mean dude, yelled out, 'No, we want more girls.' And they had a big argument and kicked the big mean dude out of the wagon train. He went back East and tried to act innocent of everything when people asked him about the wagon train. When he was asked why Brigham and the others did what they did, he answered, 'Because they wanted more, man.' And the townspeople there misunderstood him and from that day on they referred to Brigham and his followers as 'moremen, which was later Anglicized to the current 'Mormon.'"

When he finished his story, he took a large drink of Coors Light and sat back in his chair smiling. Bill never responded but the young waitress, who overheard most of the tall tale, did respond. She walked around in front of Allen and said, "Wow . . . I always wondered how it all started. Thank you."

Bill went back to typing and smiling and Allen stood up and walked around the roof admiring the scenery. Near the bar, someone had left a paperback book lying on a chair. The book seemed as though it had been left outside for many weeks. The cover was faded and worn, and the pages were frayed and dim but it caught Allen's eye and he picked it up. He turned to the first chapter, "This is the most beautiful place on earth . . . the canyonlands. The slickrock desert. The red dust and the burnt cliffs and the lonely sky—all of which lies at the end of the roads." Allen read these words and dreamed visions he'd never imagined.

He was lost in thought when an attractive middle-aged woman tapped him on the shoulder and said, "I think you have my book. Can I get it back, please?" She was a true beauty, with dark flowing hair and green eyes. She temporarily mesmerized Allen and he didn't speak. She then held her hand out and he placed the book in her palm but didn't let go of it. Neither did she take the book from him, she just kept her hand stretched out as the book lay in her palm. Maybe two days later, or ten seconds later, Allen couldn't tell, she spoke again and said, "But you can borrow it if you want to read it."

Allen still didn't speak. Not because he couldn't but because he didn't know what to say; for the first time in his life, he was speechless. For another two days, or maybe fifteen seconds, they were both silent until she said, "You just keep it and give it back to me when you're finished."

Allen's spell was finally broken and he answered, "Are you sure?"

She smiled at him and replied, "Yes. I've probably read this book at least a dozen times. Even though I know what it says, it always seems to make me stop and think and laugh and even cry at times." Allen looked down at the cover to read the title again, then looked back up at her and once again fell under her spell. She never broke their gaze and continued, "I'm here for a couple of more days. Keep it and read it. You can return it to me then. Okay?"

Allen finally composed himself and asked, "Do you live here?"

"No, I live in Cedar City. I'm a professor at the university there. Do you live here?"

Allen didn't know how to answer that question. Or even if he should answer that question. Or, if he should just ask her to marry him right now and get it all over with. So, he just continued to stare at her.

27

As he typed, Bill was so lost in thoughts of Ellen that he never noticed Allen was missing. When Allen finally made it back to his seat and sat down, Bill said, "You want something else to drink?" Allen didn't answer him, so Bill looked over at him and asked again but Allen still didn't answer. Then Bill tapped his friend's knee and asked, "You okay?"

Allen looked at him and answered, "No, I'm not okay. I'll never be okay again. My world has been turned upside down."

"Do we need to get a doctor?"

"No," Allen exclaimed, "you need to get a preacher. I'm going to marry that woman over there."

Bill looked in the direction Allen was nodding and saw a woman with dark hair standing at the bar area talking to their waitress. He asked, "Who are you going to marry? Our twenty-year-old waitress or the fifty-year-old woman with dark hair?"

"The dark-haired one. I'm going to marry her."

Bill had seen Allen pull pranks all his life . . . this wasn't one of those times. So Bill asked, "What's her name?"

Allen took about ten seconds to answer, then said, "I don't know."

"How old is she?"

"I don't know."

Bill leaned forward and half-whispered, "Does she know you want to marry her?" Allen looked back at Bill but didn't answer, so Bill asked, "Does she know how old you are?" Allen still didn't answer but he did break his gaze away and stared at the floor. Then Bill really pulled the dagger out and asked, "How do you know she's not already married?"

Eventually, Bill and Ellen stopped emailing each other and the guys went up to their room. Allen was unusually quiet as they showered and changed clothes for dinner. Before they went downstairs to the restaurant, Bill asked Allen where he wanted to go next when they left in the morning. Allen didn't answer. Bill said, "Why don't we drive down towards Moab. There are several national parks down there that sound interesting . . . is that okay with you?" Allen still didn't answer, so Bill walked over in front of him and asked, "What's wrong with you?"

"I don't know, Bill. That woman did something to me and I can't explain it. I've never felt that way before—ever!" Bill didn't know how to respond to that, so he didn't. A few moments later, Allen continued, "Don't worry about me, I'll be alright. Yeah, that morbid place sounds alright in the morning."

Bill thought for a moment, then understood what Allen meant. "It's not morbid, it's a place called Moab. They say it's beautiful."

"Okay. That'll be fine. I'll be fine. Everything's alright."

They finished up and walked down to the restaurant for dinner. Allen never put the book down. He'd been carrying it with him everywhere except into the shower. When they sat down and ordered, Bill looked at the book and said, "How are you going to get that book back to her?"

"I don't know. I guess I can leave it at the front desk in the morning." But he couldn't put the book down. He wasn't reading it—he was only holding it. Even during the meal, he laid the book on his lap, not on the table. When they finished eating, Bill suggested they stop by the bar and have an Iron Maiden before retiring. Even when sitting at the bar with a drink in front of him and a stranger speaking to him, he was still silent. Bill had never seen anything like this before.

Bill finished his drink but Allen hardly touched his. Bill suggested they head upstairs for bed and Allen dutifully followed him to the door. As they passed through the lobby, the front door to the hotel opened and the dark-haired lady came walking in with two other women. Bill noticed her but kept walking. Allen immediately stopped. She said something to the other two ladies, who walked away, then she walked over to Allen. They stood there facing each other, Allen holding the book, the dark-haired lady holding a briefcase, neither one of them saying a word.

Finally, Allen said, "I'm reading your book."

"I'm glad. Do you like it?"

"What's your name?"

"Amanda." Their eyes never left each other's gaze. Bill had stopped at the corner and was watching. She never asked Allen what his name was, she just kept staring into his eyes.

Allen then asked, "Are you married?"

"No." Allen felt as though every hair follicle in his body was exploding. Then she said, "I have to go to a meeting with my colleagues right now. Would you like to have breakfast with me in the morning?"

Initially, Allen's brain couldn't figure out how to say, "Yes." Then he slightly recovered and answered, "Yes."

"Is 9:00 okay with you?"

"Yes."

At that point, Allen heard one of the other women call out, "Amanda, are you coming?" She smiled and turned away. Allen watched her walk toward the other women and just before they turned the corner, she quickly looked back over her shoulder and caught his eye. But it was long enough for him to know what she meant.

He kept standing there staring at the empty hallway when Bill walked over and tapped him on the shoulder. "You okay?"

"Yeah, I'm fine." But he still didn't move. Then he said, "Her name is Amanda and she's not married."

At this point, Bill was thinking to himself, "Oh, no . . . this ain't good." Which was really weird because Bill never used the word "ain't."

Bill then suggested they go up to the room and get ready for bed. Allen followed but didn't say anything until they were in the room. Then he told Bill, "I'm having breakfast with her in the morning."

Bill nodded and replied, "Okay . . . what then?"

"I don't know, Bill. I just don't know. I can't answer that. But I have to meet her for breakfast. I have to do it. Is that okay with you?"

"Of course it is, buddy. You have breakfast with her, then we'll decide what to do. Quit worrying, everything will work out for the best." Bill meant every word of that. He didn't believe it but he meant it for Allen's sake. In fact, Bill was worried.

He'd never seen Allen like this. There was nothing he could do now except wait and see what happened at breakfast and go from there.

After the lights were turned off and each guy laid quietly in his bed, Allen said "Bill, I don't understand what just happened to me. But something did happen to me. And let's face facts . . . I'm not a young man any longer."

Bill didn't want to argue with him about that; heck, they were both old—but only in years. So he said, "Allen, it's never too late to be happy."

And then Allen, seeming like he was trying to convince himself more than anything else, said, "But how can things develop so fast? I don't understand."

Bill firmly answered, "I'll tell you how: Because with God, just like that! Everything can change."

Somehow, that fact calmed Allen's mind and allowed him to rest and think good thoughts, and not question why, or how, or what. He didn't pray every night, not because he didn't believe, but mostly because he either forgot or just fell asleep too fast. But tonight, he prayed to thank God for whatever it was that happened to him today.

28

ALLEN WAS UP AT SUNRISE for his 9:00 breakfast with Amanda. He was so excited that he cut his chin shaving; he hadn't cut his chin shaving since his son was born forty years ago. Bill got up with him and tried talking to him to calm him down until it was time for breakfast. He asked what Amanda's last name was—Allen didn't know. He asked where she worked—Allen didn't know. He asked if she had any children—Allen didn't know. He asked where she lived—Allen knew, but had forgotten. It was pointless; none of that stuff mattered. Bill went down to bring back coffee for them while they waited.

As he passed by the restaurant, he noticed Amanda sitting at a table by herself. It was only 8:15. He didn't know if he should stop or not. He decided he should. He walked over to her holding two cups of coffee and said, "Good morning, I'm Allen's friend, Bill." She had a puzzled look on her face and Bill realized she didn't know Allen's name. So, he added, "The gentleman you're meeting for breakfast at 9:00."

She looked up at him and said, "I thought he was meeting me at 8:00. I have a meeting to go to at 9:00."

Bill quickly replied, "He told me he was meeting you at 9:00. He probably got the time mixed up."

Then she smiled at him and Bill realized why Allen was so taken with her. There was something about her smile and her face that was extremely alluring. She added, "I thought he had stood me up. I'm glad you stopped and cleared things up for me. By the way, I'm Amanda."

Bill smiled and suddenly had either a great inspiration or a big stupid idea pop in his head. Whichever it was, he was going to follow it. He asked, "Do you mind if I sit for a moment or two?"

"No, please do. You want to ask me a few questions, don't you?"

Bill immediately thought, "How did she know that?" And then, he actually answered her, "Yes, if you don't mind."

Amanda said, “I’ll agree if you let me have one of those coffees.” He did and watched her add cream but no sugar, which impressed him. She continued, “Go ahead, ask away.”

Bill tried to ease into things and said, “It’s just that Allen is my life-long friend and I don’t want

him . . .”

He stumbled for his next words but Amanda helped him by saying, “It’s just breakfast, Bill. We’re not eloping or anything.”

Bill smiled and touched her coffee cup with his, then added, “He’s just very excited and was totally taken with you. Frankly, I’ve never seen him like this.”

She said, “That doesn’t sound like a question. But I understand how you feel. My two friends had the same concerns for me. Look . . . maybe this is just breakfast and nothing else. And maybe nothing will come of it and it won’t work out.” Then she grinned at Bill and added, “But maybe seeing if it does will be the best adventure ever.”

Bill was momentarily mesmerized and charmed by her smile and her answer. He smiled back at her and said, “That was my only question. I’ll go get Allen; he’ll be right down.” As he stood, he stopped and added, “That’s not true. I have one more question and I know it’s probably very rude, Amanda, but can you tell me how old you are?”

She smiled again and without hesitation said, “Fifty-eight.”

Bill walked back to the room thinking, “Fifty-eight? No way she’s fifty-eight? I’ve never seen a woman look that young and that good at fifty-eight.” He opened the door and Allen was pacing around holding a piece of toilet paper to the cut on his chin. Bill said, “Guess what? She’s fifty-eight years old.”

Allen immediately stopped and said, “Who?”

“Amanda. I just talked to her in the restaurant and she told me she was fifty-eight.”

“She’s in the restaurant?”

“Yeah.”

“Right now?”

“Yeah.”

Allen rushed past Bill and went out the door without another word. Bill wanted to go downstairs and spy on them, but he didn't. Instead, he said a quick prayer asking God to please make Allen sure he was doing the right thing. Then he thought, "That was stupid. God knows the right time, the right place, the right person, and the right answer. He knows, so we don't have to." He thought about that, then he added another short prayer to help his friend . . . just in case.

Bill packed up all the stuff and took everything out to the Silverado while Allen went to breakfast. He was hoping Allen would remember him and bring him a biscuit or two for the road. He remembered Amanda telling him she had a meeting to attend at 9:00 so he knew he wouldn't have to wait too long. He was wrong. 9:15 . . . no Allen; 9:30 . . . no Allen; 9:45, still no Allen. At 10:00 Bill decided to go down to the restaurant and see what was happening. He got to the entrance and saw Amanda and Allen still sitting at a corner table, deep in some private conversation, with no breakfast plates on the table, except for a couple of coffee cups. Before Bill could decide what to do, Amanda saw him and waved for him to come over to their table.

Allen never turned around to see Bill but Amanda was whispering something to him as Bill joined them. She said, "Bill, have a seat. We were just talking about you."

Bill replied, "Well don't believe anything he says about me."

Allen laughed and answered, "I only told her the truth: You are a scholar, a gentleman, an excellent sportsman, a best friend, and the best rock-thrower in the world."

Amanda laughed and Bill smiled and answered, "What do you want?"

"Huh?"

"You want something . . . what is it?"

"No . . . I don't want anything."

Everyone was awkwardly silent for a few seconds, then Bill said, "Allen, tell me what's going on." Allen looked at Amanda who looked back at him, then looked down at her lap. Finally, Allen started mumbling some incoherent thoughts until Bill chastised him saying, "Tell me!"

Allen took a sip of his cold coffee, which caused him to cough, then said, "Amanda lives down in southern Utah and it's close to several national parks: Zion, Bryce Canyon, Capitol Reef, places that are truly beautiful and awesome. We need to see places like that. We could visit a different park every day and explore places that most people have never heard of. We could . . . "

"Okay." Bill interrupted Allen's monologue, which left Allen temporarily speechless. He had this long, convincing argument for Bill to hear. He hadn't expected Bill to agree so easily and suddenly. "I've already got the truck packed; we can leave anytime."

"Well . . . there's one other little thing. Amanda can't leave until tomorrow. Can we wait and drive down with her? I'll do all the driving and stop wherever and whenever you want to. I'll unpack the truck this morning and pack it again tomorrow—you won't have to do a thing. What do you think?"

Amanda still hadn't looked up from her lap. Allen was holding his breath waiting on confirmation. Bill could see that both of them were about to burst with anticipation. He waited about ten seconds, then again said, "Okay." With that word, Amanda and Allen both jumped to their feet and each one hugged Bill, thanking him profusely for his act of kindness. Bill loved it because Zion and Bryce and Capitol Reef were on his wish list anyway. Now, he could get Allen to do all the driving while he relaxed. Win, win.

Amanda left to attend her meetings and Bill and Allen got a couple of bacon biscuits and went back to the room. Allen suggested they unhook the camper and drive around the countryside and do some sightseeing. That sounded like a good idea until they actually got on the road and couldn't find any sites worth seeing. The surrounding area was mostly flat desert with sand, rocks, and a few small bushes and cactus spread unevenly throughout. There were some mountains off to the east but they were quite a distance away. They talked about everything except the nine-hundred-pound gorilla sitting in the truck with them. Amanda's name was never mentioned.

They came to a small bridge that covered a dry wash, which was probably a river during storms or the rainy season. Now, it was just a dusty stream bed full of rocks and sand but Allen pulled off the road anyway. He got out of the truck and walked around to Bill's side, then opened Bill's door saying, "C'mon, let's have a rock-throwing contest." Bill knew Allen was only trying to amuse him and butter him up for being so agreeable with everything. Bill had a plan for that.

Allen had never beaten Bill at rock-throwing; he'd never even come close to beating him. Bill was a natural athlete and could still throw, regardless of his age. Allen could not throw. Even in high school he hadn't been nearly the athlete Bill was. Allen picked up a rock and said, "C'mon, old man, find you a rock and let's see who wins today." Bill nodded and found a nice oval-shaped rock and walked over next to Allen, who said, "I'll throw first and try not to embarrass you too much." He threw his rock over the stream bed, but not very far, even for Allen's standards.

Bill knew Allen purposely threw it short just so it would be easy to beat his throw. When it landed, Allen said, "See if you can beat that, old-timer."

Bill could have beaten that throw left-handed, but instead, he reared back and made a grunting noise and heaved his rock out well short of where Allen's rock had landed. Allen was stunned to see where Bill's rock ended up. Bill looked over at him and said, "Well, looks like everything's going your way today, buddy." He turned around and walked back to the truck while Allen kept staring out at the area where the rocks had landed, wondering if he had truly beaten Bill, or if Bill was only messing with him in a way that only Bill could mess with him.

There was absolutely nothing to see out where they were, so they turned around and drove back to the hotel and went up to the rooftop bar and ordered Coors Lights. Only when they sat down in a shady area did the subject of Amanda come up. Allen looked over at his friend and said, "Bill . . . "

Before he could continue, Bill said, "It's alright, Allen."

"But . . ."

"I said, it's alright. Quit worrying about it."

"You sure you're not mad?"

Bill took a small sip of Coors Light and answered, "I'm not mad. I'm happy for you. I just don't want you to do something crazy . . . that's all."

Allen then took a small drink himself and said, "She's beautiful, isn't she?"

"Absolutely. And very nice as well."

Allen grinned and asked, "You like her don't you, Bill?"

"From what I know of her, I think she's great." Allen smiled again, then Bill continued, "What exactly are your plans with Amanda?"

Allen looked up in the sky, then he looked down at his beer can and said, "I don't know how to answer that question, Bill. All I know for sure is that I have to see this through."

Bill nodded and replied, "What exactly does that mean, 'see this through?' I'm a little confused."

Allen sat up straight in his chair and looked directly at Bill before answering: "Anyone who isn't confused really doesn't understand the situation."

Bill figured that statement was probably the most logical thing Allen could tell him. They both settled in their chairs, leaned back and pulled the footrests out, then let nature take over. Allen quickly dozed off, dreaming thoughts of southern Utah and Amanda—not necessarily in that order—while Bill closed his eyes and hoped and prayed his friend could somehow conjure up some common sense and not do something stupid. Then, he thought of the shores of Lake Superior and Ellen—and definitely not in that order.

29

ALLEN AND BILL HAD DINNER THAT EVENING WITH AMANDA and her two colleagues in the restaurant at the hotel. All three of the women were on the staff at the University of Southern Utah in Cedar City, where they all lived. Amanda was a professor in the Geography Department and the other two ladies were in the Sociology and Psychology Departments. Bill had a great time discussing sociology and psychology with the other two women, while Allen and Amanda spent most of the evening holding hands underneath the table and staring at each other like two love-sick teenagers.

After dinner, Allen and Amanda went on a walk together leaving the other three to retire to a small bar area and have a glass of wine together. The sociology professor, who was named Lydia, tried to dominate the discussion after she started on her second glass of wine. Bill had no problem with her until she started saying some things he didn't agree with politically and religiously.

He started getting more and more upset with her idealistic views on America and society as a whole, but he waited for her to finish before he began. Then, he started, "Let me see if I understand what you're saying: We take money from people who work hard for it and give it to those who don't want to work; we support the Constitution, but only when it supports our political ideology; we have freedom of speech, but only if we are being politically correct; parenting has been replaced with Ritalin and video games; and the land of opportunity is now the land of hand-outs.

"And how do we handle a major crisis today? The government appoints a committee to determine who's at fault, then threatens them; passes a law; raises our taxes; tells us the problem is solved so they can get back to their reelection campaign." Bill paused a moment to look at both women, then finished by saying, "What has happened to the land of the free and the home of the brave?"

The psychology professor raised her wine glass to salute Bill, whereas, Lydia quickly stood up and said, "Well, I never." Then she stalked off to her room at the hotel. Bill and the psychology professor did not know what Lydia's 'never' meant, but it was clearly evident that neither of them really cared either. After another glass of wine, Bill and the professor both went back to their rooms as well. Bill was eager to check his emails for any messages from Ellen. He had only one, but it was a doozy. He was re-reading it for the third time when Allen came walking in the room.

"Hey buddy, I heard you really pissed off Lydia tonight. Great job; they all hate her anyway. Thinks she's knows everything and is always trying to tell everybody else what they should be thinking."

Bill quickly closed his computer and replied, "What are you talking about?"

"Lydia. They say you really put her in her place; that she stormed out of the bar. Amanda loved hearing that story. They work at the same school but they aren't friends . . . not by a long shot."

Allen insisted that Bill re-tell the entire story and especially the part where Lydia stood up and said, 'Well, I never.' He made Bill tell that part twice. After Bill had finished his story, he asked Allen about his evening. "It was alright."

"It was alright? That's all you're going to say? It was alright?"

"Yeah, it was alright."

"Allen, I think I have a right to know what's going on here."

"Remember on our last trip, when you met Ellen and you guys went on a five-hour hike on a deserted island that was only supposed to last an hour and a half? Do you remember that? And when I asked you what in the world you did for five hours . . . do you remember what you told me? Huh?"

Bill sheepishly answered, "Yeah, I said we went on a nature walk."

"Right. That's exactly what we did tonight . . . we went on a nature walk."

Bill answered, "But we really did go on a nature walk! What have you been doing for the last three hours?"

Allen walked to the bathroom door, turned around and said, "Nature walk, buddy. A good long, soothing, relaxing, intoxicating, seductive nature walk." With that being said, he went into the bathroom, shut the door, and took a long, hot, intoxicating, relaxing, soothing shower.

The following morning, Allen and Bill followed Amanda and the three women back towards Cedar City, Utah. They made one stop on the way to gas up and get something to drink. Allen and Amanda huddled together, while Bill and Lydia stayed far apart. At the university, the other two women separated from the group and Amanda insisted that Allen and Bill stay at her house while they visited the national parks in the area. Bill knew he had no choice in this decision, plus, a nice house and bed were better than the small cot inside their camper.

Amanda's house wasn't large but it was nice. She had two extra bedrooms, one for each guy. Allen let Bill take the larger one—he was still trying to be nice. They ordered a pizza to be delivered and Amanda had some stale Rocky Mountain watery beers in her refrigerator. After the boys had become full of pizza and thoroughly waterlogged, they all retired to the den where Amanda began to fill them in on her personal history: "Allen already knows most of this but I think I should tell you both some things I know that you're probably asking yourselves. First, I've been married three times." Allen did indeed already know this fact but Bill didn't. However, Bill didn't react, which was a credit to his self-restraint. "I met my first husband when we were both in college. We were too young and too naïve to understand what we were doing. It only lasted three years and we both agreed to move on. Him to California and I moved here.

"I met my second husband here at the university; he was an economics professor. About three years after my divorce, we married and lived here in Cedar City. We both decided to concentrate on our careers so we didn't have any children—probably a mistake, at least on my part. Anyway, I decided to surprise him at work with a fancy lunch on our tenth wedding anniversary. I went to his office and caught him and his graduate assistant having sex on his desk. He had forgotten it was our anniversary."

Bill didn't comment, so Amanda continued. "Five years after that divorce I met a man from my church who was a dentist here in town. Great guy and we really hit it off well. We dated for about two years then got married and lived in this house. He loved to golf and one day he was out playing and stepped out of his golf cart and fell over dead from a massive heart attack. It took a while to get over that, but I did. Now . . . here I am."

Bill didn't comment; he didn't know what he could say or should say, so he said nothing. Allen was also unusually quiet during this story, probably because he'd heard it before. After a few moments, Amanda asked Bill to tell her of his past history; she wanted to know all about his deceased wife, Eliza, as well as his current status with Ellen. She listened intently as Bill chronicled his entire history including his divorce, reconciliation, her death, and the current state of affairs with Ellen. Allen stayed quiet the entire evening, which must have been a world's record for him.

After everyone finished in the bathroom and went to their bedrooms for the night, Allen knocked and walked in Bill's room as he was typing Ellen an email. He didn't say anything until he sat on a chair near the bed. Bill closed his computer and Allen asked "Well?"

"She's one-in-a-million, Allen. Don't screw it up!"

Allen smiled and fist-bumped his friend. He then stood up and said, "Are you going to be alright in here by yourself, or do you want me to sleep with you?" Bill threw a pillow at him and they both laughed and felt good about life. It had been a long time coming . . . but it finally did.

30

AMANDA SAID SHE WAS GOING TO TAKE A FEW DAYS OFF and asked if she could be their tour guide as they visited the national parks in southern Utah. Since she was a local, it seemed a logical and great idea to all three of them—especially Allen. She first took them to Zion National Park which Bill had heard of but knew nothing about. When Bill asked about it, Amanda said, "Well, about a bajillion years ago, ancient iterations of the Virgin River starting wreaking havoc on southwestern Utah. Now there's a faint 'you're welcome' echoing through the canyons of Zion National Park." She looked at both guys to get their reaction . . . Bill was all ears at this enchanting introduction; Allen was still staring at Amanda all googly-eyed and didn't pay attention to anything she said. She noticed his inattention and continued, "Zion was the home-away-from-home for Adolph Hitler and the Third Reich during the Civil War. They would come here to relax and get away from all the confusion of landing on the moon." She looked at Bill who scrunched his face up and mouthed, "What?" She looked at Allen who was still smiling at her and nodding his head up and down. She then laughed and looked at Allen and said, "Pay attention!"

After Bill quit laughing, she started again, "Zion is like the set of a movie that's so grand you know it's fake, but you don't care because it's so delicious to look at; the kind of film where the art director was given carte blanche and didn't worry about believability."

It was difficult for Bill to comprehend what Amanda meant by all this . . . until they arrived in the park. It was awe-inspiring. The massive red stone monoliths, the waterfalls, the beautiful valleys, and the vistas almost left them speechless. Amanda decided to only stop at a few overlooks; they didn't have time to do any hiking, but that was enough.

The only time she stopped for any length was to walk them down to the Virgin River in the middle of the park, where the vertical walls of the canyon rose over 2,000 feet on each side of them. Bill stayed on the banks of the little shallow river but Allen and Amanda took their shoes off and waded into the middle of the river, which only came to below their knees. They didn't stay long because the water was too cold. Bill was thoroughly taken with the scenery and wished he could stay several days and explore. Allen was thoroughly taken with Amanda's legs as she rolled up her pants when they walked into the river. Amanda loved it all, and with each passing hour, she was loving Allen more and more.

When they arrived back in Cedar City, Amanda wanted to show them the campus of the university and where her office was. Bill sensed she and Allen needed some alone time so he asked them to drop him off at a pub downtown and he'd relax and wait on them. He walked into an Irish pub named The Laurels and took a seat at the bar. A waitress in her mid-thirties, and very attractive, came over and asked what he wanted. Bill said, "Coors Light, please."

She smiled and answered with a slight English or Irish accent, "One Guinness coming up."

Bill quickly responded, "No, I ordered a Coors Light."

She smiled again and said, "Coors Light, Guinness, they're basically the same thing."

"No, miss. They are nowhere near the same thing. I want a Coors Light."

"Well, six of one, half-dozen of the other."

Bill started to erupt when she leaned over and smiled at him, saying, "One Coors Light, on the house." She smiled again at Bill and he finally realized she was just messing with him. He really forgave her when she also brought him a bowl of Chex Mix to munch on with the beer.

After a few minutes, she came to check on him and Bill commented, "Judging from your accent you must be from Scotland."

"Scotland? Oh, no. I'm from Ireland. County Kerry."

Bill nodded and replied, "Ah, Scotland, Ireland, they're basically the same thing."

She immediately straightened up and quickly said, "No, sir, they are not even . . . " Then she realized Bill had just pranked her back. She saw Bill smile at her and she smiled back and shook her head, saying, "You're good."

Bill answered, "I had a good teacher."

She high-fived Bill and said, "Your second Guinness is not on the house, it's on ME."

When it dawned on Bill that Allen and Amanda might not be picking him up any time soon, he ordered a plate of nachos from the waitress, Eileen. He paid for those. When she brought the nachos to him, she asked, "Where are you from, sir? I know you're not from around here, I've never seen you before."

"North Carolina . . . have you heard of it?"

Eileen smiled and replied, "I said I was Irish, I didn't say I was stupid." They both laughed, then she asked, "North Carolina, that's where everyone's a Baptist isn't it?"

"Well, not everyone. I'm a Moravian." He could tell she had never heard of Moravians before, so he asked, "Are you familiar with Moravians?"

"Moravians . . . No. Baptists, yes."

Bill thought he might have a serious religious conversation with Eileen now. He asked her, "What do you know about Baptists?"

She came close to him and said, "I know that Baptists can't have sex standing up; they're afraid people will think they're dancing." Bill laughed so suddenly and so loud that several people around the bar looked over at him. Eileen just shrugged her shoulders and walked away.

When Bill regained his composure, Eileen came back over with a grin on her face and asked him, "You know what the difference is between kinky sex and perverted sex?" Bill had no idea but he couldn't wait to hear the answer. She said, "Kinky sex involves the use of duck feathers, perverted sex uses the whole duck." Again, Bill could not control his laughter. As everyone stared at him again, Eileen pointed at him, shrugged her shoulders, and said, "He's from South Carolina . . . you'll have to forgive him."

In between customers, he and Eileen traded stories and jokes until Allen and Amanda walked into the bar looking for him. Bill immediately noticed that Allen had a button on his shirt left unbuttoned. He didn't say anything. They asked if he was ready to go and Bill called Eileen over and introduced everyone to each other. Then Bill pointed to Eileen's left hand and said, "If I was twenty years younger and she didn't have one of those rings on her finger, I'd chase her to end of the earth and back."

Allen was stunned to hear something like that from Bill. He was more stunned when Eileen answered, "Forget the years . . . if I didn't have one of these rings on,

I'd let him catch me!" She came around the bar and gave Bill a big hug. They looked at each other, laughed, then hugged again. Allen was 100% flabbergasted!

Back at Amanda's house, Allen told stories most of the evening and everyone laughed and had a great time. Bill knew Allen was completely smitten when he agreed to have a glass of red wine with her; he and Allen hated red wine. Since Bill had already had two Guinnesses/Coors Lights, and because Amanda didn't have any Diet Pepsi, he opted to have a Diet Coke. He decided to go to bed fairly early and let them have some more alone time but Allen surprised him by knocking on his door shortly afterward. He came in and asked about Ellen; then asked about the bartender, Eileen; then asked about Bill's health; then hemmed and hawed around about nothing in particular. Bill knew Allen was beating around the bush wanting to say something . . . he just didn't know what, but he suspected it was about Amanda.

Bill listened but didn't divulge much information about Ellen; she was still private to him. Eventually, Allen got around to asking his serious question; however, it wasn't about Amanda at all. He began, "Bill, I'm feeling a little guilty about what I'm thinking and what I might do. I know I'm not perfect, and I'm not holy or anything, but I do want to be good. I don't want to do things that'll prevent me from being saved. Do you understand? I'm in a quandary." He leaned forward in his chair and stared directly at Bill waiting for his answer.

Bill wasn't prepared for such a serious issue. He took a few moments, then spoke, "Allen, history is full of ordinary people who faced adverse circumstances like you are. But they rose above them and changed their world. They weren't perfect. In fact, they were far from it. They failed often but they had great faith in God.

"Think about some of these people: Gideon was a frightened farmer and became a man of courage, Moses was a fugitive from justice, David was an adulterer, Abraham lied to his wife twice, and Sarah laughed at the Lord. But in the end, they all had great exploits of faith. Yes, they collected their scars, just like you. But God sees us for what we can become if we'll only step up and use our faith." Bill waited for Allen to comprehend all that he'd just told him.

Allen nodded but didn't say anything, so Bill asked him, "Do you have any questions about any of this?"

He looked up at Bill and asked, "So, God would forgive me if I have sex with Amanda?"

Bill thought Allen was joking around and he started to throw a pillow at him, but then realized Allen was serious. Bill said, "Is this something you and Amanda have discussed?"

"Not exactly in human words."

"Well, how do you know she wants to have sex with you?"

Allen smiled and replied, "Oh, I know alright. A man can tell, if you know what I mean."

"I suggest you and Amanda discuss this and all the implications that come with it."

Allen said, "Okay, you might be right. Thanks, buddy. But I know what she's gonna say." He got up, smiled at his friend and said, "See you in the morning."

Bill thought about his conversation with Allen until thoughts of Ellen inevitably crept in. He then wondered if he would give himself that same advice if the situation was reversed. It took him quite a while to finally fall asleep there in a strange bed, in Amanda's house, in Cedar City, Utah.

Early in the morning, Bill heard Allen in the bathroom that connected their two bedrooms. He waited until he heard the toilet flush, then he knocked on the bathroom door. Allen opened it and Bill asked, "Did you talk to her?"

"Yep."

"What happened?"

"Nothing! She said she's only interested in sex with a husband, not a boyfriend. Can you believe that?"

Bill smiled and said, "Good for her. I'm liking her more every minute. How do you feel about the situation now?"

Allen finally smiled and answered, "I guess I'll have to marry her, won't I?"

31

THE NEXT MORNING, while Amanda was preparing toasted bagels, oatmeal, and the morning coffee, Allen cornered Bill in the living room and said, "I might have a problem."

"What's wrong? You can't find your Viagra?"

"No . . . I told you I won't be needing those anyway. It's Sophie; she's started sending me topless pictures again."

Bill didn't know how to respond to that. Finally, he asked, "Why's that a problem for you? I thought you liked seeing them."

"Not now! I can't let Amanda see those pictures. She wouldn't understand."

"Understand what? That you're an adulterous, lecherous old man?"

"Bill!"

"Quit worrying about it, Allen. Just delete the pictures and email Sophie back and tell her you're not interested anymore."

Allen frowned, then did a little dance of front of Bill, before asking, "Will you email her for me?"

"No, I won't. I don't even know her, Allen. You need to do that and you need to do it now."

Allen didn't particularly like that answer, even though he knew that's what Bill was going to tell him. He said, "Okay, I'll do it. Tell Amanda I'll be right back." He walked into his bedroom while Bill went to the kitchen to say good morning to Amanda and get some coffee. About three minutes later, Allen came into the kitchen smiling and happy. He hugged Amanda and winked at Bill.

When Amanda opened the back door to take out a bag of garbage, Bill asked, "Did you email Sophie?"

"Yeah, it's all taken care of."

"What did you tell her?"

"I told her that you were forbidding me to have any more contact with her because it wasn't appropriate. I told her I'd try to pressure you into changing your mind but not to email me back until she heard from me."

Before Bill could erupt, Amanda walked back in the door. She could tell something had happened by the expression on Bill's face. She asked, "Everything okay?"

Allen quickly responded, "Yeah, it's great! Bill was just wondering where you're going to take us today."

Amanda didn't believe a word of that but she answered, "I think we'll ride over to Bryce Canyon National Park and let you guys see something quite a bit different from Zion." The bagels and oatmeal were great and the coffee was soothing. By his second cup, Bill had calmed down a little and understood that Allen was just being Allen. Then he noticed the way Amanda and Allen were staring at each other and how happy they both seemed, and everything seemed good again. He was happy for his friend.

The drive over to Bryce Canyon was itself an amazing adventure. Bill thought the entire lower half of Utah should all be a national park. Amanda had packed the car trunk with a large picnic basket and her own cooler, which was full of various drinks. She knew exactly what they would do today. She drove them inside the park and they witnessed the largest concentration of hoodoos (irregular columns of rock) anywhere on Earth. The high elevations and geological wonders defied description.

After taking in the views from several vistas, Amanda pulled into a large parking lot and viewing area called Inspiration Point. She told Allen and Bill to bring the picnic basket and cooler as they made their way through the pinyon pines to an isolated picnic table on the edge of a large canyon that was over nine thousand feet in elevation. The entire valley was full of hoodoos, colored various shades of reds, ambers, scarlet, vermillion, and maroon. It was as if Picasso had stepped from heaven and painted the landscape a surrealistic array of colors.

They set the basket and cooler on the picnic table and then found a seat on the ground near the edge where they could lean back against a tree trunk admiring the beauty below them. Amanda told them stories of hikes through the hoodoo land below and of grand adventures over the years. Her geography background gave everything a realistic and educational touch to her stories. Bill loved listening to her. Allen was so smitten she could've been speaking Russian and he'd have never known. They nibbled on ham biscuits, fruit, and snacks throughout the afternoon. She also had brought a bottle of red wine and a few Coors Lights as well. Amanda was good.

Amanda and Allen leaned back against a juniper, nestling against each other, Amanda with a glass of red wine and Allen with a Coors Light. Bill rested against a pinyon pine and wished Ellen was here with him to nestle against. They all sat and talked and stared into the valley of colorful spires. It would be hard to imagine a better day. It would also be hard for Bill to imagine Allen ever leaving Amanda's side. He didn't know what would happen in the short term, but he was certain that in the long term Allen would be with Amanda.

Amanda took them to dinner that evening at her favorite restaurant in Cedar City, Cugino Forno, which had the best Italian food in southern Utah. Bill hated it; not the food, but the fact that he felt like a third wheel. Allen and Amanda held hands and stared in each other's eyes all evening while whispering sweet nothings to each other as Bill ate breadsticks and sipped a glass of wine that wasn't half bad. Amanda made a few attempts to include Bill in their conversations . . . Allen didn't even try. He was too overwhelmed with his feelings to think about anything else.

Back at Amanda's house for the evening, Bill waited for Allen to finish in the bathroom before knocking on his door. Allen was already in bed with the light turned off when Bill walked in and asked, "You awake?"

"Umm, maybe."

"I need to talk to you. Can you turn the light on?"

Allen reached over and turned the lamp on, then sat up in bed and asked, "What's up?"

"That's what I want to know, what's up? Clearly, something is happening with you and Amanda and I'm happy about that. But I'm also concerned exactly what is happening and what is going to happen. You need to be honest with me, Allen."

"Bill, I will be honest with you . . . I asked her to marry me right now! Run off to Vegas and do it, but she wouldn't. Said it was too soon. Said she needed more time and wanted more time with me to know for sure. She would love for me to move here and be with her. Bill, we both know this is something special; something that may never come again and we don't want to lose it. When I'm with her, she's all I think about. When I'm not with her, all I'm thinking is that I want to be with her."

He looked at Bill waiting on a reaction but Bill sat there silently so he continued. "We've talked about three options: One, I just stay here and don't leave. She has a friend who rents out a condo that I could get really cheap. I could stay there and we could see each other and see where it takes us. Two, since I don't want to abandon you, I could go with you to Lake Superior and see happens with you and Ellen. If you wanted to spend time with her, then I could fly back out here and you could stay at Lake Superior as long as you wanted. And three, if things don't turn out the way you wanted with Ellen, we just drive back home and I pack up some things and fly back out here then. Bottom line is that with any of the options, I'm going to end up back out here . . . I have to, Bill."

None of these options was a surprise to Bill. In fact, he had thought of similar scenarios himself. Both guys were silent as they thought about everything and what should or could happen. Finally, Bill asked, "Tell me what you want to happen. What would be best for you?"

"Bill, I won't lie to you . . . I don't want to leave her. But I don't want to abandon you either and make you drive all the way across the country by yourself—I won't do that."

"I don't mind, Allen. I can do the driving."

"Nope, I won't do it. Ain't no way in the world you could have a good time without me showing you how. You know it's true." They both smiled and they both knew Allen was probably right. So, they decided right there on the side of the bed that option two was the best deal for everyone. They would go to Lake Superior. Bill would meet Ellen again and see if there was anything between them. If so, Allen would fly back to Utah; if not, they would drive home to North Carolina.

They sat in silence for a few moments, then Allen said, "Can you believe all of this is happening? I remember what you told me last week sometime, that with God, things can change just like that!" Allen snapped his fingers as he finished that sentence. Bill rose from the bed and smiled, then walked out of the room to go back and email Ellen to tell her things worked out exactly as he had planned.

32

WHEN THE DECISION WAS MADE for the boys to drive to Lake Superior, Allen was ready to go then. Not to drive straight through, but to get on with the journey so he could be closer to returning. However, Amanda had told them both how scenic the area around Moab, Utah, was and made them promise they would go visit on their way to Lake Superior. The next morning, Allen and Amanda took a long walk before breakfast, Allen promising he would be back soon and Amanda making him promise to keep that promise.

Bill sat in the kitchen and drank coffee by himself while he texted Ellen. He told her they'd be leaving today and she texted back, "Just tell Allen he can stay there. I'll fly down and ride back with you." Bill was tempted to accept this offer but for selfish reasons, he wanted to spend a few more days alone with Allen. He knew they would probably never have this opportunity to be alone again as friends. He texted Ellen back, "Thanks, but Allen would never forgive me if I abandoned him at this point."

Ellen asked, "So you're saying you'd rather spend your nights alone with Allen than with me?"

"Are you saying you want to spend some nights alone with me?"

"Define 'spend some nights alone with me.'"

Bill replied, "You know . . . be alone at night with each other."

"As in?"

With a feeling of relief, Bill said, "Allen just came back, I've got to run. I'll keep you posted."

"Chicken," Ellen said.

It was easy to tell Amanda had been crying. Bill had everything packed in the Silverado and made one last bathroom break as Allen promised the world to Amanda before they left. Then, Amanda came to Bill and hugged him saying,

"Please take care of him, Bill. You know how he is. Make him keep his promise to come back."

"Don't worry, Amanda. He'll be back and I'll take good care of him."

"And, Bill . . . good luck with Ellen. I hope it turns out as well for you as it has for us. I'd really love to meet her sometime."

Bill went to the truck as Allen and Amanda tried to leave each other. He was tempted to blow the horn, but wisely, he didn't. Allen finally hopped in the passenger side and rolled the window down, then held Amanda's hand as Bill started pulling out of the driveway. Allen turned completely around in his seat to watch her as they started down the street. When they turned the corner, Allen received a text from Amanda telling him she missed him already. He tried to show it to Bill, who said, "Alright, I'm stopping up here and you're getting out! I'm not driving all the way to Moab with some lovesick teenager."

"Aww, shut up, grumpy. Just keep driving and wake me up when we get to Nirvana, or wherever it is we're going." Bill smiled and Allen texted as they headed out to I-15 north on their way over to Moab, Utah.

They drove north until they soon turned onto I-70 West towards Grand Junction, Colorado. It was high desert in this part of Utah, with very sparse vegetation and a few scattered mountain ranges in the distance. After a few hours, they stopped in the little town of Richfield, not because they needed anything, just because. As Bill pulled off the interstate, he noticed a small café under a canopy of trees, which was unusual for this part of the country. Allen woke from his dream but didn't say anything until Bill had stopped the Silverado and turned the motor off. "Where are we?"

Bill answered, "In the beautiful little town of Richfield, Utah."

Allen looked all around him but didn't see anything except the café and a few cars parked in front. He said, "I like it."

Bill smiled and replied, "Let's go in and get something to eat so we can use the bathroom."

"I'm not really hungry. I'll just hit the john and we can leave."

Bill had opened his door but stopped his exit and said, "You can't go in there and use their toilets without buying anything."

"Why not . . . they won't care."

"Listen to me, Allen. If you go in there and pee, you make sure you buy something, even if it's only a Diet Pepsi. You understand?"

"What about if I only poop and not pee?"

Bill got out and slammed his door and started for the café; Allen tried his best to stop laughing but was unsuccessful in his attempt. He followed Bill in and saw him sitting at the counter but he chose wisely and sat two stools down from him. A young waitress took Bill's order of coffee and apple pie, then shuffled over to Allen who ordered a Diet Pepsi and a slice of carrot cake.

They ate in silence, Bill never once looking over at Allen until Allen asked the waitress what her name was. She answered, "Christine," then she asked Allen, "Where are you headed today, sir?"

"I'm going back home to Kansas City, Christine. I've got a lot of explaining to do when I get there."

Christine was hooked: "What kind of explaining?"

"Well, my friend and I went on a Colorado River rafting trip, Christine. He was a man about my age but a little homely. Never could keep a girlfriend because, you know, he just wasn't very good-looking." Christine was thoroughly hooked and Bill even leaned slightly closer so could hear the story better. "We were way out in the wilderness and stopped for the night, right there on the riverbank, like we usually did. We were all sitting around waiting on sunset when we noticed a small raft coming down the river with only one person in it. This little raft pulled over to us and we saw a really old, ugly Indian woman right by herself. She asked if we had any extra food and my friend, his name was Bill, he gave her a hot dog to eat. Well, she and Bill started talking with each other and then went off by themselves to talk in private. After it turned dark, we all started looking for Bill but couldn't find him or the Indian woman anywhere. We finally checked inside Bill's tent and he had left a note that said, 'I'm gone. Don't try and follow me. I've found my true love.' So, we let old Bill and his Indian lover go off together, Christine. Now, I've got to go back and explain all that to Bill's friends and family . . . it ain't going to be easy."

Christine's mouth was wide open but she made no sound. Bill eventually smiled but he never looked over at Allen. Then Allen asked Christine where the restroom was and he left her a nice tip as he walked away. Christine brought Bill's check over to him and asked him, "Did you hear that guy's story, sir? It was amazing."

Bill also left Christine a nice tip and then said to her, "Christine, cigarettes and alcohol have warning labels on them because they are addictive, dangerous, and destroy lives—and yet, some men are just allowed to run their mouths and roam about freely with no warnings." Christine nodded as Bill walked out the door and climbed back into the Silverado, where Allen was pretending to be asleep as they resumed their journey towards Moab, Utah.

Allen took over the driving as they exited off I-70 onto state road 191 towards Moab. It was getting to be late afternoon and the lowering sun starting changing the color and hues of the red rocks in the distance. The closer they came to Moab, the redder everything got. As they neared the town, Bill pointed off to the left and said, "Look at that!" Allen took his foot off the accelerator as he noticed a large red rock arch off in the distance. He pulled off onto the shoulder and they each stepped out of the truck to gaze into the back of beyond. They saw a couple of other smaller arches in other directions. Bill exclaimed, "What sort of place is this?"

It took a lot to make Allen speechless . . . this was a lot. Finally, he said, "Amanda said it was gorgeous. She wasn't lying."

Soon after they resumed the drive they spotted a sign for a campground that was apparently in the middle of nowhere. They didn't see any office or any other vehicles, only a dusty, potholed, gravel road leading off over a small rise to the left. Bill yelled out, "Take it!"

So Allen cruised over and turned onto the road, which looked like no one had driven on it for years. They went down into a sandpit and Allen had to gun the Silverado so it wouldn't get stuck. They made it up the next rise to find the land filling up with pinyons, junipers, cactus, and rocks of all sizes and shapes. It was like they were entering a fairyland of geologic shapes and forms. About two miles down this rutted, rock-strewn road, they finally came to a so-called campground. There was no office and only one other RV parked at the far end. A small sign was posted next to an old porta-potty, which read, "Park anywhere and sign in the book below."

Fine, but there was no book below; it was missing. They got out of the truck and were standing there in awe of the landscape when they were surprised by an older couple who came walking from behind a rock wall. The older man said, "It's okay.

Park anywhere, nobody cares. We've been here three days and haven't seen a soul. The toilet kind of stinks but it's worth it to be out here alone."

So, Bill pulled the Silverado up to the top of a small incline and that's where they set up the camper. Directly in front of them, about a hundred yards away, was a tremendous spear-shaped, or arrowhead-shaped rock balanced long ways on a small pedestal of rock about fifty yards tall. They stared at this incomprehensible rock formation and did not understand how such a large rock could somehow balance on top of such a small base. Each direction they turned revealed a different, yet just as amazing, scene. They were too excited to simply sit in their chairs. Each guy grabbed a Coors Light from the cooler and they started walking around the campground in a large circle to see as much as they could before the sun set for the evening.

As they passed near the other RV, they noticed the older man and woman were grilling something on a portable grill they had set up. The man yelled at them to come over and join them. When they got to the RV, the man said, "Nice to have you here in our campground, boys. Can you join us for dinner?"

Whatever it was he had on the grill smelled very good but neither guy could actually identify exactly what he was cooking. Before they could answer his question, the lady said, "We've got plenty and we're not dangerous. Pull up a chair, we've got extras over there. My name's Holly and my husband is Whitey."

Allen and Bill introduced themselves and volunteered to bring their cooler over and furnish the drinks. When they all sat down, Whitey lit a couple of lanterns and attended the grill, as whatever it was continued to smell great to Allen and Bill. Curiosity finally prevailed and Allen asked, "What are you cooking there, Whitey? It smells fantastic but I can't place it."

Whitey grinned but before he could answer, Holly said, "It's some fish he bought in town. He's smoked it, grilled it, and peppered it. He's done everything to this fish but pistol-whip it and dress it in a kilt." Allen and Bill burst out laughing at this description. Whitey held up his drink and they all saluted as they continued to whiff the unmistakable aromas coming from his kilted fish.

It tasted as good as it smelled. Whitey and Holly were generous, fun, and very talkative. Even Allen had a hard time telling stories. Eventually, drowsiness overcame them all and they each went to their own campers to await what wonders would meet them when the sun rose again at a campground, in the middle of nowhere, somewhere near Moab, Utah.

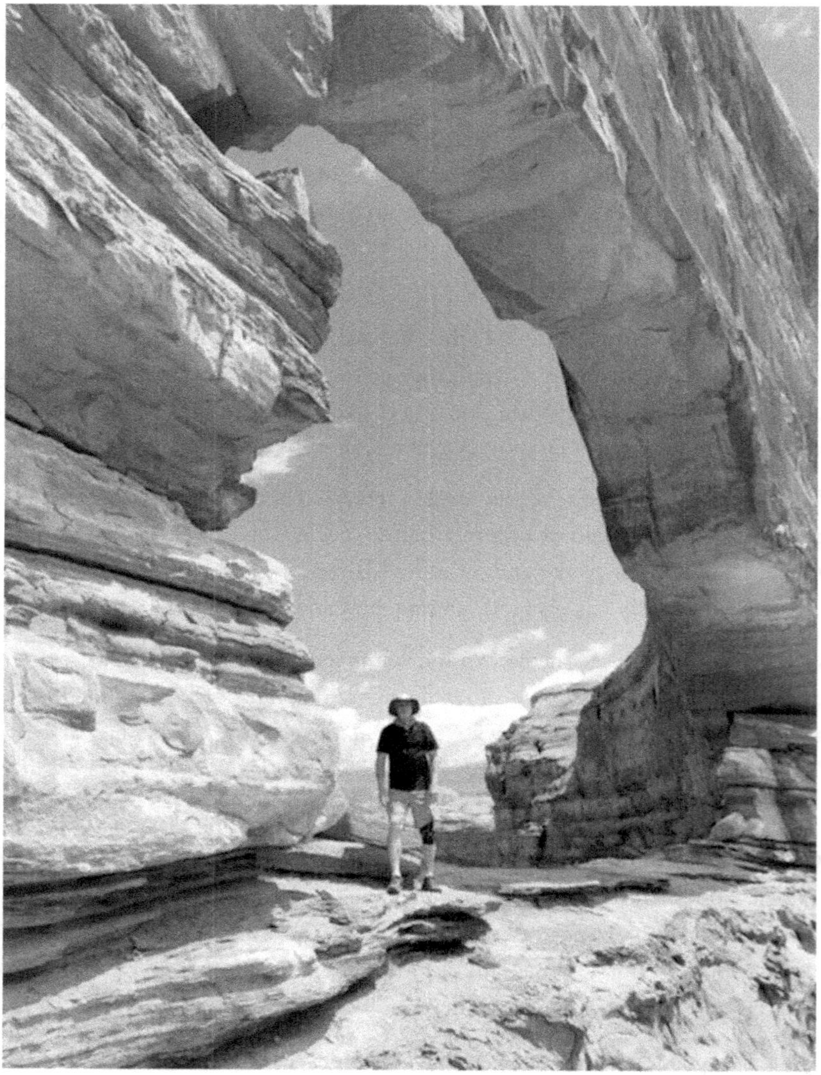

33

In the morning, after bathroom breaks, they walked around the campground again staring out in wonder. They noticed no movement from Whitey and Holly's RV, so they stayed away from their site. They detoured around to where the large pinnacled rock was balanced on its improbable base. At first, they were a little hesitant to walk near it. Allen said, "That's close enough, I don't trust that thing."

"Allen, that rock has probably been balanced up there for thousands of years. What makes you think it's going to fall now?"

"What makes YOU think it's not?"

So, they kept their distance as they circled the entire formation trying to understand how that huge rock stayed up there, balanced on that small base. On the other side of the ridge were two large stone arches right next to each other. They looked close, but it took about ten minutes for the guys to walk over to them. Allen gawked at these unbelievable formations and asked, "How does something like this happen?"

"Beyond our comprehension, son. I'm just glad Amanda told us about this place."

Hearing Amanda's name set off an alarm in Allen's head. He said, "Let's go, I need to email her and text her and let her know I'm okay." They scurried back to the truck only to find that there was no Wi-Fi service out there in the back of beyond. They unhooked the camper and started the truck to drive into town when they noticed Holly and Whitey come out of their RV. They drove over and thanked them again for dinner and told them they were going into Moab but would be back in camp that night.

Allen told them they'd already been up and walking around exploring the area. Holly remarked, "Y'all didn't get much sleep then, did you?"

Allen answered, "We were a little excited by the scenery. Normally it's good to get at least eight hours of beauty sleep each night." Then he nodded over towards Bill and said, "Nine if you're ugly." Before Bill could respond, Allen took off, waving goodbye to Holly and Whitey, while leaving a dust plume about a hundred feet tall down the old, rutted, rocky road.

Allen was hungry and couldn't wait to get into Moab and find a restaurant with a good cup of coffee. As they drove down Main Street, Bill saw a place called Desert Bistro with parking spaces right in front. It was an eclectic sort of place, not what they were expecting out here away from civilization. They sat at a small table and a very thin waitress with blue hair and piercings in her ears, nose, eyebrows, and lower lip came to take their order. She was very nice and introduced herself as Anne (with an "e" she noted). Bill ordered bacon and eggs with hash browns; Allen ordered a large stack of pancakes with bacon on the side.

Anne refilled their coffee and was very attentive but her thinness seemed to bother Allen. He asked Bill, "Do you think something's wrong with her?"

"No, she's just thin, that's all."

"I don't know, she might be amnesic."

Bill said, "You mean anorexic?"

"Yeah, that too. She's so skinny that she looks like she could be mailed first class to New York for about a dollar and a half."

The breakfast was very good, everything except the coffee. Bill and Allen just wanted coffee! Not spices and flavors and all sorts of added junk—just coffee. It wasn't Anne's fault, she only served it, so she still got a nice tip as they left. But as soon as they stepped outside, they started looking for a coffee shop to fulfill their caffeine habit. Plus, they needed a place to access Wi-Fi to check in on Amanda and Ellen. They noticed a sign for a Starbucks about two blocks up Main Street. That would do. Not all the specialty stuff they had, only plain, straight coffee—plus Wi-Fi.

They passed all sorts of gift shops and bookstores and western clothing stores on their way to Starbucks—Moab was quite a unique little town. They walked in the door and smelled the aroma of fresh coffee and it immediately put smiles on their faces. They ordered and sat at a table next to the window to email the girls and slowly sip their coffee. After the first emails were sent and others were read, Allen said, "Hey, look over there."

Bill looked up and replied, "Where?"

"Over there at that guy by himself."

Bill looked at the man, then said, "What?"

"He's in Starbucks with no iPhone, no tablet, no laptop, nothing. He's just sitting there drinking coffee like a psychopath."

Bill wanted to pick up a packet of sugar and throw at Allen but there was none on the table. So, he just said, "Shut up."

After breakfast and coffee, they went out to Arches National Park on the edge of town. They were overwhelmed. The natural arches, the fins, rock formations, and just the entire panorama of endless sights was more than they had imagined. At one overlook, Bill leaned back against the hood of the Silverado and said, "This is the most beautiful place on earth."

When Allen heard Bill say that, his memory kicked in and he scrambled in the back seat of the truck to find the book that Amanda had given him that first day. He opened it to the first page, to the first paragraph, which read, "This is the most beautiful place on Earth." He brought the book around and showed it to Bill. They were both silent for a few moments, thinking about that coincidence. Then, their minds got around to thinking about Amanda and Ellen. As much as they enjoyed each other's company, they were silently wishing that the girls could be here and see this with them. Bill finally said what they were both thinking, "I wish Ellen was here to see this."

Allen nodded, then he said, "I know, I wish Amanda was here to see this, too."

Bill turned to Allen and replied, "She's already seen it, numbnuts. She's the one who told us about it."

Allen wasn't fazed and answered, "But she hasn't seen it with me, grandpa . . . that's the difference."

Bill smiled and said, "Sometimes you make a little sense, and other times nobody understands you."

Allen pointed at a large, black bird that had just sailed through one of the arches, then said, "The older I get the more I understand that it's okay to live a life others don't understand." Then he looked at Bill and asked, "Understand?"

"Totally."

They drove through the park and came to a large parking lot for hikers who were walking out to the most famous of all the arches in the park, Delicate Arch. This arch was so famous that its image was on all Utah license plates. They got out of the truck and studied the signs and looked at the trailhead. It was about two and a half miles out to the viewing area, over some rugged terrain; then two and a half miles back. It was getting later in the afternoon and Bill asked Allen if he thought they could make the hike out to the famous Delicate Arch. Allen replied, "You can do what you think you can do, and you cannot do what you think you cannot."

Bill started to try and understand what that meant. Then he changed his mind, turned around, and started walking back to the truck. Allen happily followed him. Arches National Park had been more than either guy had ever dreamed possible. They took a couple of short hikes on the road out, nothing over five minutes, and wished they had the stamina and courage and youth to take off walking over the next ridge and see for themselves just what was out there in the back of beyond, in Arches National Park, near Moab, Utah.

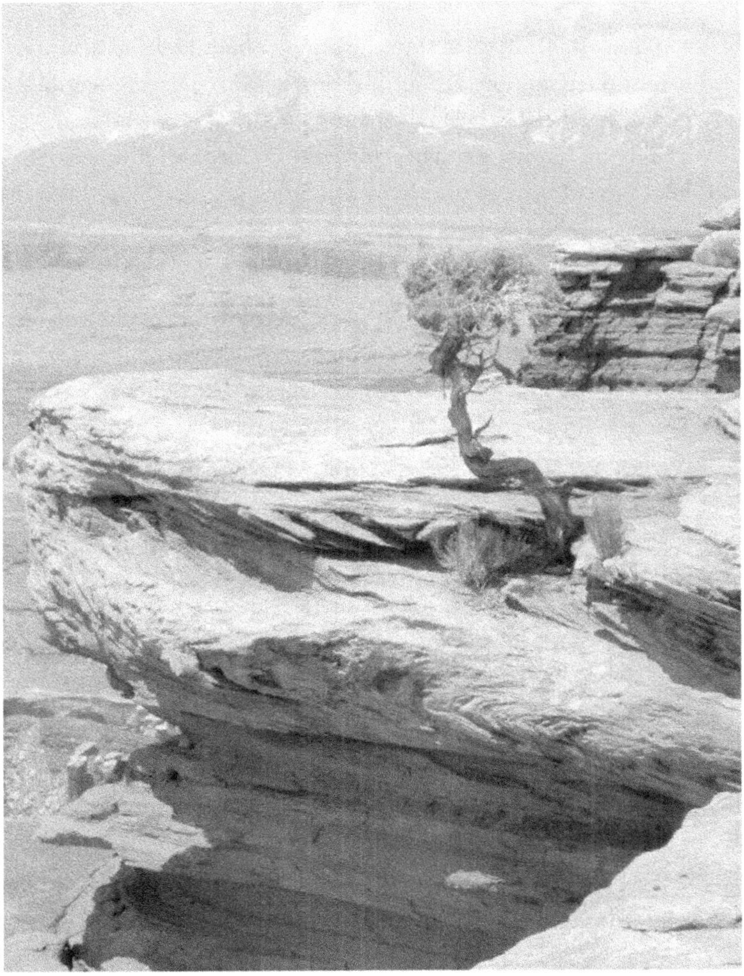

34

WHEN ALLEN AND BILL RETURNED to the campground, Holly and Whitey were gone. It was just them and the various rock formations, the balanced rock, a few buzzards floating overhead, a lone rabbit sitting under a bush, and some chirping birds they could hear but not see. They drove the camper over to where Holly and Bob had theirs located because the view was a little more dramatic. Then they set the chairs out facing the balanced rock and put the cooler between them as they planned on watching the sun drop over the horizon.

Since there was no Wi-Fi, they couldn't text or email either of the girls but they could talk about them—and that's exactly what they did. Even Bill opened up a bit and described his feelings about Ellen. Allen happily told Bill how happy he was now since God had finally answered his prayers and put Amanda in his life. Bill set his beer down, leaned forward a little, and said, "He's always answered your prayers, Allen."

"Not this one! I've been praying for Amanda for a long time and she just now came into my life."

"This was the only time He answered 'yes.' He's answered 'no' a lot of times, and probably even answered, 'slow' a few times." He knows what's good for you, son. Trust me, if He answered 'yes' to everything you asked Him for, you'd be in a world of trouble."

Initially, Allen didn't believe that or really understand it. But the more he thought about what Bill just told him, the more sense it made. Then he started remembering some things he asked God for over the years and realized that Bill was right. But he sure was happy God answered this one with a "yes."

The boys wanted to explore Moab for several more days, but they also wanted to continue their journey to Lake Superior and beyond. They decided to wind their way out of Moab by following the Colorado River as it flowed from Colorado down into Moab. They read online about a few nice, short hikes they could take on the way out. They passed a winery that was out in the middle of nowhere, right on the banks of the Colorado. Shortly after that, they saw a small sign for one of the hiking trails they had read about. Bill drove down the isolated dirt road and parked in the small parking area at the trailhead. They were the only vehicle in the lot. In fact, except for the winery, they hadn't seen another building of any kind since leaving Moab about twenty minutes earlier.

They started up the winding trail which was replete with views reminiscent of old western movies. Around every curve, they were met with landscapes that could have come straight from a movie set. They decided to make the climb to the top of the next incline, then turn around and return to the truck. Just after they went around a large rock wall they saw someone sitting on the ground with his legs crossed, staring out across the horizon. As they came closer, they noticed it was an old man—older than them. He had on some sort of military hat with a few emblems pinned to it.

They approached him slowly so they wouldn't startle him but he never seemed to notice them until they were five or six feet from him. He turned his head and looked up at them but didn't say anything. Bill asked, "Are you okay, sir?"

He looked at them both and answered, "I'm fine."

Bill and Allen looked at each other, totally unsure what they should do or say. They wondered how this old man had gotten out there. There were no other vehicles in the lot and no signs of houses or buildings for miles. And, he was old! Finally, Bill asked, "Do you need any help?"

"No, I'm fine," he answered again.

But he didn't seem fine. It seemed to the guys that he had been crying. They really didn't feel comfortable leaving him alone out here in the middle of nowhere. Bill went near him and sat down, then Allen sat down as they all stared out across the buttes and mesas in the distance. After a moment or two, the man said, "I appreciate your concern but you don't need to stay here, I'll be fine. My son operates that winery you probably passed. He dropped me off here and he'll be back in an hour or two . . . I'll be fine."

At least that answered a few of their questions. But still . . . why was he sitting out here by himself? The man must have sensed what they were thinking, so he began: "It's my birthday. It's the one day each year where I reflect on my life and why I am allowed to be here when so many of my friends are not here. Why I'm not planted in some field in France like they are. I look at all those rocks and pinnacles and buttes and mesas and think, these are the boys of Pointe du Hoc. These are the men who took the cliffs. These are the champions who helped free a continent. These are the heroes who helped end a war. They were the fathers we never know, the uncles we never met, the friends who never returned, the heroes we can never repay. They gave us our world. And those simple sounds of freedom we hear today are their voices speaking to us across the years."

They all sat in silence for several minutes. Then Allen nudged Bill and they both rose. The old man never looked up at them or made any gestures. They started back down the trail and decided they would go back to the winery and inquire inside if the old man did indeed have a son that was coming to pick him up. There was no way they could leave him without knowing someone was coming to get him. As they started down the dirt road, they noticed a dust tail from another vehicle near the entrance. Bill pulled over to the side and stepped out of the truck and waited for the other vehicle. It was the son. He thanked them for checking on his dad. He said, "My dad never talks about what happened during World War II. Never. He just wants to be alone on his birthday to think about it. This, however, will probably be the last year he can make this hike; he just doesn't have the strength anymore. Thanks again for checking on him."

The son continued up the road to check on his dad. The boys continued down the road in silence, thinking about dads and sons and friends and heroes that they both knew and never knew.

They took two more short hikes during the day and wished they had more time for others. Soon, they crossed over into Colorado and spotted a campground on the banks of the Colorado River before they got to Grand Junction. It was a newer campground that was located right next to a vineyard, which the guys thought was a little strange. Why would there be a vineyard out here in the desert? It also had a small grill next to the office that sold burgers, pizza, and comfort food most campers were looking for.

Allen picked out a spot at the end of the property and a considerable distance from the restrooms. Bill asked why he was parking so far away from the bathroom and Allen said, "Look, we're next to the grapevines." Bill saw the vineyard next to them but never thought anything about it. When Allen saw the grapevines, he immediately thought "dessert."

Bill said, "Allen, you better not steal any of those grapes."

"It ain't stealing, Bill. They expect some grapes to be lost . . . it's natural. Deer come and eat some; squirrels, crows, all sorts of animals eat them. They expect a certain amount of loss."

Bill firmly replied, "There's a big difference between animal loss and outright theft."

"Aww, don't get your panties in a wad. I'll probably leave 'em alone anyway."

Bill didn't believe him. Allen didn't even believe himself. He was already thinking about dusk when he could sneak over to the fence and grab a handful or two.

They got a couple of burgers, which were delicious, and a Diet Pepsi, then sat by the river to eat and watch nature roll by. This section of the Colorado was calm and slow, unhampered by cliffs and drastic elevation changes. It sort of reminded them of the Yadkin River back home in North Carolina. The campground somehow even had Wi-Fi, and after they finished eating both guys were typing furiously to their girls.

Allen finished his typing just as the sun fell down below the horizon. Bill was reading a message while keeping an eye on Allen. Then Allen rose and said, "I'm going to the bathroom, I'll be right back."

"Stay away from that vineyard, Allen."

"I'm going to pee, old man."

Bill watched him as he did indeed walk toward the bathrooms, then he continued reading his latest email from Ellen, for the fifth time. A few minutes later, Bill heard Allen yell out, "Owww!" He looked around and saw Allen grabbing his arm, standing next to the fence where the vineyard was. As darkness fell, Allen had misjudged the barbed wire fence as he reached through it to grab some grapes. One of the barbs stuck his arm and he yelled.

He walked over to Bill holding his arm and said, "I'm bleeding. Help me."

"I'm not helping no thief."

"I'm not a thief. I didn't steal anything."

"But you wanted to. Same thing."

Allen huffed and said, “No it’s not. I wasn’t going to steal them, I just wanted to feel them and see if they were ripe yet.”

Bill finally got up, shaking his head, and went to the truck to get the first aid kit. He bandaged Allen’s arm and said, “I hope you learned a good lesson.”

“I did. I need to find a nicer friend.”

35

THE FOLLOWING MORNING, Bill bought some breakfast burritos and coffee from the camp office and they sat by the river and discussed life as they ate. When they finished their meal, each guy spent the next half hour typing emails and reading emails. The flow of the river was nearly hypnotic and almost put them both to sleep. Bill eventually said, "I guess we'd better pack up and start moving."

"Bill, why don't we just turn around and head back to Cedar City. You can call Ellen and tell her to fly down and we'll all just stay there for a while . . . or, forever."

Bill didn't answer. He thought about it though, mostly because Cedar City sounded like a better place to live than the shores of Lake Superior did—especially in the wintertime. But it was only a dream for him and he knew it. He also knew it could be a reality for Allen, but he truly could not tell what the future would hold for him and Ellen. Yes, they both missed each other. Yes, they were looking forward to seeing each other again. But after that . . . who knows what would happen. Bill could not foresee himself living on the shores of Lake Superior—it just didn't seem possible. And, Ellen told him two years ago that she would never leave Lake Superior. So now, every time he had wistful thoughts of Ellen, he also had remorseful thoughts as well. But still, the thoughts of seeing her again brought great happiness and excitement to him. He could hardly wait.

After the truck was packed, Bill changed the bandage on Allen's arm and they were ready to go. The small two-lane road roughly followed the route of the Colorado River as it flowed from the Rocky Mountains down into Utah and eventually Arizona. The road crossed the river several times and Bill would stop and pull over so they could stand and watch the mighty river pass below them. Eventually, they made it back to the interstate and headed east towards Grand Junction, Colorado. The entire country was a wide-open desert. Not even many scrubby bushes were growing and absolutely no trees were anywhere to be seen.

The interstate also followed the route of the Colorado River and both led them into the town of Grand Junction that afternoon. As they neared the city, they started seeing billboards and signs for various vineyards. Neither guy could figure out why or how vineyards were prominent out here in the high desert. The next exit had a large sign advertising another vineyard, so Allen said, "Take this exit, Bill. Let's visit this place and see what's going on here. It doesn't make any sense."

The sign advertised the Two Rivers Winery. Before they could get to that particular winery, they passed the Desert Sun Winery, the Graystone Winery, the Debeque Canyon Winery, and the Talon Winery—all within five miles of each other. When they pulled in the parking lot of the Two Rivers Winery they saw an impressive French-designed chateau surrounded by acres of vineyards. They went in the tasting room, which was already busy with about a dozen other customers, and gawked at the impressive architecture and paintings on the walls. An attractive woman came up to them and introduced herself as Lily, the daughter of the winery's owner.

She explained the reason for so many wineries: The Gunnison River and the Colorado River meet here and this great confluence is the reason for the name of the town, Grand Junction, and is the source of water to irrigate all the wineries. They walked behind the winery and could see the Gunnison River flowing close by. Lily told them all the wineries followed the paths of the rivers. They went back inside and the boys sampled some of the local wines. Most of them were a little too dry and too red for their tastes, but they did find one that was okay.

They bought a glass of this wine and sat outside with the other tourists and watched the Gunnison River roll by. Soon, a very pretty, young girl sat at the table next to them and said hello. Allen and Bill both sat up a little straighter and tried to suck in their stomachs a little. A couple of minutes later, her boyfriend came to the table carrying two glasses of wine. Her boyfriend was either dressed in shorts that were too long or long pants that were too short—it was hard to tell which. He also had spiked hair and each different spike had a different color: blue, orange, red, green, pink, and purple.

Bill wondered how in the world this very pretty girl could be with this freaky-looking guy. Allen wasn't thinking anything; he was just in awe of the guy's hair. Apparently, Allen stared a little too long at the guy, who asked, "What's wrong old man? You were never crazy when you were young?"

Allen didn't appreciate the tone from this young man, so he answered, "Yeah, I was crazy once. I got drunk one night and had sex with a peacock and I was just wondering if you might be my son."

It took the young man about ten seconds to figure out what Allen meant. By then, his girlfriend had picked up her wine glass with one hand, and grabbed his arm with her other hand and said, "Let's go, Nigel." Nigel, either being the good boyfriend he was or the scared punk he looked like, dutifully followed his girlfriend back into the winery.

Bill smiled and said, "You ain't no good at all, are you?"

Allen took a small sip of wine and answered, "Nope."

Lily came back by their table and talked the guys into having a second glass of wine, then a third. By the time they stared on their fourth glass, Allen was telling stories to everyone in the winery. At closing time, it was evident that neither guy could be driving very far. Two blocks down the street was a Holiday Inn that Lily told them about. She also told them it was okay to leave the Silverado in her parking lot. She called Uber for them because no one trusted anyone to drive these two blocks in their condition. Their driver, Mark, seemed a little disappointed that he was called to only drive his customers for two blocks. But being the good old boy he was, he didn't complain . . . at least not until he got to the Holiday Inn and found both of his customers fast asleep in the back seat.

He woke them up and helped them get into the hotel and even carried their luggage for them. Fortunately for all of them, their room was on the first floor. Mark even opened the door for them to their room as Bill did have enough composure to fish a twenty dollar bill out of his wallet for a tip. Allen did not feel good . . . not at all. There was a big difference between two Coors Lights and four glasses of red wine. He was swaying in the hallway as Bill was getting the twenty bucks out when he knew he had to get to the bathroom quickly.

He didn't make it. Just as Bill was handing the twenty dollars to Mark, Allen tried to step between them to reach the bathroom, but instead, he vomited on Bill's hand, the twenty dollar bill, and Mark's hand. It was then a fight to see who could get into the bathroom first to wipe the puke off of themselves. Mark made it first. He grabbed a towel and ran the hot water while soaping himself down furiously. Allen stumbled to the bed and flopped down on it and immediately passed out. Bill waited with puke dripping off his fingers.

When Mark finished, he saw the twenty dollar bill lying in a puddle of Allen's vomit. He thought about it, but not for long. As he started to walk out the door,

Bill asked him to wait. Bill finished toweling off, then went to Allen's wallet and got out two twenty dollar bills and handed them to Mark. Then Bill went to his bed and flopped down, hoping that the two phrases: "Grand Junction" and "red wine" would never come up in any conversation ever again.

Allen woke up first because he was dehydrated and thirsty. The room was completely dark. He thought it must have been about five or six in the morning, so he'd let Bill sleep a little longer. He stumbled to the bathroom to get some water and looked at his watch to find that it was only nine-thirty at night. He quickly tried to piece together the events of the past few hours . . . it was a little hazy. Bill heard the water running and yelled out, "You okay?"

"Course I'm okay. Why wouldn't I be?" Then he saw a big stain on the floor and several dirty and soiled towels lying around and his memory started kicking in. Then his head started hurting. "Bill, you got any Excedrin?"

They both took some Extra Strength Excedrin and drank a glass of water, then laid back on the bed with a dim light on. Bill said, "I'm never, ever, drinking red wine again."

Allen said, "I hope I didn't do anything crazy last night . . . I mean, tonight." Bill didn't want to tell him about puking on poor old Mark. He'd wait for a more appropriate time for that. Allen continued, "I hope the Lord will forgive us for all this."

Bill, trying to get a short Bible lesson in, added, "Just be glad we're in the New Testament now and not the Old Testament, or we'd probably get lashed or stoned for doing what we did."

Allen thought, then said, "Stoned? Yep, four doobies would be a lot better than four glasses of red wine." Bill wanted to throw a pillow at his friend . . . but his head hurt way too much.

Checkout time wasn't until noon the next day. They used every minute of it to lay in bed and regret ever hearing the words "red wine." They checked out, then went to the hotel's restaurant to drink coffee. No food, just coffee. After three cups apiece, they walked out to the parking lot but couldn't find the Silverado. It took a couple of minutes for Bill to finally realize where they left the truck—at the winery. Neither of them wanted to go anywhere near that winery again. It would probably be at least a week before their heads quit hurting. And, there was no way they were going to walk two blocks back to the winery, carrying their luggage, as bad as they felt.

As they were thinking, Allen's phone dinged with a text. He'd forgotten to text or email Amanda since early last evening; she was worried about him. He texted back assuring her it was all Bill's fault, that he was fine. Just then, the Holiday Inn's shuttle van pulled in the lot and Bill went to ask the driver if he would take them the two blocks back to their truck. Sure, twenty bucks! They really had no choice, so Allen said, "Here, I got it." He opened his wallet to realize that some money was missing—two twenty dollar bills.

He looked at Bill, who said, "I can explain. You won't like it, but I can explain."

The shuttle van took them to the Silverado and they quickly left the parking lot. They got back on the interstate but didn't get far before they stopped again at a small diner to drink more coffee and take more Excedrin. This was not going to be a pleasant day.

36

THE RHYTHM OF THE ROAD seemed to settle things down and each guy's headache was beginning to lessen. There wasn't much to see or think about on I-70 until they reached the Rockies. They stopped once for gas and to stretch their legs and to take more Excedrin, and by the afternoon they were feeling better. Then things changed.

The Rocky Mountains are not like the Appalachians, where you have rolling hills for many miles before you actually reach the mountains. No. The Rocky Mountains are suddenly THERE! You see them for a long time, while you're actually driving along the flat plains. Then, Boom! You're in the mountains, no gradual, rolling hills—just mountains—big mountains. Bill was driving and Allen was glued to the windows as he stared in wonder at the scenes ahead of him. Pulling the trailer seemed to put a little strain on the Silverado as they rose in elevation quite suddenly, but it caused no problems.

In the matter of a few minutes, they were deep in the mountains. High mountains. Whether it was the thrill of the scenery or the effects of the Excedrin, or something else, but they were feeling much better and very hungry. They came to a town they'd never heard of named Glenwood Springs, which seemed to be a good place to stop and get something to eat. It was surrounded by peaks on all sides, extremely gorgeous and photogenic at its location at the confluence of the Colorado and Roaring Fork Rivers.

The restaurant they stopped at had travel brochures in front and Allen picked up a couple to read as they ate dinner. As soon as they ordered, Allen said, "Bill, they have hot springs here." Bill immediately started paying attention. "This says Glenwood Springs is considered the world's largest mineral hot springs pool. It features two enormous outdoor pools and just downstream it has sixteen smaller pools, all in varying sizes, shapes and temperatures."

He stopped reading and looked up at Bill, who said, "I'm ready. Let's do it."

Like magic, the memories of yesterday and last night were gone. All that was on their mind now was wading in some soothing, warm springs and relaxing in the waters while they dreamed thoughts of Amanda and Ellen.

Allen said, "Do you think there'll be any . . ."

But before he could finish that question, Bill answered for him, "No! They won't have adult sections here where girls are going topless. You can forget about that."

Allen set his Diet Pepsi down and replied, "If you'll let me continue, I was going to ask if you think there'll be any hotels with their own private hot springs, Mr. Prude." That's not what Allen was going to ask . . . but it sounded good, so Bill let it go.

They found a nice Holiday Inn that was actually a hotel named the Doc Holliday Lodge in the middle of town. When checking in, Bill asked the lady about the name of the hotel. She explained to him, "In the late 1800s, dentist-turned-gambler/gunfighter Doc Holliday came to Glenwood Springs seeking a cure for his advanced tuberculosis. Unfortunately, his illness was too far advanced for a cure. Even the medicinal hot springs couldn't help him. He died here and is buried in the Linwood Cemetery and we have a Doc Holliday Museum here in town. He was only thirty-six when he died. So, the hotel is named after him."

After they dropped their luggage in the room, the boys visited the OK Corral Saloon there in the hotel. The bartender and waitresses were dressed in old west costumes. They sat down at a table near the window and a fairly young waitress, dressed in an old-time western dress with extremely low cleavage, came to take their orders. She was not a very pretty young lady, but she was so well-endowed that she didn't need to be overly pretty. She impressed any and all men that she served. Especially Allen. He had been texting Amanda until the waitress came to the table, then he suddenly stopped.

Both guys stayed with Diet Pepsi as their drink of choice for the evening. As the waitress handed them their menus, the bartender called out to her, "Teri, I need you for a second." She rolled her eyes but didn't move from the table.

Bill said, "It's okay, you can go see what he wants."

Teri replied, "I know what he wants and it's not work-related." Both guys totally understood. Then she explained, "We had a date last week and now he thinks he owns me. I shouldn't have let him kiss me. I mean, he's nice and all . . . but, I don't know." And then, inexplicably, she asked Bill, "What do you think?"

Allen was pretty sure Bill wouldn't know how to respond, so he was thinking of an answer when Bill immediately said, "To let a fool kiss you is stupid; to let a kiss fool you is worse."

Teri suddenly smiled and looked back over her shoulder, then said, "Thank you, sir. That's the best advice I've ever had."

After they finished their drinks, Teri asked if they wanted dessert or anything else and Allen answered, "Do you have any gelato? That's Italian ice cream."

Teri didn't appreciate that condescending answer and told Allen "I'm not stupid, sir. I know what gelato is. Seems like all men think that women with big boobs are stupid. Well, let me ask you this, sir: Which city is farther North—Seattle or Burlington, Vermont? Which city is farther West—Atlanta or Detroit? And, which city is farther South—Charlotte or Bentonville, Arkansas? Do you know, sir?"

Allen knew but he didn't want to further antagonize Teri so he didn't say anything. Then Teri said, "I guess you don't know then do you, sir?"

Now Allen had to speak, "I certainly do young lady. Anyone with any knowledge of the country knows the answers to those questions."

"Well, tell me then."

Allen huffed up a little and answered, "All it takes is common sense in geography to know Vermont is farther north than Seattle. The same with Detroit; it's much further west than Atlanta. And of course, anywhere in Arkansas is farther south than Charlotte. Heck, I'm from North Carolina; any fool knows that!" Allen then wondered how Teri was going to gracefully make her exit.

She very politely answered, "Wrong, wrong, and wrong." Then without taking their gelato order, she left the bill on the table and walked away. Allen was fuming, Bill was laughing, and the other customers were all staring to see what the commotion was.

Allen pulled out his iPhone and started googling geography. After several minutes of frantically typing information, he said, "Let's go. I'm tired."

So, Bill followed him up to the room and listened to him mumble about Teri and her "trick" questions. After he'd vented for several minutes, Bill said, "You can't hate her for being right and knowing those answers."

Allen huffed and replied, "I don't hate her, I'm just not necessarily excited about her existence."

After showers and emailing the girls, Bill turned the lights off and they laid in bed thinking. Allen was certain of his thoughts: He wanted Amanda and nothing else mattered. Bill wanted what Allen had but was uncertain if it would happen with Ellen. The closer he was getting to Lake Superior, the more apprehensive he was becoming. He was almost as afraid that things would turn out well as he was that they wouldn't. His daily emails with Ellen were almost too good to be true. He wondered if he was only setting himself up for a major heartbreak.

Just when Bill thought Allen was asleep, he got the nightly question from him: "Bill, why do you think God waited so long to send Amanda into my life? And, why did he choose to take Barbara at such an early age? Why and why and why? I've got a whole big list of questions for Him when, and if, I get to heaven. Do you think He'll answer them for me?"

"Buddy, you just keep that list with you. Take it with you everywhere you go, and then if you die unexpectedly, you'll have it handy to pull out and ask God when you stand before Him. Somehow, that's not the way I think it'll be though. I think that when you arrive in heaven and see your Creator, in all His blazing glory, you'll forget all about your little list of questions. But maybe I'm wrong. We'll find out one day, won't we?"

Allen was either too tired to go further with this issue or he didn't know how to go further. At any rate, Bill waited until he heard Allen's gentle snoring before he turned his thoughts back to Ellen and drifted off to sleep.

The next day was spent visiting three of the town's hot springs. The first one was on the outskirts of town and was huge. Not very hot but bubbly and soothing. The second hot spring was much smaller and much hotter. They couldn't stay in the water long; it was just too hot for them. The last one was several miles outside of town and was definitely the best one. Seats had been contoured in the pool and each one was very comfortable. The water was just right, not too hot, just perfect. Plus, they served drinks to you as you sat in the pool. The guys figured an ice-cold Iron Maiden would be just what they needed to cap off the day. They were right. They argued about which hot springs were better: here, Hot Springs, Arkansas, or Truth or Consequences, New Mexico. Because of the scenery, Arkansas won.

Glenwood Springs was a vibrant little town. Shows and clubs and bars filled the downtown area. The guys decided to visit a local theater that was advertising the best Elvis impersonator in the West. Plus, they had a discount on the tickets from one of the hot springs earlier in the day. Elvis was good and they enjoyed the show. During intermission, the host came on stage and introduced the Governor of Colorado, who was also in the audience. The Governor came on stage and said a few words and Allen took this opportunity to go visit the restroom. When Allen came from the restroom, he saw the Governor standing with a small group of people, schmoozing with the public, as politicians do. Then, the Governor turned to one of his aides and starting cursing him and jabbing his finger in the young man's chest.

Allen stopped to watch this display and the Governor caught his eye. He must've thought that Allen was one of his constituents because he walked up to him and shook his hand, asking Allen if he was enjoying the show. Allen said, "Yes, sir, I sure am. I was wondering if you could do me a favor, Governor?" The Governor didn't want to seem rude in front of his followers so he asked what the favor was. Allen said, "I'm here with my friend and we're sitting over there. I was hoping you could just walk by our table and say, 'Hello, Allen, good to see you.' You know, just act like you know me. My friend would really get a charge out of that."

The Governor thought that was a simple gesture, so he agreed. Allen shook his hand again and went back to the table with Bill. When Allen saw the Governor start coming his way, he started talking to Bill, asking him a question about God. The Governor stopped at the table and said, "Hello, Allen, good to see you again."

Without batting an eyelash, Allen turned to the Governor and replied, "Geez, Governor, can't you see I'm busy here?" The Governor was so flustered he didn't know what to say or do. Allen turned back to Bill, waiting for Bill to answer his question, and Bill . . . poor Bill didn't know what the protocol was for someone who had just insulted the Governor of the State of Colorado.

37

GLENWOOD SPRINGS WAS NICE. The boys enjoyed their short stay but they needed to be moving. Back out to I-70 East and on the road again. Bill was driving while Allen was texting Amanda and admiring the mountain peaks all around them. After one text message was sent, he saw a mileage sign for Vail, Colorado, and asked Bill, "Vail, isn't that where Gerald Ford used to live?"

"I'm not sure if he lived there full-time but I know he used to ski there a lot. Do you know his son, Mike Ford?"

Allen quickly looked over and answered, "How in the world would I know the son of a President of the United States?"

"Because he lives in our hometown and goes to the same YMCA that we go to—or let me rephrase that—the same YMCA that I go to but that you're only a member of."

Allen huffed up and said, "What's that supposed to mean?"

"It means that you don't actually go to the Y . . . you're just a member. Correct me if I'm wrong."

Allen opened his mouth and started to argue but quickly realized he had no argument, so he continued with his texting. After a few minutes, he then asked Bill, "So you know Mike Ford?"

"I know who he is and I've spoken to him a few times, that's all."

"So you've spoken to the son of a President of the United States and you never told me?"

"Look, when we get back, and you actually go to the Y, I'll introduce you to him when he comes in."

"Bill, I really, really don't think I'll be around. I miss Amanda so bad it's all I can do to not hop out of this truck and start hitchhiking back to Utah right now."

Bill nodded and totally understood. He correctly concluded to stay quiet and not say anything else as they traveled along the interstate towards Vail, the home of Gerald Ford, former President of the United States of America.

They each thought Vail would be a small, ski resort type of place. It wasn't. Vail was large and spread out. They could see the ski lifts and ski runs down the sides of the mountains as they drove along the interstate. They had to stop if nothing more than to say they'd been to Vail before, so they found a restaurant to have lunch and take a break from the road. They soon discovered that Vail was also expensive and a touch snooty as well. At the restaurant, Allen ordered a Diet Pepsi with his lunch but the waiter replied, "We don't serve those here. We only have mineral water and Perrier, unless you'd like a cocktail."

Allen started to tell the waiter exactly what he wanted but Bill reached over and grabbed his arm. Then he told the waiter that mineral water would be fine. There was nothing on the menu that really appealed to two southern boys. Bill finally decided on a Cobb salad and Allen ordered prosciutto. When the waiter brought their food and set it down, Allen asked, "What's this?"

"That's your prosciutto, sir."

Allen looked at Bill, then back at the waiter and said, "Okay, but what is it?"

Before the waiter could respond, Bill answered, "It's thinly sliced ham."

Allen looked up at the waiter and asked, "Has this even been cooked?"

"This is the way prosciutto is served, sir. If you don't want it, I'll be glad to bring you something else."

"Will it be cooked?"

Bill jumped in, trying to diffuse this conversation. "Let it go, Allen." He looked at the waiter and said, "That'll be all."

The waiter sauntered away while Allen picked up a piece of the paper-thin ham and held it up, saying, "Look at this! Who would eat something like that?"

Bill tried not to laugh as he asked, "What did you think prosciutto was?"

Allen honestly answered, "I thought I was ordering a pizza."

Bill picked at his salad and even ate a thin piece of Allen's prosciutto. They drank most of their mineral water then paid the bill and left. When they were outside the restaurant, Allen said, "Find us a McDonald's, old man. One that serves all-American meat and Diet Pepsis."

Bill only nodded . . . he didn't want to tell his friend that McDonald's only served Cokes.

There were pull-offs on the interstate where cars and trucks could safely pull over and take in the panoramic scenery. Allen and Bill stopped at nearly every exit they passed. At one viewing area they were sitting on a picnic table overlooking a tremendous valley with several peaks in the distance. Cars and trucks from all over the country were in the lot, with the passengers roaming around taking pictures and selfies. One lady and her husband, who was wearing suspenders, asked Bill if he'd take their picture for them. She sounded like she had a southern accent, so after he took their picture Bill asked them where they were from. "South Carolina," she answered. "Spartanburg."

Bill smiled and replied, "We're from North Carolina. Don't see much scenery like this back home, do we?"

The lady didn't answer but her husband said, "We got plenty of mountains back where we live—better than this."

Allen was listening to this conversation and asked the man, "Your mountains in South Carolina are better than these?"

"Yep, better, higher, and more altitude, too."

Bill tried to head Allen off from pursuing this conversation, but to no avail, "So you're saying that your mountains in South Carolina are higher than these mountains here? Is that right?"

"You said it, not me."

Bill replied, "Sir, your mountains in South Carolina aren't even as high as our mountains in North Carolina—and we don't even come close to these."

The man said, "Well you probably count your mountains in millimeters! We count ours in feet, by God!" Allen almost started to rebuke the man, but didn't have time as the man grabbed his wife's arm, looked at Allen and Bill, and said, "Let's go, Myrtle, at least we ain't . . . " He started walking away mumbling something that Bill and Allen couldn't understand but were pretty sure what the implication was.

Near the end of the day, they came to another town they'd never heard of named Frisco, Colorado. It was chilly up in the mountains and neither guy especially wanted to camp, so they pulled off in Frisco and found a nice Holiday Inn near the center of the little town. It was actually a motel named the Rigby Lodge, named after one of the town's founding fathers. As luck would have it, there was a microbrewery at the next corner down from the hotel. But unluckily, they didn't serve Coors Lights, only their original brands. However, they did have some excellent tasting Rocky Mountain Burgers with home fries.

Looking out the brewery window, the guys could see one peak in the distance and about half of a large lake nearly a mile away. After eating, each guy started texting. They looked like two teenagers in old men's bodies. When they finished, Allen asked Bill, "How are things with Ellen? You still happy?"

Usually, Bill was hesitant to discuss his personal affairs but tonight was different. He looked directly at Allen and said, "Allen, I'm scared."

"Scared of what?"

"Scared that things might not be like I'm hoping they'll be, and scared that they might be exactly what I want them to be." He went on to explain things in depth to his friend, and to Allen's credit, he listened intently and didn't judge. That's why they're best friends. Friends listen and empathize and console and encourage. Bill needed to talk and he needed Allen to be there for him—which he was, there in a brewery, in Frisco, Colorado, deep in the heart of the Rocky Mountains.

38

BEFORE HITTING THE INTERSTATE THE NEXT MORNING, they stopped at a local diner near the highway. They needed coffee and bacon before the next leg of their trip. They hit the jackpot! This little place had the thickest slices and best-tasting bacon they'd ever had. And there was something about the coffee that made them drink four cups—knowing that it would make them stop to pee all morning. They didn't care, it was that good. They told the waitress how much they enjoyed the meal and asked her to pass along their compliments to the chef.

A few minutes later, the chef came from the kitchen to greet the boys. He was the prototypical chef: big and round, wearing a greasy apron, and a goofy-looking hat on a semi-bald head. Allen introduced them and then told him that his bacon was the best they'd ever had and that his coffee was addicting it was so delicious.

The chef smiled and thanked them and told them to fill their thermos before they left—no charge. Then Allen asked him, "What's in that coffee to make it so good?"

The chef looked all around him, then leaned over and in a low voice said, "We put a small pinch of cocaine in each pot to get you hooked on it." He waited about three seconds, then burst out laughing at his punch line. Allen and Bill weren't sure if he was serious or not . . . but the coffee sure was good.

They sat in the truck and looked at a map to see where they should go next on their way to Lake Superior. They knew that when they left the Rockies there was really nothing left to see across Nebraska, Iowa, Minnesota, and Wisconsin. It made them a little sad. The scenery from California, Nevada, Utah, and Colorado had spoiled them. They had the map spread out between them on the seat, each one staring at different spots on the map: Allen was only staring at Cedar City, Utah, and Bill at Monterey, California. Then, Bill shifted his gaze over toward Lake Superior when he spotted something they hadn't noticed before: Rocky Mountain National Park, just north of where they were now.

Allen quickly texted Amanda and asked her if she knew anything about this park. She texted back one word, "Go!" So, they started in that direction and actually drove almost an hour before they had to stop at a rest area and visit the bathrooms. But they didn't complain; the cocaine coffee was that good. They arrived at the park in early afternoon and felt like they were driving on top of the world. They were close. The road they were on was named Trail Ridge Road and crested at over twelve thousand feet. There were sections of that road that only had a flimsy guardrail on the road's edge to stop a vehicle from plunging one or two thousand feet straight down the mountain. Allen was glad Bill was driving.

The first campground they came to was full. The second one had some sites still available. Upon checking in, the ranger told them to watch out for wildlife and to be prepared for some bad weather. Bad weather? It was sunny and nice outside . . . he probably gave all visitors that same warning. They bought some snacks from the park office and went to set up before darkness fell. As Bill was backing in their spot, seven or eight bighorn sheep ambled across the lot, with not a care in the world, nor paying attention to any of the humans in their park. Allen whistled for them and Bill scolded him saying, "They're not dogs, Allen." Allen didn't care, he whistled again.

The view from the campground wasn't awesome but it was nice. They sat out in their chairs and ate some snacks while sipping a Diet Pepsi, breathing it all in. Then, they heard a faint rumbling—a long way away. They ignored it. Before they finished their soft drinks the rumbling became more ominous and much, much closer. Allen walked out to an opening in the trees and looked in one direction and saw only blue sky. He walked a bit further to see the other direction and only saw dark, apocalyptic, sinister, and lightening-filled clouds. He hustled back to Bill and said, "Pack up everything and get in the truck."

"What's wrong? It's too late to be going anywhere."

Allen excitedly exclaimed, "We ain't going nowhere! We just need to get somewhere safe. It's coming, Bill, and it's coming fast."

Bill knew the sky was darkening quickly. He didn't argue, as they packed up the chairs and cooler, then closed the camper and got inside the truck. No sooner had they closed the doors than they started hearing and seeing lightning bolts flashing all around them. It was as if Thor himself were waging war against them. Flash! Boom! It alternated with these for nearly forty-five minutes, then almost as if someone had unplugged everything from the wall, it was over. Limbs were strewn across the camp, other camper's tents were toppled over, and water was running down the roadway. But they were safe.

They waited several minutes just to be sure it was over. Then they brought the chairs back out but had to move them from underneath the trees so the water wouldn't drip on them. And they switched from Diet Pepsi to Coors Light as they still felt a little electricity in the air. About twenty minutes later, a lone elk strolled through camp, ignoring everyone just as the bighorn sheep had done. Allen whistled for him too, but the elk obviously wasn't trained because it kept on walking.

The rest of the evening was glorious. A little chilly but they dressed for cooler weather while sitting out in the crisp evening. When they retired for the night and things were quiet, Allen again asked Bill a question he'd been thinking about all day. "Bill, I know all men are basically good; I understand that. My question is why do good men start having bad thoughts? And how can you control that or even stop it?"

Bill answered immediately, "You're wrong, Allen. The Bible doesn't teach that man is basically good. Instead, it teaches that man is basically sinful. He's born sinful and sin comes naturally to all of us. It also tells us that humans are capable of very evil things. In spite of all our advances in technology, we still can't change the human heart.

Bill was going to further explain this when Allen interrupted and asked, "Well, what do you do when you come to a verse in the Bible that you don't agree with?"

"You change your opinion because you're wrong. Who are you, a mere human being, to argue with God? Look, Allen, if you don't agree with the Bible, then change your outlook—because the Bible is always right. Who are you going to trust, Allen? You, who is always getting himself in trouble? Or, God, creator, and savior of the world?" Bill wondered if Allen would believe any of what he just told him. Allen didn't ask any more questions, but he did reflect on Bill's words and even questioned whether or not he could change. One thing he knew for sure, though: Bill would never lie to him.

Bill drove them around Rocky Mountain National Park all morning. They stopped and watched waterfalls, then stopped to watch several bighorn sheep cross the road, and finally pulled over simply to enjoy the captivating beauty of the mountains and the valley that spread out before them. Allen still didn't feel comfortable driving, so Bill took them around and eventually back out to the exit toward I-70.

Both guys were fairly quiet as they drove. Each was a little nostalgic about the scenic parts of their trip being over, but also excited about the romantic parts of their lives being closer. Allen had become a texting machine. Bill wondered what in the world he would be saying to Amanda all day . . . then he realized it was Allen, not some normal human being, so it all made sense. Each guy was starting to feel a little headachy when they realized they never had their coffee that morning. The thrill of the mountain scenery made them forget all about their caffeine fix. Their heads were now reminding them.

They were looking for an exit to take and saw a sign for Golden, Colorado. Allen screamed out, "Golden! That's the home of Coors, Bill. Take that exit!" Bill did. Golden was less than twenty minutes away and each guy suddenly got very excited at seeing the home of Coors Light, their favorite adult beverage.

The Coors Brewing Company was HUGE! The town of Golden itself was located along the banks of Clear Creek. It was a scenic little town with a very wide main street containing many bars, taverns, souvenir shops, and clothing stores, none of which would probably be in existence without Coors. Bill drove straight to the brewery, which offered tours all day long. They didn't have to wait long before they were on their way with tourists from across the country. The facility was so large that a tramway was available to take the group from one vantage point to the next.

After about eighty minutes, the tour ended in the tasting room, which was actually a huge bar set up to hold at least three hundred people. All the tastings were free and the boys indulged appropriately. However, they learned a lasting lesson from their night in Grand Junction and did not indulge more than their bodies could handle. Each guy bought several souvenirs: hats, t-shirts, mugs, and key rings to commemorate this occasion. They decided they should further enhance this experience by staying the night at the Golden Inn, which was an architectural tribute to Coors and the beer that put Golden on the map.

The doors to all the rooms were shaped like beer cans; the bedspreads on all the beds had Coors beer emblems on them, as did the shower curtain and the carpet in the bedroom. They had dinner in the Coors restaurant and ordered beer-flavored steaks, which were delicious. The menu offered sixteen different Coors beer selections, which included all the specialty brands they made, as well as their seasonal brews. Allen told their waiter they'd been on the Coors Brewery tour and tasted several of the brews. The waiter asked him which were his favorites, which gave Allen the opportunity to give the answer he'd been saving all day, "Coors Light in a bottle, Coors Light in a can, and free Coors Light."

The waiter replied, “Coming right up!” Then he took two steps towards the bar, stopped and half-turned around, saying, “Not the free one though, we’re out of those.”

After dinner and showers, safely back in the room, they each texted and emailed the girls. Each guy gave varying descriptions of the same events they’d experienced that today. Each guy was thankful he had his best friend in the world to share these moments with but was also thinking of a time in the future when a woman he loved would be sharing time with him as well. Then they closed their computers, took their nightly medicines, and dreamed heavenly thoughts, there in the Golden Inn, in Golden, Colorado, on the eastern slopes of the glorious Rocky Mountains.

39

EVERYTHING EAST OF DENVER, coming out of the mountains, was flat. Flatter than flat. Boringly flat. Allen was driving while Bill was texting Ellen, and he suddenly said, "I can't take it anymore. This is terrible. You have to drive some, Bill, and let me sleep through this."

"No can do, buddy. Your turn, fair and square."

"What's fair got to do with it? Can't you see I'm losing my mind here, Bill?"

"A little too late for that, wouldn't you say?"

Bill never stopped texting. They still had over a half tank of gas and neither guy was hungry but Allen pulled off the next exit anyway. He said, "I need a break."

There was an old convenience store at the stop sign, with two gas pumps out front and an old spotted dog laying across the doorway. After Allen parked the Silverado, they walked up to the door but the dog never moved or opened its eyes. Allen said, "Maybe it's dead."

"No, you can see it breathing."

Allen was going to reach across and open the door but it opened for him and a thin, middle-aged guy said, "Don't worry about him, he's harmless. C'mon in."

The store was like a movie set: Everything was old, including the floor which creaked with each step, and it even had a wooden barrel set up with a checkerboard on top of it. The guy said, "What can I help you with, gents?"

Allen thought, "How do I tell him we're bored to death with his state?" Instead, he said, "Nothing really, we just needed a break from the road. Maybe we'll get something to drink."

The thin guy said, "Pretty boring drive isn't it?" Allen and Bill both started laughing and the thin man said, "I get that a lot from people passing through."

Allen asked the man, "You lived out here all your life?"

"I grew up outside of Denver but moved here nearly twenty years ago."

Bill found that news fascinating, so he asked the man, "You moved from Denver to out here in the middle of nowhere?"

"Well, sort of. I was a ballplayer and had been in Montreal and then Seattle and I was just tired of the traffic and the congestion, so I just bought this place and have been here ever since. I don't make much money but I was lucky enough to save a good chunk from my playing days."

Allen said, "A ballplayer? What kind of ball?"

"Baseball . . . I signed with Montreal back in the day, then got traded to Seattle. I only played five years in the majors but I loved it."

Bill, who was a big baseball fan, asked, "What's your name, sir? I probably know you."

"I'd seriously doubt that. I was never a star. Name's Brian Holman." The man was right, Bill had never heard of him. The man said, "My major league record was 37-45, but back in those days, Seattle was not very good."

They talked baseball for about twenty minutes and then talked about life out here on the plains of eastern Colorado for about twenty minutes. Bill knew it was probably rude but he had to ask this next question or he'd always regret it: "And you're happy out here, Brian?"

Brian looked at both guys, then answered, "I spent so many years in big cities and crowded clubhouses, this just seems like a vacation to me. My dad told me something just before he died that I've never forgotten. He said, 'Brian, be fearless in the pursuit of what sets your soul on fire.' He was talking about playing baseball . . . but for me, this is it."

The boys shook hands with Brian Holman and wished him well. Then Bill volunteered to drive so Allen could text Amanda and take a nap as they continued their journey across the flat plains of eastern Colorado.

By the end of the day, they were sick of driving. They came to a little town in Nebraska named Hastings and they pulled off the interstate to look for a place to spend the night. They had in mind a comfortable Holiday Inn but as they were driving down the road, they spotted a nice campground next to a small river. Rivers nearly always won out over Holiday Inns. There was a teenaged boy at the office and he told them to park anywhere, stay as long they wanted, and simply pay when they left. It was on the honor system.

Bill parked two spots down from the restrooms and within thirty steps of the little river. They didn't see the name of the river but it was clean, fairly wide, and flowed pretty swiftly to be out in the plains like it was. They had bought some pre-wrapped sandwiches and snacks from Brian Holman's country store and had also stocked up the cooler for the evening. Nothing to do now but text, email, and sit by the river and talk. The teenager had given them a Wi-Fi password, which made them both happy, and Allen set the chairs out on the banks of the river in a grassy area. Bill rolled the cooler over and brought some food with him, too. Each guy popped open a Coors Light and immediately started typing. Allen giggled as he typed and read his emails from Amanda. Bill seemed to be in another world as he typed and read his emails from Ellen.

They finished before the sun started fading for the evening. They watched the river and listened to the birds and crickets chirping at each other. As the sun sunk below the horizon, a few camp lights automatically turned on which left a small glow on the area where the guys were sitting. The sound of the water from the river was about as soothing as anything they could imagine. They were content just to listen and contemplate the silence, their friendship, and their girls. After they'd eaten a sandwich and some Oreos, Bill asked, "So, you really think you'll end up living in Utah, huh?"

"Bill, I'd live on the moon or even in Chapel Hill if I could be with Amanda."

Bill knew exactly what he meant. He just didn't know if he could make that commitment to leave his lifetime home in North Carolina and move to Lake Superior where Ellen was. That worried him. Allen asked, "You and Ellen will be coming to visit us, won't you?"

"Not if you're living in Chapel Hill."

"Shut up! You know what I mean."

"I don't know, Allen. I don't know what's going to happen with us. You know she said she's not going to leave Lake Superior. And how in the world can I ever leave Winston-Salem and move up there? I just can't see that happening."

Allen didn't want to belabor that point, so he wisely let it pass. They switched the conversation to Monterey and Reno and the Rockies, which made them both smile as they finished their second Coors Lights. They heard something splash in the river but couldn't see anything because of the darkness. The moon rose in the sky and cast a light orange glow on the little river. They were both quiet again, left to their thoughts and memories. Even though both guys were happy and excited about the prospects of life with Amanda and Ellen, they both still thought about their deceased wives and missed them terribly. That would never change. They didn't want it to ever change.

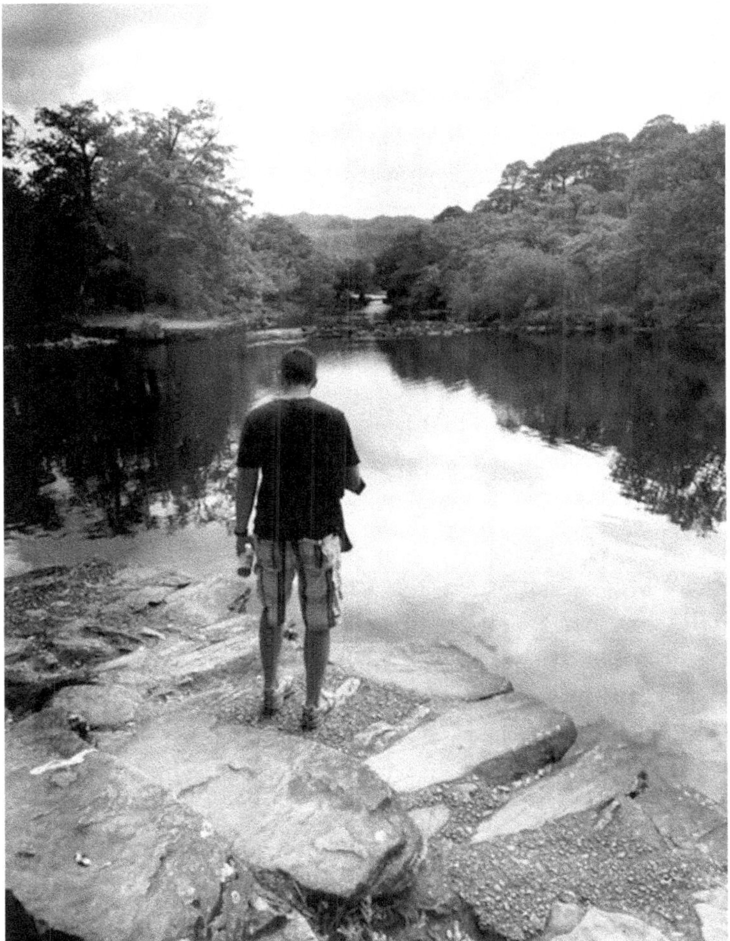

40

THEY LEFT HASTINGS PRETTY EARLY and drove all the way to Omaha, Nebraska, the next day. They could've driven farther but were intrigued by the city and the Missouri River running through it. They drove through town and stopped in a large park that was right on the river. Each guy was surprised by how big the Missouri River was and how fast it was flowing. In the city park was a sign commemorating the Lewis and Clark expedition in 1804, which passed through this site. As they read the sign, Allen asked, "So they went up this river towards the Rockies, right?"

"Yep."

"How? How did they do that, Bill? Look at the current out there and how fast it is. They didn't have motors back then. How did they get their boats up this fast-flowing river, against the current, carrying all their supplies and all the men? I don't understand it."

Bill said, "Well . . . " But he didn't understand it either. He thought to himself, "How DID they do that?" They both gazed out at the fast-flowing river for several minutes, then decided to go to a restaurant and get something to eat and ruminate on that question. There were several restaurants along the river banks that had outdoor seating. In fact, Omaha had done a good job of revitalizing the entire downtown area and taking advantage of its location on the Missouri River.

Bill chose to stop at the World Series Chop House, named in honor of the Baseball College World Series, which was held each year here in Omaha. The outdoor patio area was about ten feet above the river, which gave them great views up and downstream. They were fortunate enough to have a very pretty young lady as their waitress, whose nametag read Elizabeth. Elizabeth had a brilliant smile and wore a short skirt that drew attention to her shapely body. The guys were impressed. They ordered Diet Pepsis as they looked over the menu; at least Bill was reviewing the menu. Allen was reviewing Elizabeth's legs and rear end.

When she returned to their table, Allen asked her, "Elizabeth, my friend and I were wondering how Lewis and Clark took their boats up that river. Can you help us?"

Elizabeth's smile vanished as she answered, "Who?"

"Lewis and Clark. You know, back in 1804."

Elizabeth half-smiled and replied. "Oh, them. Yeah, I remember them."

Allen continued, "How did they get their boats up that river as fast as it's flowing?"

Elizabeth's smile returned and she said, "Hold on a minute."

She walked away and a couple of minutes later an older woman came to their table and said, "You guys ready to order yet?"

Allen started to say something but Bill interrupted him and asked, "What comes with your country fried steak?"

The older woman answered him then looked at Allen who said, "Same thing."

When she left their table, Bill looked sternly at Allen and said, "See what you did? You ran off that pretty girl and left us with her." Allen didn't say anything, so Bill asked, "You happy now?"

Allen disgustedly said, "Dang!"

They found a nice Holiday Inn right on the river's edge that was named The Carolinian. As they were checking in, Allen told the well-dressed clerk that he was from North Carolina. The clerk nodded and said, "Oh."

Allen added, "You know, North Carolina, like in Carolinian."

"Oh!" It had dawned on the clerk what Allen was referring to, "The hotel isn't named for the state, sir; the owner's wife's name is Caroline." Allen then took this opportunity to ask this well-dressed man how Lewis and Clark went UP the river, against the current. The man set his pen down, thought a few seconds, then asked, "Are you sure they went upstream? They probably went with the current. That would have been much easier, I'm sure."

Bill grabbed Allen's arm and tugged it before Allen could say anything that might seem inappropriate. Bill then added, "Thanks for your help. Room 137, right?"

"Yes, sir, enjoy your stay."

After checking in the hotel, they walked down the busy street and spotted a nice tavern, also on the riverbank. A college-aged young man took their order and returned quickly with two Coors Lights, then asked, "Anything else you need?"

Allen immediately asked, "Yes, young man. How did Lewis and Clark get their boats upstream, against the current, way back in 1804?"

The young man answered, "I guess they had motors on their boats. I don't know." Bill again grabbed Allen's arm, just in case. After that, they sat back and enjoyed the evening. Each guy texted and each guy dreamed. It was nice. They only had one beer because they were still rather full from the country-fried steak earlier. As they were leaving and walking down the sidewalk, they came to a stoplight and Allen told Bill he was going to google how Lewis and Clark went upstream as soon as they got back to the room.

Behind them, someone said, "They used push-poles. Each guy on board had one and they walked down the sides of the boat with the poles and pushed the boat forward with the poles on the ground in the water."

They both turned quickly to see an old, dirty, homeless man who looked like he hadn't bathed in three months. He was holding a sign that read, "Please help, if you can."

Allen reached in his pocket and pulled out ten dollars and gave it to the man saying, "Sir, you're the smartest man in this entire town."

As they crossed the street, Bill said, "You didn't need to give him ten dollars for that. He'll probably just use it for drinking."

Allen quickly replied, "So? That's what we were using it for, weren't we?"

Omaha had some pretty good coffee the next morning; not as good as the cocaine coffee in Frisco, but pretty good. After breakfast, they found the interstate again and started northward, following the Missouri River toward Sioux Falls, South Dakota. Except for the river itself, there wasn't much to see. It took about three and a half hours to drive to Sioux Falls and they were both ready for a break and lunch when they arrived. The city itself is located on the Big Sioux River and seemed larger than Allen or Bill thought it was. It was also at the crossroads of two interstates, where they would now change directions and start heading for Minnesota and Lake Superior.

Allen saw a billboard advertising the Falls Restaurant not far off the interstate. They found it and it was indeed located next to a small waterfall called Sioux Falls. They took a window seat overlooking the falls and were so mesmerized by the scene that they didn't notice the waitress when she came to their table. She knocked on the table to get their attention and they saw her smiling at them. She was about forty, forty-five maybe, with light brown hair and a pretty face. She also had on a name tag that identified her as Billie. Allen noticed her name and said, "Hello, Billie, my friend here is named Bill, but you're much prettier than him."

She smiled and replied, "Thank you, sir. And what is your name?"

"My name's Allen. We like your restaurant. It's a great location."

Billie stopped smiling and said, "My last name is Allen; I'm Billie Allen." That coincidence made all three of them stop momentarily to think about it. Then Billie asked, "Where are you guys from? You don't sound like you're from South Dakota."

Bill answered, "We're from North Carolina, Billie. Have you ever been there?"

A momentary glaze came over Billie before she answered, "No, I haven't. But my husband was from North Carolina. A little place called Clemmons."

Two things immediately startled the guys: First, Billie said her husband "was" from North Carolina. Is she not married to him now? Or, was that only a small error in Billie's grammar? And second, Clemmons is a small town that is virtually a part of Winston-Salem, their hometown. Allen recovered first and asked, "What do you mean, he 'was' from North Carolina?"

Billie sadly replied, "He died about three years ago of liver cancer. I still miss him."

Allen felt a sudden fog overcome him and he almost lost his bearing. He then said, "My wife died about three years of liver cancer. I miss her too."

All three of them stared at each other. No one was able to say anything else. Each person was afraid to say anything else. Just then, the restaurant manager walked by and noticed all three people staring at each other, not ordering anything, so he stopped and asked if everything was okay. Only then was the spell broken.

Billie took their orders while Bill and Allen stared at each other unable to say or ask anything. When Billie brought their Diet Pepsis to the table, she apologized for the awkwardness of everything. Then she said, "It's just been a hard year for me. My

Mom died less than a year ago, too. She'd been sick for a few months but it's still hard . . . you only have one mom."

Both guys nodded, remembering their moms, then Allen asked what her name was. Billie said, "She had an old-fashioned name that everyone remembered easily, Eliza."

Bill immediately blurted out, "That was my wife's name!"

Billie knew what he meant when Bill said "was." She started crying. Allen and Bill both rose from the table and they all hugged each other. The manager started to come back over but didn't. Several other customers were wondering why in the world three people were hugging and crying in the restaurant.

Eating their meal was difficult even though they were hungry. When they finished, they each gave Billie another hug, then each guy left her a twenty-dollar tip. She followed them to the door and watched as they climbed in the Silverado and pulled back onto the highway. Each guy was silent as Bill drove back onto the interstate. After a few minutes, Bill said, "Dang."

That jolted Allen back to reality and he replied, "Yeah, I know. That was weird."

"No, not that. We're going the wrong way. We're headed back to Omaha." Bill took the next exit and turned around. Allen didn't say anything . . . which was very unusual. It would be a long, long time before either of them would ever forget Billie Allen of Sioux Falls, South Dakota.

41

THE GUYS DROVE INTO THE METROPOLIS of Minneapolis/St. Paul, Minnesota just at rush hour. Traffic was a mess and they were exhausted. They finally made it through the urban sludge and came out at a place north of the Twin Cities called Coon Rapids. They saw a sign for a Holiday Inn and quickly pulled off the road; however, there was a more appealing place next to it called the Coon Rapids Kempton that was located near a little river and that's where Allen parked the truck. The Kempton had a restaurant and a bar so they wouldn't have to drive anywhere—thank goodness.

They took showers and checked emails from the girls. They returned emails and texts to the girls, then they sat in their chairs and thought about the girls. When they finally made it to the restaurant, they asked their waiter what the name was of the little river outside the window. "That's the Mississippi, gents."

Allen looked out the window at what might be considered a small stream back in North Carolina and asked, "Not the real Mississippi?"

The waiter was proud to say, "The one and only. It has to start somewhere." Both guys turned and stared out at the Mississippi River, remembering what it looked like when they crossed over the huge and mighty Mississippi River in Memphis. The waiter's name was Scott, not Allen or Bill or Barbara or Eliza . . . Scott! They liked his name. He suggested the seafood special of the day and they both agreed. Scott then suggested a nice white wine to accompany the fish—they both declined. Instead, Iron Maidens seemed appropriate for all they had seen and done today. Iron Maidens it was!

As dusk settled in during dinner, some outside lighting came on to illuminate the river. It cast a shimmering glow across the water and made a very nice picture to remember. Bill declined dessert but Allen ordered pecan pie with ice cream. When it came, it looked so good that Bill then ordered one and immediately felt a little guilty. He was trying to control his waistline and weight for his upcoming meeting with Ellen. Now he'd probably have to skip breakfast in the morning.

One Iron Maiden was usually their limit but today was special. In the bar after dinner, they both ordered another one. They watched the lights bounce off the little river and discussed Billie Allen again and tried to understand how all those coincidences could happen. Allen asked questions about Ellen and Bill asked questions about Amanda; not so much to hear the answers but more so to let their friend talk about his girl and describe what was on his mind. For the first time in a long time, during the entire conversation, neither guy mentioned their deceased wives. Not that they didn't think about them . . . not by a long shot. Instead, they were thinking of the future rather than the past.

They sat and watched the little Mississippi flow on by them for quite a while. Finally, sleep was calling them and they retired to the room. They sent more emails to the girls and read emails from them—repeatedly. Finally, the lights were turned off and almost instantly Allen asked his nightly question to Bill, almost as if he couldn't wait for the opportunity to arise.

"Bill, something has been on mind all day, ever since Billie told us about her husband dying."

"Everybody dies, buddy. It's sad and we don't always understand the timing of it . . . "

"No, Bill. That's not what I meant."

"Well, what do you mean?"

"I understand him dying, just like our wives died. And I know that our wives are in heaven now—I'm sure of that because like you've always told me: Jesus said, 'I am the way and the truth and the life. No one comes to the Father except through me.' I believe that, Bill."

"Well, what's your question, then?"

"I'm pretty sure Billie's husband had heard of Jesus before. Don't know if he believed or not, but I'm sure he heard of Him. What about people who have never heard of Jesus? People who have no clue? Just because they weren't able to hear the word, are they condemned to Hell?"

"Allen, that is an incorrect view of God. You're thinking that God, somehow, would want to send someone to Hell. But that's not the God of the Bible. If we learn nothing else in the Bible, we learn that God loves humanity and longs for fellowship and friendship with us. God doesn't want any person to go to Hell. We will all be judged according to the light we have received. We will not be held accountable for what we do not know. God will reveal Himself to the true seeker. God searches for us. He cares for us. And He wants us to know him."

After a few silent moments, Allen said, "Thanks, Bill. I needed to hear that." Bill thought about God for a few more minutes. Then he thought about his deceased wife for a few minutes, knowing she was with God. Then he thought about Ellen and wished God could answer all his questions about her, and him, and what was going to happen with them. The closer they came to Lake Superior, the more concerned, distressed, and frightened he became.

After breakfast, Allen wanted to walk down to the banks of the Mississippi River and touch the water. Bill asked, "Why?"

"Because . . . that's why." So, he did.

Allen dipped his hands in the river, then he picked up a rock and threw it upstream as hard as he could knowing that Bill was watching him from the window. When he walked back up, he stopped and smiled at Bill, who remained silent. Then they went to check out at the front desk. Allen took this opportunity to ask the desk clerk, "Why Coon Rapids?"

The clerk never looked up and answered, "Why what, sir?"

"Why is your town named Coon Rapids?"

Then the clerk looked up and answered, "I don't know, it's always been named that."

Bill once again pulled Allen's arm, which meant, "Let it go, Allen." And he did until they passed the concierge desk on the way out and Allen stopped and asked,

"Excuse me, sir . . . can you tell me why your town is named Coon Rapids?"

"Certainly, sir. It derives from the clay pools that once surrounded this area. Most of them have dried up but there are still a few around." This answer made no sense whatsoever to either guy but the concierge had turned and answered a telephone call.

When they walked outside a valet asked them if they used the valet parking. They had not but Allen took the opportunity to also ask him about the city name. He said, "I think it was named after an Indian tribe or something, maybe. I'm not really sure."

Allen was dumbfounded. How could these people not know why their city was named what it was? He quickly asked the valet, "Is it possible there were a lot of raccoons here when the first settlers came and stopped, and that's why they named it Coon Rapids?"

The valet looked at Allen as though he was speaking Chinese. He then thoughtfully answered, "I don't think so, sir. If that was the case, our city would be named Raccoon Rapids."

Bill quickly grabbed Allen's arm and pulled him out into the parking lot. Allen looked at Bill and said, "Is it just me or are these people crazy?"

Bill kept pulling him towards the Silverado and said, "It's definitely you."

42

THEY COULD'VE EASILY MADE THE SHORES of Lake Superior by the end of the day, but they decided to spend the night in Duluth, Minnesota. There were several things they needed to discuss before they drove to the state park where Ellen worked. On their previous trip, they also stayed in Duluth and remembered the hotel where they stayed. It was on the shore of the lake and had a restaurant and bar on the top floor overlooking the vast expanse of water. After they checked in, Allen spent the next forty-five minutes emailing and texting Amanda. Bill waited; he didn't want to tell Ellen he was within a couple of hours drive from her. He and Allen had some decisions to make before his meeting with Ellen and he wanted to make certain they were discussed and agreed upon.

When Allen finished his emails, they went up to the top floor to the restaurant. They had forgotten how magnificent the view was up there. The sun was setting away from them and they were looking out at the lake with the sun glowing across the waters like some sort of painting. They decided to go sit in the bar first so they could properly watch this scene unfold before them, with a Coors Light in their hand. They remembered Ellen telling them that all the other Great Lakes could fit inside Lake Superior—it was that big.

They probably sat there ten or fifteen minutes without saying anything. Finally, Bill asked, "What did Amanda have to say?"

"She said she misses me and can't wait to see me."

Bill took a sip of beer and replied, "Did she know it was you she was emailing?"

Allen smiled, then asked, "Do you know what your plans are tomorrow?"

"I don't know, Allen. From all the texts and emails, I'd have to say things look great. But you never know how it will be in person. I mean, it's been over two years since we've seen each other."

Allen nodded, then said, "Well, you've got a point there. You are a lot uglier now than you were two years ago. Heck, when she sees you now she might just start screaming and run out into the lake to get away from you." Bill wished the little table they were sitting at had some packets of sugar he could throw at Allen, but it didn't. Allen continued, "Quit worrying so much, old man. Everything will be fine. You know she likes you, even though I don't know how."

Bill looked up and asked, "How do you know she likes me?"

"It's obvious, isn't it? The way you two email and text. The way you're always smiling when you think of her. The stuff she says to you. You can't hide that, Bill."

Bill thought really hard about what Allen just said, then asked, "How do you know anything she's said to me?" Allen stumbled a little, then tried to change the subject, but Bill cornered him, "Allen, how do you know anything she's said to me? You haven't read any of my emails, have you?"

"Bill, I can't believe you'd think that I would do that. That really hurts my feelings!"

Bill stared hard at his friend, trying to convince himself that Allen would indeed not do that. Allen was holding his breath wondering how Bill found out he had sneaked and read some emails while Bill was in the bathroom. Allen was on the verge of breaking down and admitting everything, when Bill finally turned away, saying, "Well, okay . . . I'll believe you then."

Allen, however, just couldn't let it end: "I can't believe my best friend in the world would think I'd do something like that."

Bill turned back quickly and replied, "You'd better quit while you're ahead." They finished their Coors Light in silence, then walked over to the restaurant for dinner and to discuss more serious matters.

The food was too good and the noise in the restaurant a little too loud for them to talk seriously, so they waited until after Allen had key lime pie for dessert, then they retired back to the bar. They both ordered Iron Maidens and waited on each other to start the conversation. The silence was getting a little awkward when Allen finally asked, "What do you want me to do tomorrow?"

"I don't know how to answer that, Allen. I guess I'll need you to stick around a little bit until I can tell how things are with me and Ellen. After that, we'll see."

That didn't help Allen at all. He said, "Well if everything is good, are you going to stay there at the lake with her for a while? Or, do you want her to drive with you to North Carolina? Or, do you want me to drive with you to North Carolina? I'll do whatever you want me to—you know that."

Bill took a small sip of his drink and said, "I know all that, Allen. I know you'll do whatever I need you to do. The problem is that I just don't know what to do. Hopefully, after Ellen and I meet tomorrow, I can answer that question. Look, if you want to catch a flight and go back to Utah, it's okay. Even with the worst-case scenario, I can drive back home by myself."

Allen looked at his friend and answered, "No, you can't! You'd never be able to make that drive all broken-hearted like that. I ain't leaving till I'm sure what's going on. That's settled." Bill didn't respond but he sure was glad Allen said what he did. They looked out at the lake even though it was dark and they couldn't actually see anything. But they knew it was out there. Bigger than all the other Great Lakes combined.

After showers were taken and emails were sent and read, they laid in bed with the lights off. This was the usual time when Allen asked his nightly question. Things were different tonight though, because Bill asked the question. "Allen, I'm scared. I don't know what is going to happen tomorrow. I don't know how I'll feel or how she'll feel when we actually see each other." Since he really didn't ask a question, Allen was silent, which was hard for him to do, so Bill continued, "I just have so many questions . . . so many."

When Allen was sure Bill had finished, he started, "Bill, I want you to trust me when I tell you this . . . the way I see it, there are only two great questions we all must answer, just two: What is worth living for? And, what is worth dying for? The answer to both, of course, is love."

Bill was too nervous to eat breakfast in the morning. Allen had a short stack of pancakes, bacon, and two eggs over easy. He wanted grits but these uneducated people up on the shores of Lake Superior hadn't been enlightened yet to the finer points of correct breakfast etiquette. It was all Bill could do to drink his coffee without spilling it on himself. He then started rambling: "What's going to happen if things don't work out? Or, if she doesn't want for anything to happen? And, maybe I won't feel the same way. What's gonna . . . "

"Stop!" Allen dropped his fork, which had a large chunk of pancake on it, and continued, "Bill . . . stop thinking too much. It's alright not to know all the answers."

After Allen's breakfast, they packed up the Silverado and Allen said, "Give me the keys. There ain't no way in the world I'm letting you drive today." Bill started to argue but he knew he'd lose. Allen got them pointed in the right direction and off they went to the state park where Ellen worked, and where Bill's future life was waiting in the balance.

When they were within twenty minutes of Ellen, Allen pulled the truck over to a gas station. Bill asked why they were stopping, Allen answered, "So you can go in and brush your teeth and change your shirt. That's why."

"Change my shirt?"

"You're not seriously considering wearing that shirt to meet the girl of your dreams, are you?"

"What's wrong with it?"

"Look at it, Bill. It's got little pictures of palm trees all over it. Ain't no way I'm letting my best friend ruin my reputation by letting him wear something like that."

Bill looked down at his shirt, completely flummoxed, and said, "Well, you didn't have to be a jerk about it."

Allen said, "You always want me to be honest with you until I am honest with you, then I'm a butt-hole." Bill got out of the truck and went to his suitcase to find a suitable shirt, then started for the restroom. Before he'd taken three steps, Allen yelled at him, "And brush your teeth!"

43

ELLEN SERVES AS A VOLUNTEER, part-time ranger at a state park on the shores of Lake Superior. She gives interpretive lectures on the history of the area and the lake. This is where she and Bill first met. She has lived here since her husband died about seven years ago. When she and Bill met, she told him that she would never leave Lake Superior. She has since re-evaluated that statement. She loves the summers when she works and gives talks and guided tours around the lake, but she doesn't love the winter months because there are no tourists and it's much too cold. And, she has missed Bill. He made her feel like she was young once again, like she was special, like she remembered feeling all those years ago.

When Allen and Bill pulled into the parking lot of the state park where Ellen was working, they saw her car parked in front of the office building. Allen cut off the engine and they sat there staring at the car and the building. After a few moments, Allen said, "Well?"

Bill didn't answer or move. Allen decided to let him have another few moments of silence before saying anything else. Then, they noticed a door open from the side of the building and Ellen came out and started walking their way. Only then did Bill move. He opened the door and started walking towards her.

They met at the edge of the parking lot, next to a Winnebago camper from Macon, Georgia. Allen couldn't hear anything they said but he could see them stop and hold hands; first one hand, then both hands. Seconds later, they hugged and rocked gently back and forth. Then they kissed twice and hugged even tighter. Allen was extremely happy and relieved . . and a little jealous. His mind immediately started thinking of Amanda and how soon he could get back to her.

After several minutes, Ellen walked back into the offices and quickly came back out holding a coat. They both started walking over to the Silverado, so Allen got out and greeted them with a big smile on his face. Ellen hugged him and said, "So good to see you again, Allen. Thanks for bringing him back to me safely. But I must tell you, I'm not going to let you take him away from me again."

Allen replied, "You can have him! I was getting sick and tired of him anyway." Everyone laughed and Ellen grabbed Bill's hand as though she'd never turn it loose. She asked Allen if he would follow them to her house, where they could all talk and relax. Allen nodded and answered, "Can I trust you two to be alone in the car together?"

Ellen said, "Probably . . . but if you get lost, we won't come looking for you." It was less than a five-minute drive to Ellen's house on the lake. She had a small yard and a back porch that had an unobstructed view of Lake Superior. She told them to go sit on the porch and she brought out a pot of coffee for them to drink. Allen had a cup but all Ellen and Bill could do was hold hands as they sat next to each other. Allen reviewed some of the things they'd done on the trip. He omitted the topless hot springs and his foray into the brothel, but he gave a fairly accurate rendition of everything else.

Then, Ellen said, "Allen, it's okay if you want to fly back to Utah. I'll take care of him."

Allen looked at Bill, then back at Ellen, and said, "I know you will. Let me call Amanda and check on things and see what I can arrange." He went into Ellen's house to use the phone and after a few minutes, he came back out and said, "There's a flight I can catch first thing in the morning if y'all don't mind. But what about the truck and the camper?" Each had been rented in North Carolina and had to be returned.

Bill answered, "Ellen's going to drive with me back home and I'll get everything taken care of. Don't worry about it."

Allen smiled and said, "Oh, I'm not worried about the truck, but I am worried about what's gonna happen in my camper with the two of you all alone in it."

Ellen blushed a little at that reference, then Bill said, "It ain't your camper, now is it?"

Allen said, "Ellen, that's only the second time in my life I've heard him use the word 'ain't.' You're already having a bad influence on him. Congratulations!"

Ellen took them to a nice restaurant on the waterfront for dinner. Allen did most of the talking, reliving experiences from the trip and explaining all he knew about Amanda. Ellen and Bill mostly held hands and looked longingly into each other's eyes. Ellen insisted the boys stay the night at her house. She had the room and she wasn't about to let Bill out of her sight again. As soon as they arrived, Allen feigned tiredness and retired to the bedroom, while Ellen and Bill sat on the couch in the living room and whispered sweet nothings to each other and dreamed of . . . well, you know what they were dreaming of.

Allen emailed and texted Amanda. He would text her in between emails. Somehow, which he didn't understand, it was easier to be a little "dirty" in his conversations via text messages and emails, than it was actually speaking into a telephone. He liked it. Apparently, so did Amanda. She even made Allen start sweating a little with a few of her typed messages. After all the texts and emails and lustful dreams, Allen took a shower, brushed his teeth, and took his medicine, but Bill and Ellen were still on the couch. He turned off the light and thought of a couple of things he'd like to ask Bill. But, he would never have that opportunity again. That thought made him a little sad as he laid in the dark, in Ellen's house, on the shores of Lake Superior . . . all by himself.

44

ELLEN AND BILL DROPPED ALLEN OFF at the airport the next morning. Ellen hugged him and thanked him again. Bill and Allen first shook hands, then they hugged each other and patted each other on the back for so long that each guy was starting to cry a little—though they'd never admit it. Finally, Allen's flight was called and he picked up his luggage and started to walk away, then turned and looked back at Ellen and said, "Ellen, whatever you do, please take good care of . . . my truck." Then he turned and walked to the plane.

They stayed at the little airport and watched Allen's plane take off and fly away towards Utah. As they lost sight of the plane, Bill said, "Well, I guess it's just you and me now."

Ellen smiled and replied, "Forever."

The End

www.ingramcontent.com/pod-product-compliance
Lightning Source LLC
Chambersburg PA
CBHW070824180626
46818CB00001B/388
* 9 7 8 1 9 4 9 7 5 6 9 6 8 *